SEEK
AND
DESTROY

D0890866

ALSO BY ALAN McDERMOTT

Tom Gray Novels

SEEK
AND
DESTROY

ALAN
McDermott

THOMAS & MERCER

This is a work of fiction. Names, characters, organizations, places, events, and incidents are either products of the author's imagination or are used fictitiously. Any resemblance to actual persons, living or dead, or actual events is purely coincidental.

Text copyright © 2018 by Alan McDermott
All rights reserved.

No part of this book may be reproduced, or stored in a retrieval system, or transmitted in any form or by any means, electronic, mechanical, photocopying, recording, or otherwise, without express written permission of the publisher.

Published by Thomas & Mercer, Seattle

www.apub.com

Amazon, the Amazon logo, and Thomas & Mercer are trademarks of Amazon.com, Inc., or its affiliates.

ISBN-13: 9781503904989
ISBN-10: 1503904989

Cover design by Tom Sanderson

Printed in the United States of America

SEEK
AND
DESTROY

JANUARY 2018

CHAPTER 1

The thermometer on the wall said the outside temperature was 87 Fahrenheit, but to Farooq Naser it felt like a delicious 65 degrees. Three air conditioners hummed in chorus as they battled the Hyderabad heat—and, being the best that money could buy, they were doing a sterling job.

The house boy knocked on the door and entered, carrying a tray bearing a teapot and cup. He put it down on the desk and left without a word. Farooq poured himself a cup and sat back from his computer, one of three he'd splurged on after getting his share of the money he'd helped to steal from the ESO.

Eight million dollars went a long way in India.

At times, he wasn't sure that Hyderabad had been the right choice of destination. He'd picked it because it was the birthplace of his parents, but upon seeing it for the first time, he'd wondered if he'd made a big mistake. It was as far removed from the United States as one could get. Simply getting off the plane had been an experience in itself, the heat enveloping him in a stifling blanket the moment he emerged.

Traffic was another thing that was going to take some getting used to. There didn't seem to be any laws, except every man for himself.

Tuk-tuks and motorcycles darted in and out of traffic like salmon heading for their spawning grounds.

There were pluses, though. Everything was dirt cheap compared to the States: having young Arnav at his beck and call cost a mere seventy-five bucks a month. Elsewhere in the house, he had Riya, the young woman who did the cooking and cleaning. That set him back another hundred. With the rent coming in at only a thousand US dollars per month, he could afford to live like a king here for the rest of his life.

He'd chosen the three-bedroom apartment purely because of the location. It was close enough to the center of Hyderabad that he could be anywhere within half an hour, even when pitted against the sea of vehicles that washed over the city every day. The place was bigger than he needed, with three reception rooms and two bathrooms, but its relative quiet allowed him to get on with his work.

Not that he considered it work, by any means. It certainly didn't pay anything.

Not yet, at least.

Farooq's passion was ones and zeros. When it came to writing code, he had few equals, which was why the CIA had hired him years earlier. His time with the Agency had come to an abrupt end when a supervisor with a grudge had planted a bottle of whiskey in Farooq's desk drawer and canned him, but not before Farooq had written a back door into their computer systems. It was from the CIA's coffers that Farooq had stolen fifty million dollars, money that had originally been meant to fund the Agency's illicit programs. Instead, he'd used the cash to help Eva Driscoll in her fight against the Executive Security Office, the most powerful organization on the planet.

Henry Langton had been at the helm of the ESO for a number of years, as had many Langtons before him. They were the dark, shadowy men behind the governments of the world, the ones who kept 95 percent of the world's population a paycheck away from poverty, while siphoning off the rest for themselves. They controlled the banks, the

US Senate and House of Representatives, and their worth ran into the trillions. More than enough to bribe lawmakers to do their bidding. Many of the world's conflicts were initiated by the ESO, who financed and armed both sides at great profit. The ESO's sway had also been sufficient to force the United States' intelligence services to do as they demanded, as Farooq had found out the hard way. With Langton now dead and the US president personally overseeing the investigation into the ESO, Farooq's only concern was which application to build next.

He'd already updated and renamed his Taurus messaging app, which took cryptography to a whole new level. Even the NSA, with all its state-of-the-art hardware, wouldn't come close to decoding the messages his users shared. Not that there were many users. He had a copy, as did Eva Driscoll, Carl Huff, Rees Colback, and the two Englishmen Eva had hired to help her bring down the ESO.

Farooq was currently working on a piece of software that would enable him to take control of cell phones. It was proving troublesome, but he loved nothing more than a challenge. Once he'd knocked off for the day, he'd take another shot at getting back into the CIA's servers. It wasn't something he expected to pull off, but it helped him relax in the evenings. Without that little distraction, it would be too easy to return to the bottle. Having given up alcohol—with Eva's help, two years earlier—he didn't dare give himself a chance of backsliding.

He heard another knock at the study door and glanced at his watch. It was too early for his dinner, and he'd given his staff instructions not to disturb him unless it was important.

"Come."

Arnav walked into the room and handed Farooq a flash drive.

"What's this?"

"A man came to the door and told me to give it to you, sahib." Arnav placed the drive on the corner of Farooq's desk and turned to leave.

"Wait." Farooq had only made the acquaintance of a handful of people since arriving in the city, and only Samar knew where he lived. He couldn't think why Samar would drop off a memory stick without bothering to offer an explanation. "Who was this man? What did he look like?"

"I have never seen him before, sahib. He was young, maybe twenty, but looked like you in body."

That didn't sound remotely like Samar. His friend was in his mid-forties and had an expansive waistline. A far cry from Farooq's rake-thin frame.

"Okay. Thank you."

Arnav left, closing the door behind him, and Farooq picked up the drive, turning it in his fingers. There was no way he was going to insert it into his main computer—it could easily contain a virus—but he had a backup PC with a virtual machine mounted, which could be deleted and replaced with ease.

Farooq fired up the second computer and inserted the mysterious drive. He ran a virus scan, which came back clean. The drive contained only one item, an MP4 file. Farooq double-clicked on it and the screen instantly showed a familiar scene.

The local market was in full swing, with merchants hawking their various wares. The video had been taken from across the road, with vehicles breaking up the scene intermittently. After a few seconds, the camera focused on his friend, Samar. He looked to be haggling over the price of a copper pot; eventually he put it in his bag and handed over a few bills.

Why would someone send me a recording of Samar shopping?

Samar strolled through the market, stopping occasionally to check out some of the stalls. The camera zoomed in on his face for a few seconds, then panned back out, leaving Farooq with no doubt that Samar was the subject of the video.

For three more minutes he watched his friend meander through the market until he came to the road and waited for an opportunity to cross. The video panned out even more, and Farooq could see a bus approaching from the left. It wasn't traveling at a great speed, due to the traffic on the road, but it was moving faster than a person could walk. Samar waited patiently for it to pass, but as it got to within five yards of his position, the unexpected happened.

Samar's hands flew upward and his body lurched into the road. He looked like he was going to fall to his knees, but the bus hit him before he could do so. Unable to take his eyes off the horror before him, Farooq watched as Samar's body bounced off the front of the vehicle then fell beneath the front wheel. The scene started to jiggle and the screen pointed at the ground as the cameraman ran across the road, then it focused once more on Samar.

Blood seeped from a wound on his head, but the real damage had been done to his torso. His chest had been flattened and a crimson pool was forming underneath him, like the wings of an angel unfurling in preparation for its final journey.

As Farooq moved to close the video, the screen faded to black and words began to appear in place of the horrific death scene. He watched as the blurred letters came into focus, revealing a message that was both succinct and terrifying.

WE FOUND YOU

CHAPTER 2

Eva Driscoll linked arms with Carl Huff as they left their apartment on Widenmayerstrasse and strolled along the riverbank until they came to Maximilianstrasse, the artery that fed into the heart of Munich. Normally they would have taken a tram from there, but the gray skies had vanished, and as the sun was making its first appearance of the year as January came to an end, they decided to walk the final mile.

Munich had been Eva's idea. She'd visited the place once during her stint with the CIA. It had been a surveillance mission, and in those few days she'd developed a good feel for the city. It helped that she had a rudimentary knowledge of the language, and when you want to hide out in the open from the most powerful organization in the world, Munich is as good a place as any.

Not long ago, Eva thought she'd never see the outside of a prison cell again, never mind strolling the streets with her lover on her arm. She'd spent weeks looking for the people who ran the ESO, the men who had ordered the murder of her brother, only to wind up in a maximum-security prison facing life plus 150 years for multiple homicides. Fortunately, the president of the United States, Leonard "Leo" Russell, was not one of the ESO's stooges. He'd begun an investigation into the syndicate and had granted Eva and her friends secret pardons.

Things might have been different if Bill Sanders, then head of the CIA, had sent Carl to kill her rather than save her. But Sanders had been looking out for number one, much as she'd suspected. If she'd died, his career and marriage would have gone down the toilet thanks to the incriminating video she had of the two of them.

She'd taken it during her CIA training, when Sanders had been head of clandestine services and Eva a raw recruit. Sanders had invited her to his cabin in the woods, and while no reason had been given, she hadn't been naive enough to think it was for extra credit. She'd recorded their lovemaking and, days later, Sanders had received a copy with a warning that if she were ever considered disposable, his indiscretion would be laid bare to the world.

Eva often wondered what had become of her cohorts. When they'd been released, President Russell had told them that new identities awaited them in Kansas City. Ever the skeptic, she'd made them all stop off in Louisville, Kentucky, to get more false papers from her long-time associate, DeBron Harris. Armed with two new names each, they'd gone their separate ways, with Eva warning them not to share their new identities with anyone, not even each other. She and Carl Huff had stayed together, but what happened to Farooq Naser, Rees Colback, and the two Englishmen, Sonny and Len, was a mystery.

Which was the whole point. If she didn't know where they were, she couldn't give them away, and vice versa.

While none of them were technically fugitives from the law, they still had to keep their heads down. The ESO wasn't just some old boys' club that met once a week to discuss sports; these were the people that shaped the lives of everyone on the planet. They started wars when it suited their purpose, they interfered with elections in every major country, and they controlled 99 percent of the world's money. They were above the law in every way, and despite Russell's promise to shut them down, Eva was under no illusions. An organization that had been able to effectively run the planet for the last eighty years was not going to be disbanded by a president who'd barely been elected to the White House. If Russell's opponent hadn't been implicated in the death of a prostitute during the campaign, Russell would have become the forgotten man.

Eva and Carl reached their first stop of the day, the Louis Vuitton shop, where they bought a couple of shirts for him and scarves for both of them, then they wandered the streets, looking for somewhere to have lunch. In the few weeks that they'd been in Munich, they'd rarely eaten at the same place twice. Today they found a small restaurant tucked out of the way, and took seats at a table covered in a red gingham tablecloth.

Carl removed his hat and rubbed his bald head. That, along with the goatee beard and moustache, meant he bore little resemblance to his former self. At first Eva had objected to him shaving his head, but she kind of liked the way he looked now. He also blended in well with the locals. For her part, Eva had dyed her hair platinum and cut it into a bob, also a common look in Munich.

A waitress appeared and took their orders, then returned soon after with the bottle of white wine Carl had chosen.

"I was thinking," Eva said as she sipped her wine, "maybe we could drive down to Kitzbühel for a few days. Take in the slopes, cuddle up by a nice warm fire afterward."

"I don't see why not." Carl smiled. "I think we can afford a week off."

For those that tried to engage them in conversation, Eva and Carl gave the same story each time. They were graphic designers who worked from home. In truth, Eva had stolen enough from the CIA slush fund to keep them comfortable for the rest of their lives. Farooq had been given his share—eight million—as had Rees Colback. She'd also given the English guys a couple of million each to help them disappear. That left just shy of thirty million dollars to feed, clothe, and house them for the rest of their days. With a budget of half a million a year, they figured they could just about manage it.

"I'll book a hotel room as soon as we get back," Eva said, rubbing her foot up the inside of Carl's leg.

Their food arrived, and Eva tucked into her sea bass while Carl tackled the house wiener schnitzel.

"After we leave here, I'd like to go and buy some luggage. It'll be—"

Eva's phone sang in her purse, a tune that almost stopped her heart. She had set a specific ringtone for this particular application, and her hands trembled slightly as she reached into the bag. As she took the cell out, her worst fears were confirmed. The notification on the locked screen was from Farooq's Shield messaging app.

"Tell me that's not what I think it is."

Eva looked up at Carl, and the concern on his face mirrored hers.

She entered her PIN into the phone and opened the message. "It's from Farooq." She read the missive twice, then handed the cell to Carl.

"I guess that's Austria cancelled," he said, passing it back. "We have to warn the others."

"If this is who we think it is, we'll have to do more than just give them a heads-up. We'll need a plan."

Eva opened Shield and composed a response to Farooq's message. After hitting Send, she put her phone on the table, waiting for him to get back to her. It wasn't a long wait. She replied once more, then put the phone back in her bag. She took a few bills from her purse and left them on the table. "We have to go. Right now."

They walked quickly back to Maximilianstrasse and took a cab to their apartment. Carl entered the code for the communal door and, once inside, pulled a SIG from inside his jacket. Eva took her pistol from her purse and followed him up the flight of stairs. The landing was clear, and no one had disturbed the small piece of paper she'd put in the crack of the doorway. Carl used his keys to let them in, and after checking the apartment for threats, they began stuffing clothes and essentials into their bags.

Not that there was much to take. They hadn't been naive enough to believe Munich would be their final destination, and so the apartment was virtually bare. They had the essentials, but there was nothing to turn a set of rooms into a home.

Apart from the bear.

They'd spotted it at a flea market a couple of weeks earlier and Eva had fallen in love with it. It was the size of a coffee mug, but flat and with a clock set in its belly. It reminded Eva of a similar trinket she'd had as a kid. Hers had sat on the table next to her bed and would wake her for school, but the mechanism in this one had failed a long time ago. Carl had caught the look on her face when she saw it, and that had been enough to convince him to part with a whole euro for it.

Carl took the bear from Eva's nightstand, put it in with his clothes, and walked through to the bathroom.

"I wonder how they found Farooq," he said as Eva emptied the medicine cabinet. "He spends a lot of time on his computer. Maybe he got sloppy at some point."

She looked at him and shrugged. "I'd expect that of the others, but not Farooq. My guess would be that the identities Russell gave us are compromised. Maybe the ESO has someone in his office that he doesn't know about."

"Then we should tell the others to do what we did and use the passports you got from DeBron."

"First, we need to find out which ID they've been using. If they're using the one Russell gave them, they could be in danger. Farooq will have to keep traveling under the name he's using now. They'll be following him, and if he switches to the other ID, that'll be burned too."

"So where do you want to rendezvous?"

"With Farooq? Lyon. We can drive there in about eight hours. Once we set off, I'll let the others know where to meet us and book them rooms on Airbnb."

With their bags packed, Carl left the apartment first, and Eva locked the door behind them. She put the key through the letterbox. Downstairs, they got into the BMW they'd rented and Carl set the satnav for their destination, while Eva arranged their accommodation and alerted the others to the imminent danger.

CHAPTER 3

Eva's response came back within a minute, but it seemed like hours.

Which ID are you using?

Farooq's fingers worked on auto, and he sent the short reply.

The one POTUS gave me.

A moment later, Shield beeped once more.

Fly to Lyon NOW. Address to follow. USE POTUS ID ONLY!

Farooq was still in the grip of panic. The video had shaken him, and now he faced the prospect of traveling thousands of miles alone, without Eva to protect him. He wasn't built for fighting and had always found confrontation difficult at best. The prospect of navigating his way to France with killers on his trail was enough to turn the knot in his stomach to pure acid. He had no weapons and no idea what the opposition looked like. They could be waiting outside at this very moment . . .

Fly to Lyon NOW.

Farooq's analytical brain kicked in. He set the scrub program on his two computers and went to get ready for his trip. He fetched a bag from his bedroom and put his laptop inside, then took the cash he had in his safe and counted it. Nine thousand US, give or take. He threw a few clothes in for good measure. He left a short note to the staff and a couple of hundred dollars' severance pay.

Farooq took the stairs to the street two at a time. Outside, he hailed a tuk-tuk and tossed his bag into the back.

"Take me to the Park Hyatt."

Farooq scanned his surroundings, looking for any sign of a tail, but with so much traffic on the streets it was impossible to tell if someone was following him. By the time he reached the hotel, he still had no idea if the killers were on to him. He paid the driver, then went straight to the taxi rank and got in the first cab.

"The airport."

Farooq turned so that he could see out of the rear window. The driver tried to engage him in conversation but gave up when he got no response.

It was a long journey, stop-start all the way as the taxi fought against the tide of vehicles. Twice they had to navigate around crashed cars, but eventually they made it to the airport.

Farooq paid the driver and carried his bag to the Emirates desk, where he booked the next flight to Lyon via Dubai. He had four nervous hours to wait, and the temptation to hit the bar was almost too much.

Just one quick shot to calm the nerves.

He shook the thought away. One would lead to many, as it had in the past, and he needed his wits about him. Instead, he found a quiet corner and watched the other passengers going about their business, trying to spot anyone who looked out of the ordinary. The trouble was, everyone looked suspicious. The man pushing the cleaning trolley caught his eye for a moment, and Farooq almost soiled himself when the man reached into the cart, only to then pull out a rag and start wiping down a handrail.

Pull yourself together.

Waiting and watching was increasing his panic levels, so Farooq went in search of food. He found a café and ordered coffee and a sandwich, paying an exorbitant price for the substandard fare.

As he ate, he tried to think what might have tipped off the ESO. It couldn't have been his online activity. In that respect, he was extremely careful and could cover his tracks better than anyone. Likewise, his phone. It was a prepaid unregistered cell, and only a couple of people had the number. Could they have found a match to his voice while he'd been on a call to Samar? It was a possibility, but the most likely scenario was that someone knew about the new identities President Russell had given them. Whatever the reason, he would have to be extra careful from now on.

After eating, Farooq wandered the departure hall, once more seeking his tail, but it appeared he'd made it to the airport without attracting unwanted attention. He began to relax, a little.

Shortly after seven in the evening, the baggage check-in desk opened. Farooq collected his boarding pass and passed through security, then spent half an hour in the duty-free shop before proceeding to his gate.

As he sat scanning the faces, none looked familiar. He hadn't seen any of them hanging around him earlier, and he finally felt safe. No one would have the audacity to try to kill him in the airport, not even the ESO.

His section was eventually called, and he carried his hand luggage on to the plane and found his seat. Ahead of him lay a four-hour flight, followed by a short stopover and another seven hours to Lyon. With a little time before takeoff, Farooq composed a new message for Eva, giving her his ETA in France.

He hoped that when he got there Eva would have a plan.

CHAPTER 4

"*. . . the cross comes in, and there's Jones with a brilliant header! Two-nil United, and three points in the bag.*"

"I'll say one thing for the British, they sure can play soccer."

Rees Colback raised his glass in agreement. Not that he'd been paying much attention to the game. He was there solely for the beer, but once the big Texan had heard a fellow American speak, it was like they were best buds for life.

Note to self: find a new drinking hole tomorrow.

That was one of the good things about Gran Canaria—there were bars everywhere.

"About time I was heading home, Hank. The little lady's waiting on me for dinner. Catch you next time."

Hank did his best to convince him to stay for just one more, but Colback was insistent. He drained his glass, then slapped his compatriot on the back and left the bar.

In truth, he didn't much feel like going home.

Colback strolled along the second-floor walkway, ignoring the restaurant staff trying to coax him into their establishments. He found the bar he was looking for and ordered his fourth beer of the evening.

The "little lady" was actually his sister, and her constant complaining about his daily drinking had begun to grate on his nerves. But what else was there to do? He ran five miles each morning and swam fifty lengths of the pool every afternoon, but apart from that, he'd found little to occupy his time. He'd seen the whole island during his ten weeks here, and it wasn't as if he had friends he could socialize with. Eva had been clear on that point: avoid forming bonds with people. You begin to trust them, and one slip could be your undoing.

It wasn't much of a way to spend the rest of his days. He had millions in the bank, but Eva had been clear when she'd transferred the money: Don't splurge on fast cars and fancy houses. This money is to last you the rest of your life.

Some life. I might as well be back in that prison cell.

Colback put the empty bottle on the table and headed home. It wasn't far to the apartment he shared with Kayla, but he was in no hurry to face her, so he took his time and made the most of the deliciously warm evening.

Kayla had come with him to the Canary Islands reluctantly. It hadn't been easy, but he'd managed to convince her that the ESO might try to use her to get to him, and that her life could be in danger, no matter what steps the president took. He'd tried convincing his parents, too, but they were adamant about not abandoning their Florida home. When Kayla grudgingly agreed to move to Gran Canaria with him, he'd paid another visit to DeBron Harris to secure new papers for her. She'd given up her life as a nurse to join him in the Spanish archipelago, but it was only once they'd landed at Las Palmas that she'd found out that the new life came with strings attached. She, too, was struggling with the reclusive lifestyle; what had until recently been a close brother-sister relationship was becoming increasingly fractured by the day.

When he reached home, he found Kayla sitting on the couch wearing shorts and a bikini top, sipping a lemonade. She looked disgruntled, much like every other day.

"You got a message," she said, her eyes never leaving the television.

Colback habitually left his phone at home these days. The only person likely to call was his sister; it wasn't as if he had friends to chat with.

He picked the cell up from the dining table and saw the Shield notification. His hands trembled as he opened it.

Which ID are you using?

The message was a few hours old. He sent her a response, and wasn't surprised to get a reply seconds later.

Fly to Paris NOW. Address to follow. Use DEBRON ID ONLY!

Colback was already using the passport he'd purchased from DeBron Harris, having decided to keep the one from the US president as a backup. Did Eva's message mean someone had managed to get wind of the other one? If they had, it was now worthless.

Of more concern was Eva's urgency. She was not given to histrionics, so there had to be a damn good reason for telling him to get on a plane right away.

"Kayla, we have to leave."

"I don't feel like going out. Haven't you had enough already?"

"I don't mean leave the house, I mean leave Gran Canaria. Tonight."

Kayla put her glass on the coffee table and stood, facing him. "What have you done now?"

"Nothing," Colback replied. He walked into the bedroom and began putting clothes into a bag. "Eva said we have to move, so we're moving."

"But where?"

"Paris. France."

Kayla crossed her arms and stood in the doorway. "Can you please tell me what's going on?"

"No, because I have no idea myself. She told me to get on a plane and she'll send the rendezvous address later."

Kayla turned and stomped back into the living room. "Well, I'm not going," she said.

Colback sighed. For a twenty-six-year-old, his sister could play the role of a teenager to perfection. He followed her into the main room and turned her to face him.

"Look, I'm sorry, but if Eva felt the need to contact me, it must be serious."

"I don't care. I'm not going to spend the rest of my life running like some criminal. I haven't done anything wrong!"

"I know you haven't, but it's not safe here now."

"Did she say that? Did she say we're in danger?"

"No," Colback admitted, "she didn't. She said to get to Paris as fast as I can and only use the passport I bought in Louisville."

"There you go. If those passports are okay, I can keep using mine here."

It was a fair point. If Eva thought the papers were still secure, surely she wouldn't have told him to use them. That aside, he still didn't like the idea of leaving his sister behind. Not until he knew what the emergency was.

"Okay, we'll compromise. I'll go to Paris and see what the problem is. If Eva thinks it's safe to leave you here, great. Otherwise, I'll send for you. I'll have a letter sent to the Ocean Beach Club on Playa del Cura with your name on it. Go there every day after five, have the all-you-can-eat buffet, then ask if you have any messages. Try not to ask the same staff member twice. Is that good enough?"

Kayla pouted, then her arms loosened and fell by her side. "Fine."

"Good. Before I go, I'm going to give you some ground rules."

"No friends, no socializing, no leaving the house, no breathing—"

"Hey! I'm being serious. If you don't do as I say, it could get you killed."

His outburst did the trick. The attitude was suddenly gone, and his mature sibling stood in front of him once more.

"I'm sorry. I just don't like this situation."

"Me either. Now, while I pack, I need you to look up flights to Paris."

~

"*Storms battered the coast as Jake Strong pulled his sea canoe out into the dark water. The swell of the sea threatened to tear it from his grasp, but he kept it steady before climbing awkwardly aboard. Fires raged behind him, and he could still hear gunfire as the enemy fighters shot at unseen targets. He unclipped the paddle and began rowing into the darkness, feeling . . .*"

Feeling what?

Len Smart got up from his desk and went to make yet another cup of coffee.

When reading novels—and Len was an avid fan of fiction—he found the words flowed from the page. As a writer, it wasn't quite the same. Any dreams of having his first book finished by the spring were fast evaporating. He'd been hard at it for seven weeks now and had barely reached five thousand words. How people managed to churn out five or six books a year, he had no idea.

Perhaps it was time to consider plotting it out first. He'd read about authors known as "pantsters," who began typing on a blank page and went from there; while others had to outline the entire story ahead of time to the nth degree before they even considered starting to write. Len was using the first method, and it wasn't going well.

Still, there wasn't much else to occupy his time.

His job at Tom Gray's firm Minotaur Solutions was history, and not just because of his run-in with the ESO. It had been a financial basket case for some time now, as competitors squeezed the market for every dime. The decision had finally been made to wind it up, and not a moment too soon. Gray had managed to walk away with a healthy amount in the bank, and Len had declined any suggestion of severance pay.

With the two million he'd been given by Eva Driscoll, he didn't need it.

What he did need was to finish this chapter and then decide what Jake Strong was going to do next.

He sat back down at the computer and reread the last couple of paragraphs, making changes as he went, then returned to the struggle of adding more words.

Feeling . . .

The cell phone on his desk vibrated, and he picked it up to see a message had been sent to him.

Eva Driscoll . . . *Not a good sign.*

He swiped the combination that unlocked the phone, then clicked on the notification. After answering that he was using the passport DeBron had made for him, he hit Send. A moment later, he received instructions to get to Geneva as soon as he could.

In a way, he'd half expected this day would come. From what he'd learned about the ESO during his stint with Eva, he knew that cutting and running wouldn't be so simple. The ESO were the most serious of players. It had only been a matter of time before they found one of his group. Len was just surprised that it had taken this long.

"Sorry, Jake, but I'm gonna have to leave you freezing your arse off in the Atlantic, feeling . . . whatever."

Len saved the document, closed it down, then emailed a copy to himself. A simplistic backup method, true, but it was one way of ensuring his work wasn't lost if his laptop got lost, stolen, or damaged. He could easily replace the hardware, but not the time he'd invested in his novel. Now he could simply access his email account online and down-load a copy anywhere in the world.

Next, he booked a ticket to Geneva, for a flight leaving in a few hours' time, before throwing essentials into a small suitcase.

As he left the house in Calgary, his padded winter coat zipped up to protect him from the bitter cold, he was glad he'd decided to rent a car rather than rely on public transport. His place was at least two miles from the nearest shop—an easy jog at any time, but to get to the heart of the city would be a nightmare on foot or even by bus in these icy conditions. He would hand the Ford back in at the airport before his flight across the Atlantic.

Jubilant!

That was it: "*. . . feeling jubilant after another successful mission, though he wasn't home yet.*"

Len rummaged around in the glove box, but couldn't find what he was looking for. "Never a pen and paper when you need one."

Knowing he'd forget before he had a chance to update his manu-script, he started the engine and set off on his own adventure.

~

DeBron's.

Simon "Sonny" Baines hit Send, then waited for Eva to get back to him. When she did, he punched the air as he read her reply through the Shield application.

The last two and a half months had been almost intolerable: as bad as his spell in prison beforehand.

Many people would kill for a ton of money and never to have to work another day in their lives, but for Sonny it felt more like a punish-ment. He'd made the most of his new life soon after reaching Milan, eating out every lunchtime and evening, but the novelty had soon worn off. Even the thought of sipping beer in a bar full of beautiful women had lost its appeal.

Sonny's trouble was that he was a talkative drunk, and he knew it. His fondest memories were of reminiscing with the guys about battles ancient and recent, everyone boasting of their exploits. Now he'd been reduced to chit-chat with strangers, unable to tell them what was really going on in his head. Until after a few beers . . .

A couple of times recently he'd referred in conversation to his experiences in Africa and elsewhere. It was only the following morning that he'd realized how stupid he'd been, but by then the damage was done.

Soon after his last transgression, he'd gone to a hardware store and purchased a safe with a time-release locking mechanism. Whenever he felt the urge for a drink, he would throw his house keys in the safe and set the timer for eight hours later, then grab a few from the fridge and sit in the apartment with only the television for company.

He still ventured out now and again, but usually only for lunch in one of the chic restaurants in the area. In the evening, he cooked. Not the egg and sausages from days gone by, but what he now liked to call proper food. He'd invested in an array of kitchen equipment, from blenders and mixers to a *sous vide* water bath, and after many hours watching reruns of *MasterChef* on TV he could produce meals that he would have happily paid good money for in a restaurant.

Within a couple of weeks of his new routine, he'd stopped buying beer at the supermarket. He wasn't programmed to sit alone and wallow in despair, so he'd upped his exercise routine instead. His morning jog became a five-mile run, followed by three hours at a gym and daily swimming. It was the perfect complement to his new healthy-eating lifestyle, but while it was good to get the endorphins flowing, life still didn't feel complete.

He missed socializing. Specifically, being around his friends, sharing tales, swapping jokes.

What he really craved, though, was action.

He'd been a soldier for most of his life, and only really felt alive when the bullets were flying. He'd been fortunate enough to have seen his fair share of battles and emerged unscathed, and the job he'd had for the last few years, working for Tom Gray, meant he'd gotten to play with guns to his heart's content.

When Gray had made the decision to liquidate Minotaur Solutions, a part of Sonny had died. His role as training officer had given him immense pleasure over the years, allowing him to evaluate the new recruits while keeping his own skills sharp on the range. Nothing in civilian life, he knew, could ever possibly compare.

Eva's message, though, gave him a new lease on life. Strange how the direst emergency could feel like a life preserver. At least to a dyed-in-the-wool soldier like Sonny Baines.

He checked the map on his phone and saw that the drive from Milan to Geneva would take him four hours. Eva would likely have sent him an address by then. If not, he'd find a hotel and check in for the night.

It didn't take long to pack what he needed. Within fifteen minutes of receiving the news, Sonny was in his car and heading west.

CHAPTER 5

Henry Langton stood in the control room of his mansion, overseeing the next phase of the operation. Willard Eckman, with his white open-necked shirt and cropped hair, had been tasked with tracking down Eva Driscoll, and would be the one to issue orders, but everyone in the room knew that Langton was in charge.

Not that they knew him by that name. The plastic surgery he'd undergone a few months earlier had changed his appearance enough that barely anyone would recognize him from the few photographs available. As far as the world was aware, Henry Langton had died of a heart attack the summer before. To the people in this room, the seventy-year-old man standing with them was an ex-NSA official by the name of Charles Danby. But this mission wasn't government-sanctioned, and they knew it. If it had been, they would be operating out of a facility in or near Washington, DC, not on an island in the middle of nowhere. The only people with an interest in killing Eva Driscoll were the ESO, but for the money they were getting, no one in the room cared who they were working for. All that mattered was that Driscoll and her team were on the loose once more, and it was their job to track them down and eliminate them.

"Nest, this is Eagle One. I have eyes on."

"Roger, Eagle One," said Eckman. "We have visual."

The camera carried by the operative using the call sign Eagle One showed a weary-looking Farooq Naser walking through the arrivals hall at Lyon–Saint Exupéry Airport. He was carrying just one bag as he made his way to the exit, following the signs for the taxis.

"Stay with him, but not too close. We don't want to spook him."

One wall of the control room had a sixty-inch monitor mounted on it, and it showed Naser joining the line for a cab. Surrounding that were six smaller screens displaying the profiles of Driscoll and her friends. The images had been burned into Langton's memory months earlier, but some of the people under his command were new to the mission. The mug shots were there as a constant reminder of the people they were hunting.

Apart from Langton and Eckman, there were four other personnel sitting at computers, each with three screens on the go. Art Barnaby was skinny as a rake, while Edwin Masters was the polar opposite. He weighed close to four hundred pounds, and always had either a chocolate bar or a squeezy toy in one hand. Marcus Granger was the youngest at twenty-five, half the age of navy veteran Dennis Turner.

"Nest, Eagle Two. We see the target and are waiting to tail him."

Eckman acknowledged the report and asked Eagle Three for a status update. They replied that they were still four hours out from Lyon. No way they would make it in time.

The minutes ticked past slowly, and Langton kept his eyes on the monitors. Either Driscoll was going to pick Naser up at the airport or meet him somewhere in the city. The latter was more likely, as he could see that Naser was nearly at the front of the line and there was no sign of her.

"Check the drivers of those cabs. See if any of them are Driscoll."

Eckman passed on Langton's order, and Eagle One started walking the line, pointing the camera in his briefcase toward the cars. One by one, the drivers were eliminated as suspects.

"She's not going to show," Langton told Eckman. "Make sure you don't lose Naser trying to spot her. He's our only hope."

Once Langton had learned of the president's decision to give Driscoll and her cronies new identities, he'd quickly put measures in place to uncover the false identities that they would be using. It hadn't taken much money to convince a White House staffer to divulge the information, but to Langton's dismay, only one of the six had decided to use the new papers. There had been no travel booked under their original names either, leaving Naser the only method of getting to the others.

The operative in Hyderabad, Ali, had easily found which flight Naser had booked at the Emirates desk. Ali had bought a ticket on the same flight and followed Naser to Dubai, aware that he might be laying a false trail and intending to purchase another ticket to a different destination. That hadn't been the case. Naser had continued on to Lyon as expected, and now he was about to get into a cab with a dozen eyes on him.

~

Farooq Naser was exhausted. He'd never enjoyed flying and found sleeping on a plane impossible. He slumped into the back of the taxi and handed the driver a piece of paper with an address on it. His French was awful and he knew he would make a mess of trying to enunciate it.

The cab pulled away, and Farooq closed his eyes for a few moments. He was tempted to sleep until he reached his destination, but he knew he wasn't safe yet. Eva had sent him the address and asked him which ID he'd been using. He'd responded that it was the one President Russell had given him, and she'd told him to keep using it. No doubt that's how the ESO had found him, and they were probably not very far away. He turned and looked out the rear window. There were no ominous black SUVs to be seen, but they could have learned their lesson and be using standard vehicles to follow him instead. The trouble was, everyone seemed to be heading into the city, and he wouldn't be able to tell if anyone was tailing him until they got closer to the center of Lyon.

After half an hour, they encountered a labyrinth of streets, all of them one-way traffic. The taxi came to a stop and the driver turned to give Farooq the price. A few euros changed hands, and Farooq got out and looked around. The driver wound down his window and said something that he didn't understand, then started pointing down a street guarded by No Entry signs.

Farooq thanked him and began walking, checking the shop names on the narrow street for one that matched the one Eva had given him. As he strolled farther, he heard a buzzing sound coming from ahead. It got louder, until a dirt bike screamed into view and powered toward him. Farooq was frozen like a rabbit caught in headlights, and the bike stopped a yard away, the rider looking straight at him. The figure was dressed all in black, and he couldn't see the face beneath the tinted visor.

When the mysterious figure took a pistol from inside the leather jacket, Farooq closed his eyes and waited for the fatal shot. But when the gun fired, he felt nothing. He wasn't blown off his feet and felt no searing pain to announce the strike of the bullet.

"Get on!" Eva shouted as she lifted the visor.

Farooq opened his eyes, still frozen to the spot.

"Move!"

Farooq snapped into action. He leaped on the back of the bike and Eva burned rubber as she pointed the machine in the direction it had come and gave it full throttle. He managed a glance behind him and saw a man lying on the ground, a gun in his hand. People were tentatively gathering around him, but the scene disappeared from view as Eva reached the main road and spun the bike right, then made a quick left. She gunned it once more, barely slowing at the next junction.

They flew down the narrow street, then came to a major intersection. Eva fed the bike through a gap between a car and a bus, then flew around the next corner.

"When we stop, you'll see a black Audi," Eva shouted above the whine of the engine. "Get in and keep your head down!"

Farooq tapped her on the shoulder to acknowledge the order, then clung on for dear life as she braked hard to take a sharp right. Fifty yards later, the bike screamed to a halt next to an Audi. Farooq jumped off and dived in the open rear door as Eva sped away.

"Get under the blanket and keep your head down," Carl Huff said as he gently pulled the vehicle into traffic and drove in the opposite direction from Eva.

Farooq was happy to do so. "What about Eva?" he asked from under the blanket.

"Don't worry about her. She's got it covered."

～

"Man down! Man down!"

Eagle One gunned the engine of the Citroën and gave chase. After seeing his partner gunned down and Naser climbing on to the bike, he knew it had to be Driscoll on the motorcycle. He also knew that losing her would be a bad career move.

She was on the street paralleling his, and at the next junction he turned to intercept her. But she flew past his position before he got to the intersection, and by the time he was behind her she was gone again. He'd seen the way she'd gone, though, and sounded his horn as a pedestrian thought about crossing in front of him.

"Nest, I've got Driscoll! She's on a motorbike. I need backup, now!"

Ten seconds later he took the same turn as the bike. He could still see her heading toward the end of the street, but there was no sign of Naser. Had he fallen off? More likely he'd jumped off and hidden somewhere, but he was of no interest now. Driscoll was the one they were after, and she was getting away.

"Nest, Eagle One. I'm on Place Louis Pradel. She's just turned left. Where's Eagle Two?"

"Two streets over. They'll be with you in thirty seconds."

~

"Sir, if we can get the satellite overhead . . ."

"No satellite," Langton growled. He'd told Eckman that it had been tasked to an NSA mission, but in truth he simply didn't have access to it anymore. It had taken a lot of his remaining influence—and a shit-ton of cash—to gain access to the databases of the NSA, CIA and FBI without the full approval of the ESO. The organization—one that *his* family had run for two centuries—wouldn't have sanctioned his mission if he'd asked, which was why he hadn't. He still had enough in the bank to buy whatever he wanted, with the exception of access to a few billion dollars' worth of space technology.

Eckman could follow his vehicles on the screen thanks to the on-board trackers, but the lack of satellite meant he had no imagery of their target. So his directions for Eagle Two—the aim being to get ahead of Driscoll and cut her off—relied on Eagle One's best estimate of Driscoll's location.

"She's just crossed the bridge," Eagle One reported. "We're closing in."

Langton saw the dots representing his two cars take the same direction, and wished he could at least provide video to help coordinate the chase. He rued not having it even more when the next call came in.

"Shit! She's gone off road!"

~

Eva reached the end of Pont Morand just as the traffic lights on the far bank turned green. Instead of turning right on to the one-way street, she kept going straight and bounced the bike up the curb and into the park. She knew that the cars on her tail would have to take the long way around, by which time she'd be out of sight.

She didn't count on them following her.

Metal screeched as a Citroën leaped into the air and crashed back down twenty yards behind her. Eva gave the bike gas as the car bounced once more before the wheels gained purchase. She zipped between two trees and across the grass, while the Citroën was forced to stick to the path, almost demolishing a flower stall as it raced parallel to her.

Seconds later she was back on the road, heading the wrong way up a one-way street. Her hope was to prevent the car following, but traffic was light and the Citroën was still on her tail. It had the horsepower advantage, but the bike was all about maneuverability. Eva headed straight for a truck, then jinked right at the last moment. The truck slewed sideways, blocking three of the four lanes, but the Citroën sneaked past and stayed on her tail.

A police siren sounded in the distance; the last thing Eva needed was more people on her case. She nipped down a side street, again heading into oncoming traffic. This road was narrower, only two lanes, and she soon opened up a gap between her and the pursuing Citroën as she squeezed between vehicles.

No sooner had she lost one car than a second flew out of a side street and missed her bike by inches. She scooted ahead of the car's fender and on to the sidewalk, scattering pedestrians as she searched for a way out. As the car turned to continue the chase, Eva opened up a sizable lead, turning on to a one-lane street and staying off the main road.

She could still hear the sirens, but they were behind her now. She hoped the police would concentrate on her pursuers. She had a rendezvous to make, and falling into the hands of the police would be almost as bad as the ESO's men catching her.

Eva took a right and steered the bike on to a path toward Place de l'Europe, the bollards preventing any cars following her. A minute later, she doubled back on herself, then flew the wrong way across Pont

Lafayette. She navigated the back streets until she came to the fountain at Place des Jacobins, where she stopped the motorcycle under a tree and dumped the helmet on the seat. She walked over to where Carl Huff had parked the Audi.

"Any problems?" he asked as she got in beside him.

Eva shrugged. "Nothing I couldn't handle."

She glanced in the back seat at the partially blanket-covered Farooq. "Did you ditch your phone like I said?"

"Yeah. Left it in the restroom at Dubai Airport."

"Good. Keep your head down until we're out of the city."

"Where are we going?"

"To meet the others," Eva said. "First Geneva, then Paris."

She put a cap on and sank into her seat as Huff drove north to pick up the main road to Geneva.

CHAPTER 6

Henry Langton had never been one to suffer fools gladly, though he could usually keep his temper under control. The incompetent performance he was witnessing was testing his patience to the limit.

"She's gone right on . . . Rue Duguesclin."

Langton saw the street highlighted on the map, and the two glowing dots trailing in the invisible Driscoll's wake. She had clearly picked her route in advance and was leading them on a merry chase.

"She's gone off road. It says Place de l'Europe. We can't follow. Where does it come out?"

"Take a right on Cours Lafayette," Eckman said over the comms.

"Shit! We've got cops on our ass!"

The situation was turning into a farce, and Langton was approaching apoplexy. He grabbed the mic from Eckman and pressed the Speak button. "Never mind the cops! If you lose her, you're next on my list! Get that bitch!"

He threw the microphone on to the table and fumbled in his pocket for his cigarettes. His hands were shaking as he lit one, and he glanced around, looking for someone who objected to the smoke. Sensibly, they all concentrated on their screens.

"I'm on Cours Lafayette," Eagle One announced. "There's no sign of her."

"Eagle Two, report."

"We lost the cops, but no sign of Driscoll."

Langton picked up a coffee cup and threw it against a wall. "You've got to be kidding me."

"We only had two units available at such short notice," Eckman said, but Langton wasn't buying it.

"Bullshit! How many assets have we got?"

"A hundred and twenty, sir."

"And you only managed to get four to Lyon in the last . . ." he looked at his watch " . . . eighteen hours?"

"With respect, we thought she would be in a non-extradition country. The likelihood of her being in Europe was slim. The majority of our people are in South America and Africa."

Langton had agreed to that assessment, but it didn't change his mood. He certainly didn't appreciate having it thrown back in his face. At the time, it had made sense to place his teams in regions where Driscoll would be most likely to show. Her file said she spoke fluent Spanish, making South America her most likely destination, but she'd always been unpredictable. He should have known she would throw them a curveball.

"Nest, we lost her."

Langton cursed, then stormed out of the control room. He walked up the marble staircase to his room and sat in front of his computer. When he entered his password to unlock it, he saw Driscoll's CIA file on the screen. It had been there for months, her face waiting to greet him every time he logged in, but now she seemed to be mocking him.

Langton closed her file, then looked at the folder containing the details they had on the other five. He'd used Naser to flush Driscoll out once, so she wasn't going to fall for that ruse again. However, the rest of her team were not in Driscoll's league. Actually, Carl Huff might be, so

Langton discounted him. Naser, too, was crossed off the list. That left Rees Colback and the two Brits, Len Smart and Simon Baines. They'd already looked for Colback's sister to use as leverage, but she and her brother had disappeared from the face of the earth, so it was time to focus on the two men Driscoll had recruited in England. He'd learned all about them during their widely televised trials, and getting access to their jackets—personnel files—had been a piece of cake.

He opened the file for Len Smart and read his history again.

Born an only child in 1976 in London, went to a typical public high school, worked in a sports center for one year before joining the army at nineteen. After three years in the parachute regiment, he'd passed SAS selection. A tour in Iraq followed by two in Afghanistan. Left the regiment in 2005 and immediately went to work for Viking Security Services.

It was all standard fare, until 2011.

Smart had taken part in a siege led by Tom Gray, who had held the UK to ransom. He'd taken five criminals hostage in the countryside while threatening to release a biological weapon if the British government didn't listen to his demands. At the time it had been big news all over the world, but it hadn't impacted Langton's financial interests— and, for that simple reason, he had forgotten the entire episode.

He clicked on the link to show Smart's known associates. There were not very many. Simon Baines was obviously one, as was Tom Gray. The latter had been Smart's boss at Viking Security Services, and they'd served together in the SAS, with Gray serving as Smart's sergeant.

Langton switched to Baines's file. It was much the same as Smart's: an only child with a military background and few friends to speak of, the most notable being Tom Gray.

He opened another window and logged into the CIA database. Once in, he searched for Tom Gray and entered his date of birth. There were three hits, but only one had served in the SAS.

Gray's profile made for interesting reading. Much of it had been gleaned—off the record—from conversations with an MI5 operative named Harvey.

Gray's dramatic demands—for tougher sentences for repeat offenders, plus the reintroduction of national service and the death penalty—had made him a hero to the right wing. After his stunt ended badly, Gray had been whisked away to the Philippines and given a new identity. Reconstructive surgery had also been necessary. The last thing the government had wanted was Gray dictating the course of the upcoming general election. A man named James Farrar had been assigned to Gray, under the pretense of inviting him back to serve his country, when in fact the plan had been to eliminate Gray and the people who had helped him bring the country to a standstill.

Gray had managed to survive Farrar's duplicity and returned to England, a hero to some but a terrorist in the eyes of many. Since then, he'd become close to MI5 agent Andrew Harvey. There were unsubstantiated rumors suggesting that Gray and Harvey had worked together on special operations on more than one occasion since.

Langton sat back in his chair. Tom Gray was the ideal choice to flush Smart and Baines out into the open, yet he seemed to have a habit of surviving the most challenging situations. Much like Driscoll.

Targeting Gray would involve risk, of that there was no doubt. Killing Farooq Naser's friend had been no problem, but someone with street smarts like Gray would be a different proposition. It would be difficult to take him out and make it look like an accident, but Smart and Baines would be more likely to attend his funeral if they didn't suspect foul play. That done, it would be easy to tail them and learn their new identities. From there, it would be a matter of setting up around-the-clock surveillance and following their trail if they contacted Driscoll. If they didn't, he might be able to retrace their previous steps. There had to be something in their pasts that would lead to her.

Langton was about to return to the control room to pass instructions on to Eckman when another thought struck him. He sat back down in his chair and lit a cigarette.

Instead of killing Gray, why not just make an attempt on his life?

The more he thought about it, the better it sounded.

Langton memorized Gray's file number, then went back to the control room. He moved one of the operatives out of the way and typed the number into the CIA database.

"I want you to find everything you can on this man," he said. "I want his phones tapped, Internet intercepted, everything."

The picture on the screen showed a man in his forties with short brown hair combed with a side part. There was a hint of a scar on his cheek, and the nose looked like it had been broken more than a few times.

"No problem," Eckman assured him. "We'll install a keylogger on his computer and break into his cell phone, too. Is Gray our next target?"

"Don't tell me 'no problem' when you just lost the main target," Langton said. "I want no fuck-ups with this one."

Eckman's gaze dipped to the floor. "Yes, sir."

Langton let his words sink in, then continued. "Once we have his communications covered, I want a couple of men to attack Gray, but they are not to kill him. Am I clear?"

"Understood. Gray is not to be killed," Eckman replied. "But then . . . what is the objective?"

"I want him frightened. Mess him up a bit, then find a reason to pull back. Maybe have the police turn up or something. I'm confident Gray will try to contact Smart and Baines. They're extremely close to Gray, so they'll have some way of staying in touch."

"We'll get right on it," Eckman said.

The others turned to their stations and began searching for all they had on Tom Gray.

"I recognize this guy," the skinny operative named Barnaby said. "He's the one that had that voting website for those juvies a few years ago."

"That's right," Langton said. "And he nearly pulled it off, so don't assume we're dealing with some dumbass here."

It didn't take long to come up with his current address based on credit card use and land registry records.

"Gray's in Italy. San Giovanni in Fiore. He lives with his daughter, Melissa, five years old, as well as his dead wife's aunt and uncle, Mina and Ken Hatcher. We've also got bank accounts. Do you want us to empty them?"

"No," Langton replied. "Just get a team over there and secure all of his communications. Who's closest?"

"We've got four men arriving in Milan in the next hour. They could be there in . . . six hours. There's a flight to Lamezia Terme Airport leaving in two hours. Lamezia Terme is about a sixty-mile drive from Gray's place."

"Book their tickets and tell them to pick 'em up at the airport desk," Langton said. "I want this done tomorrow at the latest. And warn them: Gray is ex–special forces, so don't expect him to be a pushover."

He strode out of the room and down to the kitchen. It was almost three in the morning, eleven hours behind Lyon time. While Driscoll was operating in Europe, he would have to sleep during the day and work through the night. He found his personal chef and instructed him to prepare lobster for what was, in effect, breakfast.

Driscoll might have slipped from his grasp this time, but Gray was a way back in. He would lead them to Smart and Baines, and ultimately to the woman responsible for his son's death.

But that wasn't even the driving force behind his efforts. Six months earlier, he'd been the head of the most powerful organization in the world, and now he was just another schmuck. He still had a huge pile of cash, but without the influence money bought, he might as well be a street bum.

The situation didn't sit well with a man used to holding sway over presidents and prime ministers, but Henry Langton had never been one for dwelling on what couldn't be changed.

Until now.

Killing Driscoll wouldn't bring back his son or the power he'd once enjoyed, but it would satisfy the urge burning a hole in his soul.

CHAPTER 7

The four-man team reached San Giovanni in Fiore at seven in the evening. They followed the rental car's satnav as it took them through the twisty, narrow streets of the village, and eventually came to the small bed and breakfast place they'd booked earlier.

"What makes a guy want to live in a place like this?" Glenn Durston asked as he climbed out of the car. Most of the buildings were gray, and those that had been painted vibrant colors must have been done years earlier, with the majority in need of a touch-up. It reminded him a little of a Kosovan village after the war.

Feinberg grimaced. "It's a shithole, that's for sure."

"I think it's quaint." Hank Pendleton smirked, picked up his bag, and took it into the small reception area, where a woman in her sixties, cigarette dangling from her mouth, was sitting behind a counter watching a small TV set.

She looked up at them, no emotion on her face, as if seeing four fit men with buzz cuts was an everyday occurrence. Pendleton gave his name. He was the only Italian-speaker among the quartet, and five minutes later they were making their way up a narrow staircase to their accommodation on the third floor. The rooms were small but had en-suite showers, with beds that looked as if they'd survive the night. They were just about large enough for four big guys and their luggage.

"Stow your gear and meet back here in five minutes," Durston said.

Chuck Dubowitz and John Feinberg disappeared, and Durston began sorting through his own belongings. Inside his bag he had a change of clothes for the surveillance stage the following day, and among the contents were the tools of his trade. He placed the pick kit to one side and took out the electronics package. He checked the charge on the transmitter that would be affixed to the telephone wires outside Gray's house, then made sure the device that would hijack Gray's cell phone was in full working order.

Dubowitz and Feinberg knocked on the door, then entered.

Durston handed them the device. "I want you three in the town center at daybreak. Make sure you get into his phone before you initiate contact. I'll stake out his place and let you know when he leaves the house." That wasn't going to be an easy job. Gray lived with two elderly relatives and his daughter on the outskirts of town.

However, the satellite images showed no neighbors for a few hundred yards in any direction, which meant Durston would be able to watch the house without being detected.

"I'm going to do a walk-by," Durston said. He needed to find somewhere to wait unseen for Gray and his folks to leave, somewhere that wasn't wet. The forecast was for rain, and he didn't want to be breaking in and leaving telltale signs all over the house.

"Want me to come with you?" Feinberg asked.

"No, I got it. You go and find us something to eat. I'll be back in a couple of hours."

Durston put his jacket on and left the building. The street lights ended at the edge of town, and he followed the road in darkness. It was three miles to Gray's house, and during the twenty minutes it took to jog there, only three vehicles passed him on the road. That was good news, but the rain that started halfway through the journey was not.

If it kept up through the night, he would have a hard time not leaving wet footprints all over Gray's place.

The GPS on his phone showed that he was three hundred yards from Gray's house, and he could see lights in the distance confirming that he had arrived at his destination. He stuck to the side of the road as he neared the building, a white two-story affair with a terracotta roof. There were lights on the ground floor, and on the upper level a small window lit up for a few moments before returning to darkness. Durston assumed it was the bathroom.

He kept walking, putting a couple of hundred yards between himself and the house, then climbed through a hole in the hedge that lined the road. The ground was soaked, and when he reached a patch of mud it sucked at his feet. Durston thought about buying a pair of rain boots, but that would mean waiting for the shops to open the next morning, and he might miss his chance to gain entry to the house. He'd enter barefoot if necessary.

He had no idea what the occupants did during the day. The boss wanted this done in the next twenty-four hours, which gave him no time to build up a dossier on the movements of Gray, his daughter, and the Hatchers. If they didn't leave the house the next morning, then he would have to go to the backup plan, which was to find a safe place nearby and wait for Gray to go online. When he did, Durston would hijack the Wi-Fi connection and jump on to the network. Once connected to Gray's computer, he could install the spyware remotely. He preferred not to do it this way for many reasons, mainly because there was no guarantee Gray would go online. They really needed him to go into town so the team could work him over, forcing him to contact the others.

If this were America, they would be doing everything from the safety of an air-conditioned office. Unfortunately, the NSA's reach didn't include the ISPs and telephone exchanges of other sovereign nations.

Durston circled the perimeter of the building, taking his time and ensuring his feet didn't fall on anything that could give him away, such as twigs or squeaky dog toys. He hadn't seen anything about a pet in Gray's file, but it hadn't been updated in quite some time. A dog would be bad news, whichever method he used to complete his mission.

At the rear of the house, hidden in the tree line, Durston took out his night-vision binoculars and scanned the target. The back yard was protected by a wall made from local stone. At four feet high, it would be enough to hide behind while he waited for someone in the house to connect to the Internet. It was only twenty yards from the house, which should be within range of the Wi-Fi. It also gave him a good view of the car parked out front.

Having seen all he needed to see, and not wanting to push his luck, Durston made his way back to the road and jogged back to the guest house. He wanted to eat and be asleep by eleven for a 5 a.m. start.

CHAPTER 8

"It has to be somewhere . . ."

Tom Gray wondered if every child had the magic ability to lose a shoe five minutes before leaving the house each morning, or if it was only Melissa. He joined Mina and Ken Hatcher in searching for the missing footwear, and eventually found it in her toy box. He tried once again to explain that there was a place for everything, and putting everything in its place made it easier to find, but Melissa had moved on to choosing a companion for the ride into town. She was having a hard time deciding if Peppa Pig or the strange blue Igglepiggle creature should accompany her.

"Come on, darling, get your shoe on and pick one friend so we can go. Grandad needs to get to the doctor."

Ken Hatcher was actually the uncle of Tom's wife, Vick, who'd died four years earlier, but he and Mina had been happy to take on the role of grandparents for Melissa.

"I don't know what to take."

"Take them both, darling," Mina said, ending the standoff and lighting up the little girl's face.

Mina took Gray by the arm and led him toward the door. "You could try a little compromise like that now and again," she whispered.

Gray looked back down the hallway at his daughter. "I don't negotiate with terrorists."

It earned him a light-hearted smack on the arm, and he couldn't help but smile. His world revolved around Melissa, and it would for the rest of his life. He was torn between wanting her to grow so that he could see her develop, and having her remain a child forever. There would undoubtedly be tough times ahead—the teen years, boyfriends, moving into her own place. All the joys of parenthood, things he would have to face alone.

That was one of the drawbacks of living in such an isolated community. There were plenty of parents in the town, but few had a good grasp of English—and Gray's Italian needed a lot of work. The peaceful atmosphere more than made up for the lack of a social life, but Melissa needed friends to play and grow with. At some point she would outgrow her dolls and turn to other interests, such as the Internet and boys.

It didn't bear thinking about.

With her shoes now on, Mina helped Melissa don her coat and Gray handed her a Noddy-themed umbrella, then opened the front door. Melissa squeezed between his legs and was first to the car.

As Gray watched Melissa skip down the drive, he pined for her mother. Vick had been murdered when Melissa was only a baby, and his daughter's wavy blond hair and bubbly nature made him think of her every day.

Mina drove, as she always did. Ken had given up his license after his eyesight had deteriorated, and Gray preferred to jog the three miles to town. It was short of the five miles he used to run each day, but his days in the SAS were well behind him. Three was enough for a man on the wrong side of forty.

They reached the center of town minutes later, and Gray and Melissa got out at the ATM. The rain had stopped, but it was still bitterly cold.

"We'll get some food in, then meet you at the doctor's in about forty minutes," Gray told Mina. He closed the door and waved the couple off.

~

The moment Gray and the others left the house, Durston got on comms.

"Looks like they're heading out. Wait one."

He was relieved that he wouldn't have to sit outside the house for hours. The rain had stopped during the night, but the temperature had plummeted since his last visit. He'd already spent three hours watching Gray's home from behind the garden wall, and hadn't relished spending the rest of the day at the mercy of the elements.

He waited for the car to leave the grounds and turn right toward town, then informed his colleagues, who were waiting in their own vehicle for news. He gave them the car's make, color, plate number and direction of travel, then broke cover and ran through the garden to the back door. He had it open in seconds. He took off his boots and walked through the kitchen and into the living room. There was no sign of a computer, so Durston checked the other rooms on the ground floor.

One door led to a small office. Durston saw a laptop and a bunch of file folders, and when he opened one and checked the contents he saw that they related to Minotaur Solutions Ltd. This was definitely Gray's room. He went to power up the laptop but saw that it was already on, though locked. He clicked on the screen, and when it prompted him for his credentials, he opened his phone and checked a list of backdoor passwords that he'd lifted from the dark web. He tried the one that matched the make and model of Gray's machine, and it accepted it. Durston took a USB stick from his pocket and inserted it into the slot, then navigated the directory and opened the relevant folder. He clicked on the .exe file and waited until the software was installed on the laptop. Once it was, he removed the stick and locked the computer again.

The best part was that, while connected to Wi-Fi, the laptop would act as a transmitter to every other device in the immediate area. If Gray had another phone in the house, the moment he turned it on, the malware would be downloaded over the wireless network. Once it identified the type of device, it would install the keylogger and anything else that was compatible. In the case of a cell phone, it would record and transmit the data and metadata for all calls and texts.

Durston wiped down everything he'd touched, then went upstairs and checked the other rooms for electronics. Finding none, he retraced his steps to the back door and put his boots back on, then called his colleagues.

"All set. He's all yours."

"Roger that. We're going in."

Durston closed the back door, then set off for the rendezvous point.

~

As Gray stepped up to the ATM machine, he looked around out of habit. He'd known a couple of people who had been the victim of distraction thefts, so he always made sure there was no one near him when he used the machines.

That was when he saw the Renault pull up on the other side of the street. The buzz cut and leather jacket of the driver grabbed his attention, setting him immediately on edge.

"Daddy! You're hurting me!"

Gray looked down at Melissa and let go of her hand. He hadn't realized he'd been squeezing it so hard. He knelt in front of her and kissed her tiny fingers. "I'm so sorry, darling," he said, with one eye on the Renault.

Two men had climbed out of the back seat, and they were heading his way. He recognized the look they shared and pegged them as military, either former or current. Whichever it was, they reeked of trouble.

Gray took Melissa by her other hand and led her away from the ATM. He needed to get her somewhere safe, and the only place he could think of was the café. If something bad were about to happen, he didn't want Melissa witnessing it, and the owner was a friend who could handle himself. Like Gray, Marco had spent time in the armed forces. Unlike Gray, Marco was built like a tank.

Gray led Melissa to Marco's place, and when he glanced back he could see that the two heavies were still following him and had closed to within twenty yards. He opened the door and saw his friend behind the counter, preparing a sandwich.

"*Ciao, Tom. Come va?*"

"Marco, I need help."

The big man's forehead furrowed. "Problem?"

"Maybe. Can you keep an eye on Melissa for a few minutes?" When Gray saw the confusion on Marco's face, he resorted to what many people do in foreign countries. "You watch Melissa? Five minutes? I go?"

"*Si, si, non c'è problema.*" Marco smiled.

Gray tried returning the expression but suspected that it came out as a weird grimace. He turned and left the café just as the two strangers mounted the curb. There was no emotion on their faces, and Gray wondered if they were simply heading inside for something to eat, but that thought was quickly dispelled.

"Courtesy of the ESO," the first one said, and launched at Gray, aiming a boot at his chest. Gray easily parried it and countered with a punch to the man's jaw that connected with a satisfying crunch. He followed up with a left, but it glanced off his opponent's forehead. The other man joined in, catching Gray on the side of the face with a fist that felt like a hammer, and Gray's legs barely kept him upright. He'd never been hit so hard in his life, and wasn't about to let it happen again. He shook his head to clear it, then spun and delivered a roundhouse kick that almost tore the second thug's head off. The man went down, and Gray turned to face the other just in time to block a fist traveling at speed toward his face. He struck out with his open palm and caught the man in the sternum. The crack of bones echoed the pain on the man's face.

"Sonofabitch!" he grunted, but kept coming. A vicious uppercut sent Gray staggering backward, and he fell over the café's wooden advertising board and ended up in a heap on the ground. He tried getting to his feet, but kicks started flying in. One caught him in the temple, and he collapsed once more, curling into a ball to prevent damage to his major organs.

The assault stopped abruptly, and Gray heard shouting and the sound of a distant siren. He opened an eye and saw Marco chasing after one of the thugs with what looked like a meat cleaver. The two attackers were sprinting to the car they'd arrived in, and they managed to get inside the moving vehicle before Marco could take a swipe at them.

Gray sat up, trying to make sense of it all. A single word jumped into his head.

Melissa!

He staggered to his feet and stumbled into the café, and relief flooded over him when he saw his daughter behind the counter tucking into a chocolate slice.

"*Stai bene?*" Marco asked as he returned to the shop.

Gray flexed and checked for broken bones, but the only damage seemed to be a nasty headache. "I'm okay," he replied.

"I call *Polizia*," Marco said, which explained the noise bearing down on them. He handed Gray a wet cloth to place on his swelling temple and offered him a seat at a table. "I bring tea."

A minute later, two police officers entered the café and spoke to Marco. The exchange went on for a few moments, then Marco pointed to Gray and the officers sat down opposite him.

"Signor Gray, can you tell me what happened?"

Gray was grateful that at least one of them spoke English. He explained that he'd seen the car arrive and the two men get out and assumed they were up to no good.

The cop asked how he knew.

"Their build, the way they carried themselves. They seemed focused on me for some reason."

"Do you have any idea who they were?"

Gray shook his aching head and immediately regretted it. "Never seen them before."

He did, however, know who they were working for, but if the tales he'd heard from Sonny Baines and Len Smart were true, then the last thing he wanted to do was tell the police about his suspicions.

He'd met Sonny and Len in London shortly after their release from the American prison. They'd turned up at Gray's hotel unannounced, armed with Cheshire cat grins and bottles of cold beer. The tales they'd told that evening chilled Gray to the bone, not least how easy it was to track his movements. Their parting words had been to trust no one, not even the police.

Especially not the police.

The policeman asked Gray for his account of the confrontation, which though it took a while to describe, had in fact been over in less than a minute. He gave the cops vague descriptions of the attackers and their car, and the officers promised to get in touch if they had any leads. The one who spoke English handed Gray a card as they left.

Marco brought Melissa over to Gray's table and put a bowl of ice cream in front of her.

"What happened, Daddy?"

"Nothing, sweetheart. I tripped over the sign, that's all."

"Silly Daddy," she giggled, and tucked into her dessert.

"Yeah, silly Daddy indeed. Sit here for a minute, darling. I just have to have a chat with Marco."

Gray walked to the door and gestured for the owner to follow him outside.

"Have you seen those men before?" Gray asked.

Marco shrugged. "No. Not from here."

Gray had suspected as much. The one who'd spoken had sounded American.

"Okay, thanks. What do I owe you for the food?"

"*Niente*, my friend. On house."

Gray thanked the big man and followed him back inside, where Melissa was just finishing up her ice cream.

"Time to go shopping, sweetheart."

On the way out, Gray dropped a twenty in the tip jar and gave Marco a wink. "*Ciao.*"

Shopping was the last thing on his mind, but he had to act normally for his daughter's sake. They pushed a cart around the supermarket for half an hour, then carried the bags down the road to the doctor's surgery. Mina and Ken were already sitting in the car.

"What happened to you?" Mina asked.

"Daddy tripped on a sign," Melissa said.

Gray got a stare of disbelief from Mina. He gave her an "I'll tell you later" look in reply.

All the way home, Gray toyed with his phone, but Len had been adamant that he should never try to contact them using that number. Instead, they had set up a shared email account in which he could create a draft of an email that they could access. The plan was for them to check it every day. That way, no messages were actually sent. They'd used the same thing years earlier, when Gray had taken the criminals hostage, and it had worked like a charm.

He missed his best friends, but understood their need to disappear. After all they'd been through, they would be marked men for life. And simply being in contact with them could spell trouble for Gray.

Is that what this is all about? Had the ESO come after him as a way of punishing Len and Sonny? If so, would it end here, or would they be back at some point to finish the job?

The car doors opened before Gray even realized they were home. He helped Melissa out of the car, then took her into the living room and let her choose a DVD to watch.

"Can you keep an eye on her for a while?" he asked Mina. "I have to do something in my office."

"Sure, just as long as you tell me what's going on."

Gray hesitated, then realized he would have to let her know eventually. He led her into his office and closed the door behind them.

"Remember what happened to Sonny and Len last year?" he asked.

"Of course. Those poor boys didn't deserve to go to jail."

"Well, they're no longer in prison. The US president let them out a few days after sentencing and gave them new identities. He's investigating that organization called the ESO that they helped to expose."

"They're free?" Mina asked.

"Yes. They have been for a couple of months now. I met them the last time I went to London. I don't know where they are, but I have a way of contacting them. The thing is, today someone attacked me, and said it was courtesy of the ESO. I think they tried to hurt me to get back at Len and Sonny."

"Oh, Tom! That's terrible! Why would they do that?"

"To be honest, I really don't know. That's why I have to let Len and Sonny know what happened and see what the Driscoll woman thinks. She knows more about the ESO than anyone."

"But I thought the president shut them down and arrested them all."

"No, he got one of the top guys, but it looks like the rest are still active and out for revenge."

Mina looked worried, and Gray felt the same way. If they'd come for him, who was next? Mina and Ken? Melissa?

"Let me contact Len and see if he knows anything."

Mina reluctantly left the room and Gray sat in front of the laptop. He entered his password, then opened a browser window and clicked the bookmark for the email account. When it asked for his password, Gray started to enter it, then paused.

How easy was it to track a person's online activity these days? Gray had known the British security services had that capability when he'd prepared his siege back in 2011, and the draft email idea had worked to circumvent their abilities. But that was seven years ago, and technology had come a long way. Would the ESO know the draft email trick? Sure they would. He'd told Andrew Harvey of MI5 all about it, and the intelligence services of the world had had years to come up with countermeasures, one of which would be to monitor his computer.

Gray left the laptop as it was and walked into the kitchen, where Mina was preparing lunch.

"I have to nip out," he said. "Can you keep an eye on Melissa?"

He hated to leave them unprotected, but he had to get in touch with his friends to find out what was going on. Taking his family into town with him wasn't a good idea. The goons might still be around, and he didn't want them in harm's way. At least at home they could lock the doors and windows.

"Of course. Are you going to be long?"

"No, I just need to run an errand. While I'm gone, keep the place locked up, and call me if anyone turns up. I need to borrow the car."

Mina told him where to find the keys and Gray slipped out without disturbing his daughter.

He drove into town, one eye on his rearview mirror in case the goons showed up again. He parked outside an electronics store and went in, emerging minutes later with a new, unregistered cell phone. Back in the car, he drove back to within half a mile of the house. He couldn't see any signs of danger and Mina hadn't called, so he powered up the burner phone and went online, logging into the dead-drop email account. After what had happened, he didn't want to wait a day for a reply, so he composed a short message.

Call me at the following number. Urgent. ESO after me.

He added the burner phone's number, then saved the message as a draft. All he could do now was wait. He didn't know when Len or Sonny would see the message, only that they checked the account daily. It could be in the next ten minutes, or ten hours from now.

It was only a quarter of an hour later when the new cell phone rang.

"Whose phone are you using?" Len Smart asked.

"Mine. I just bought it."

"Did you register it in the shop?"

"No," Gray replied, "it's clean."

"Good. Just had to check. Where are you?"

"Half a mile from the house."

"Turn off your Wi-Fi," Len said. "Just use the phone's data."

"I'm using the data."

"Good. Tell me what happened," Len said.

Gray told him all about the encounter, including the thugs' reference to the ESO. "A friend helped me fight them off and the police arrived, so they ran. Do you think they'll be back?"

"I don't know. I'm going to check with Eva and I'll get right back to you. Stay where you are."

The phone went dead, and Gray wondered how far this was going to go. He would probably have to take Melissa and leave Italy. Whether the Hatchers would be willing to sell up and move was another thing. They'd planned to live the rest of their lives here. It was unlikely that they would just up sticks and move, based on a possible threat and no more.

Gray wasn't taking any chances, though. When he got home he would start looking for somewhere else to live. If Ken and Mina wanted to move, too, that was fine, but they were old enough to make their own decisions.

The phone rang again and Gray picked it up.

"Have you got a pen and paper?" Len asked.

"Give me a second." Gray rifled through the glove box. "Shoot."

Len reeled off a string of digits and letters. "That's the web address of a messaging app. When you get to the page, you have thirty seconds to enter the password."

Gray wrote down the sixteen-digit code.

"Once you're in, the app will automatically download. Use that from now on, and only on this phone. And remember, never turn on the Wi-Fi."

Then Len was gone once more, and Gray opened the browser on the phone and entered the seemingly random address. When the page loaded, the only items on it were a password box with a button underneath. Gray carefully entered the code he'd been given, then clicked Done. His phone informed him that installation was in progress, then a small check mark showed that it had completed. He closed down the browser and saw the Shield icon on the screen. When he pressed it, the app opened. It looked like any other messaging program he'd used in the past, only this one asked him for his initials. Gray entered TG, then typed his first message.

What now? And is this secure?

The reply took a minute to come through.

Yes, it's secure. Eva believes they targeted you so that you would try to make contact with us. You did right not to contact me directly, but they'll probably try again. You and Melissa are not safe. They killed Farooq's friend to get him to lead them to us.

The final sentence was like a stake to the heart. The thought of them hurting his daughter stirred the beast inside him.

Where should we go?

He sent the message, then realized it wasn't the right question to ask. The big concern was how to get out of Europe without the ESO tracking his movements. He could easily drive to another country within the EU, but then renting accommodation would be tough, as would getting money out of the bank. Every transaction would leave an electronic trail for them to follow. He would need a new identity if he was going to stay out of the ESO's reach in the long term.

Once he overcame that hurdle, *then* he would have to decide where to live. Perhaps the Canary Islands. His Spanish was much better than his Italian, and there was a large expat community he could disappear into. There would surely be a local school that taught in English and Spanish for Melissa, and the year-round sunshine would be an added bonus.

Gray was warming to the idea when Len Smart's reply came in, shattering the illusion into a million pieces.

Eva said you have to come with us. Help us to find them and put an end to this.

CHAPTER 9

Gray read the message over and over.

Eva said you have to come with us. Help us to find them and put an end to this.

Unpleasant as the thought was, he had to accept that simply moving to another country was no solution at all. He wasn't running from a debt collector or the tax man; these people ran most countries in the world and had technology he could only dream of. They would find him in a heartbeat, and Melissa would be squarely in the line of fire.

Eva was right. Gray had to help them end this; otherwise he and his family would spend the rest of their shortened lives looking over their shoulders.

The first thing he needed to do was find somewhere safe for Melissa. He couldn't leave her with Ken and Mina, and he certainly wasn't going to take her with him. The bullets would inevitably start flying, and he wanted her nowhere near him when that happened. He needed someone who was comfortable with kids, and preferably someone he knew and trusted.

Only one name sprang to mind.

Gray replied to Len's message.

Ok, I'm in. Meet with Andrew Harvey and ask him to arrange a new passport for me and a way to get out of Heathrow unde- tected. I'll send flight details later.

Smart replied in an instant.

Will do. Send me a recent photo for the new passport. See you soon.

With that message, Gray's quiet life was over. He'd been in a few scrapes since leaving the SAS all those years ago, but this promised to be one of the toughest challenges yet.

He looked up flights to Heathrow and bookmarked one for that evening. It had a stopover in Milan but would get him to London by 11 p.m.

Gray checked the area, then drove back into town. His first stop was the ATM, where he withdrew his daily allowance, then to the bank to draw another thousand euros over the counter. After that was the travel agency, where he purchased the plane tickets in cash and used the name Grayson. He still had a valid US passport in that name, as did Melissa. Andrew Harvey had given it to him when he'd wanted to disappear and start a new life in America. A venture that had lasted only a few short weeks.

With the tickets purchased, he went to a different store and bought another cell phone, then drove back to the cottage, where Mina was dishing out lunch.

"Something's wrong, isn't it?"

"Yeah, about that," Gray said. "Can we go outside for a minute?"

He handed Mina her coat and they walked into the garden.

"We have to leave," Gray said after closing the door.

"Who? All of us?"

"Me and Melissa, definitely, but I'd feel safer if you and Ken disappeared, too. Some very powerful people were behind the attack this morning, and I've been told they may be back. I think they're using me to get to Len and Sonny, and if I'm gone, they might take it out on you."

Mina looked stunned. "But . . . where would we go?"

It was a good question. If they didn't have new identities, the ESO would track them down in minutes. They needed to disappear, completely off the grid, for as long as it took to bring down the ESO once and for all.

Gray thrust his hands into his pockets and looked around the garden, hoping for inspiration. He didn't find much, just a reclaimed iron table and four folding chairs. The rest was a large square of grass surrounded by a border of flowers. His eye was drawn back to the chairs. They'd taken them on their last holiday, to a campsite on the southern coast.

"Does Ken still have the tent?" he asked her.

"Yeah, it's in the loft."

"Great. Then you two are going camping. I'll look up a suitable location within driving distance, but first, a few crucial ground rules. Leave your phones in the house when you go. I've bought you a new one and I'll put Andrew Harvey's number in the contact list before I leave. If you have any worries, give him a call. Until then, keep it turned off, and never connect it to Wi-Fi. And don't use your computer before you go. You need to stay offline from now on."

"Are you sure all this is necessary?"

"Trust me, your life could depend on it. And don't tell anyone you're leaving."

Gray immediately regretted saying it as tears welled up in Mina's eyes. He pulled her close and hugged her tight.

"I'm sorry I dragged you into this, but I'm going to do all I can to end it."

Mina got herself together, then nodded and wiped her eyes. "I guess I should start packing."

"Yeah. Me too."

They walked back inside and split up, Gray going to tell Melissa that they were going on a trip, and Mina to break the news to her husband.

Two hours later, the quartet were in the car. Gray drove to the airport, just in case the bad guys showed up again, but the journey was mercifully uneventful.

He followed the signs for departures and pulled up at the drop-off point. Melissa bounced out of the car, thrilled at the prospect of another plane ride. Gray took their bags from the trunk and said his final good-byes to the Hatchers as they got into the front of the car.

"Remember what I told you. Only use the cash, and don't give the campsite your real name."

Gray had given Mina fifteen hundred euros from the money he had in his safe, leaving him a shade under four thousand for his own use.

"Please, just get this over with as soon as possible," Mina said, on the edge of tears once more.

Gray stooped next to the window and kissed her on the forehead. "I'll be in touch as soon as I can. Don't let the bedbugs bite."

He turned and took Melissa by the hand and led her into the terminal, then found the check-in desk for their flight. It was due to open in another twenty minutes and a line had already formed, so Gray took his place at the back. He used the time to check for anyone likely to be with the ESO, but all he saw was the normal mix of passengers, some heading out on business or holiday, others returning home.

Once through security, Gray relaxed completely. They had a sandwich and a drink in an eatery, then walked to the departure gate. Gray scanned the faces for trouble, but no one looked as if they wanted to kill him.

It was a short flight to Milan, then a quick change and they were on their way to Heathrow.

He only hoped Andrew Harvey had been able to make the necessary arrangements. Len hadn't got back to him on that point, and the ESO was sure to know which plane he was on.

He would find out in a couple of hours' time.

~

As Gray led Melissa to passport control, he kept an eye out for anyone who looked out of place. If the ESO were going to make a move, it would be soon, though he expected it to be outside the airport, not where armed police officers could intervene.

He joined the queue for non-EU passengers, and when he eventually reached the front he handed over the two US passports in the names of Tim and Melissa Grayson. The official studied the documents, then ran them under a scanner and looked at his screen. He looked back up at Gray, then picked up his phone and said something Gray couldn't quite hear.

Another member of airport security came over and looked at the documents, then at Gray.

"Could you come with me please, Mr. Grayson?"

It was more an order than a question, and Gray wondered if the ESO had infiltrated the UK Border Force. If they had, then disappearing into a room with this man would be a big mistake.

Gray was sizing up the options when the tension was broken.

"Mr. Harvey is waiting," the officer said, his manner devoid of threat.

Gray released the breath he'd been holding, then took the passports back and followed the man down a corridor and into a room with no windows.

"Good to see you, Tom." Andrew Harvey smiled and held out his hand. He was Gray's height but wearing a couple of extra pounds, and the brown hair was a little longer than military regulations would have allowed. Gray shook it, and Melissa wanted in on the act.

"Uncle Andrew!"

Harvey crouched down and gave her a hug. "Someone's getting to be a big girl."

"I'm five now," she beamed.

"Thanks for helping out," Gray said.

"Any time. Len said you were in a tight spot. He dropped a note at the reception at Thames House, and I met him briefly at a deli around the corner. He said he'd explain more once you got here."

"Then let's not hang around."

Harvey led them out of the room and through a maze of corridors to a fire exit. He pushed through and they found themselves outside. Harvey's car was parked a few yards away, and they all got in. Harvey had thought of a booster seat, and Gray strapped Melissa in before getting in the front.

"Where to?"

"I booked a hotel room," Harvey said. "Len and Sonny are already there."

Harvey drove them out of the airport via a service road, and showed his ID when he got to the gate. It was then a quick drive into the heart of London, and they made idle chit-chat for Melissa's sake.

"Congratulations on the new arrival," Gray said. He'd sent a card when Harvey's daughter Alana had been born, but this was their first time face to face since the MI5 man had become a father.

"Thanks. Still getting used to it."

"I'll bet. They turn your lives upside down from the minute they appear."

Harvey managed a strained laugh. "Couldn't have put it better myself. Though if you asked Sarah, she'd say you were playing down the situation."

"Not coping well?" Gray asked.

"It hits some people harder than others," Harvey said. "Poor Sarah's always tired—which is understandable—but she stresses over the littlest things. Suddenly the house isn't clean enough, or the TV is always too loud, or the rooms are too cold."

"That's normal, mate. They want the perfect conditions for the baby. I remember spending most of my time in the dirt when I was two years old, playing marbles or building roads for my Dinky Toys. It helps to build the immune system, but tell that to most mothers these days and they'll eat you alive."

"Amen to that. But I don't dare mention it to Sarah. She'll tear me a new one for even suggesting it."

They pulled up at the hotel, which turned out to be The Ritz, where Harvey had booked a junior suite. When they got to their floor and used the key to get in, Gray saw that Len and Sonny had already made themselves at home.

It was good to see his friends again, though not under these circumstances.

Len was sipping a glass of wine, his ubiquitous Kindle resting on the arm of his chair. He'd brought a little extra baggage with him, most of it concentrated around his waist. Wherever he'd been for the last couple of months, he looked like he'd enjoyed himself.

Sonny was halfway through an ice-cold bottle of beer, but the only change Gray could see was a huge improvement in his dress sense. Gone were the jeans and T-shirt; he now sported smart slacks and a designer polo shirt.

"Looking good, Tom. And who's the little lady?"

Melissa giggled and ran over to Sonny, who picked her up and plonked her on his knee. "How old are you now? Fifteen?"

Melissa was loving the attention. "I'm five."

"And it's after midnight," Gray said. "Time you were in bed."

He let her say goodnight to everyone, then took her through to one of the two bedrooms in the suite. He pre-empted her stalling tactics by making her go to the bathroom while he filled a glass of water for her, then helped her into her pajamas after she'd brushed her teeth.

"Can I have a story, Daddy?"

In his haste to leave Italy, Gray hadn't thought to pack a book for her, so he fell back on an old favorite she'd heard a thousand times. He got as far as the big bad wolf blowing down the house made of sticks when her eyes closed and he heard the soft purr of her sleeping.

Gray crept back into the living room, took a bottle of beer from the fridge and popped the top off. "Sorry to drag you guys into this," he said.

"Nonsense," Smart replied. "If we hadn't taken the job with Eva, this wouldn't have happened. They only came for you to get to us. We're the ones that should be apologizing."

"That's right," Sonny agreed. "We never imagined it would come to this. If we'd known, we'd have blown Eva off. The last thing we wanted to do was put Melissa in danger."

"I know. No worries. So, what's the plan?"

"I think, first of all, we should fill you and Andrew in," Len said.

For the next hour, Sonny and Len recounted their experiences in America the previous summer. After being recruited by Eva Driscoll to help find the men behind the ESO, they'd found four names. One was Henry Langton, the leader of the group, and another his son, who was also a member. They also learned about Alexander Mumford and Joel Harmer. The former had been killed by Eva, and the latter was arrested on the US president's orders. Langton Jr. had been killed by the authorities, and Henry Langton had died of a heart attack shortly after being arrested. Unfortunately, Len and Sonny had been taken in by the police, too. Despite being the ones who had exposed the ESO's activities, including the murder of a group of schoolchildren committed in order to flush Eva out, they had been tried for murder themselves, and sentenced to spend most of their remaining lives in prison. They'd actually only spent six days behind bars before President Russell had granted them secret pardons and given them false identities.

Now, it seemed, the ESO had not only survived, but also recovered sufficiently to seek out Driscoll and her associates. Farooq's friend had been murdered, and he himself had been tailed to Lyon, where the ESO had tried to get to Eva. That attempt had failed, and so they'd turned their attention to Gray.

"If it wasn't you guys telling me this story," Gray said, "I'd have called that tale a huge pile of conspiracy theory bullshit."

"Trust me," Len said, "it's real."

"Thankfully, when they targeted Tom, he had his head screwed on and didn't get straight on the phone or email us, otherwise we wouldn't be sitting here now," Sonny concluded.

"They probably know I'm in London," said Gray. "I used the American passport Andrew got for me a couple of years ago. I'm sure that's in the CIA database, so they must have known I'd be on that flight."

"Not necessarily," Harvey said. "That was a favor between friends. I asked Doug Wallis over at the CIA station in the London embassy to keep it off the books. If he was true to his word, then you're safe. The document relates to a real person, otherwise it would flag up at immigration, but it shouldn't have any ties to you."

"For now," Gray said, and took a pull on his beer. He looked at Len. "It took you and Sonny a couple of weeks to identify the people at the top last time round. This time they're going to be a lot more careful. How do you plan to root them out?"

"I was hoping Andrew could help us there."

All eyes turned to Harvey.

"It depends on what you need."

"Names," Len said. "The ESO isn't just a US phenomenon. They have major influence in just about every country in the world, including England. We need to know who they are."

"We're talking about powerful people," Sonny added, "with lots of influence in government, banking, and major industry. People who put their own interests over those of their nations."

"Sounds like everyone in the Houses of Parliament is a suspect," Gray joked.

"You might not be wrong," Len said. "Not all, but a lot will be doing the ESO's bidding. I mean, if someone proposes a bill that makes it law for a rental property to be fit for human habitation, and over three hundred MPs vote against it, they aren't exactly out to benefit the people. Especially when over a hundred of them are landlords themselves."

"We have to think bigger than just MPs," Sonny said. "The ESO might have them in their pockets, but they're just pawns being manipulated like everyone else. Henry Langton was probably the richest man on the planet. We need to start thinking in those terms."

"So, we just eliminate everyone on the *Forbes* list," Harvey quipped.

"Not even close. Langton never appeared on that list, even though his fortune made the top ten combined look like paupers. If we want to get to the men at the top, we need to focus on old money, not Silicon Valley's finest."

"I could probably get you a list of those people," said Harvey, "but it wouldn't prove their guilt."

"That's fine," Len said. "We just need a starting point."

"Okay, but I'll have to run it past Veronica. She's been . . . difficult the last few weeks. Wants everything done by the book and recorded in triplicate."

"Do you think she'll let you get involved?"

Harvey shrugged. "All I can do is ask."

"There's one other favor I need from you," Gray said. "Can you look after Melissa until this is over?"

Harvey sighed. "I wish I could, but I'll be at work all day and Sarah is struggling to cope with Alana. She hasn't slept in six months, and having to look after Melissa, too . . ."

"I understand," Gray said. "What if we got a nanny in to look after both girls? You could vet them, and make sure they're qualified and not some whack job."

"I thought about that, but it's well outside our budget. I'd have to sell a kidney, and that would last us about week and a half."

"Sonny and I can help on that score," Len said. "If we said fifty grand, would that be enough to hire one for, say, several months?"

"Sure," Harvey said, "but where would you get that kind of money?"

"Let's just call it a productivity bonus from our last assignment," Sonny smiled.

"That's settled, then," Gray said. "I'll bring Melissa round to your place in the morning."

"Better leave it a couple of days," Harvey suggested. "I still have to square this with Sarah. In the meantime, you'll be safe here."

"No worries." Gray grinned. "As long as I'm not picking up the tab for this place—and that includes the room service—you can take as long as you like."

CHAPTER 10

Andrew Harvey stifled a yawn as he swiped his badge against the security panel to gain access to the office. He'd left the hotel just six hours earlier, and had arrived home just in time to hear Alana screaming for attention. He'd taken care of diaper duty while Sarah warmed a bottle, then fed her so that his wife could catch up on her sleep.

He had a feeling she'd be catching up for a few decades to come.

With only three hours of sleep under his belt, he turned on his computer, went to the staff kitchen, and made himself a coffee strong enough to blow away the cobwebs. Back at his desk, he yawned again, then entered his password and checked the internal messaging system for the latest updates.

Veronica Ellis entered the office an hour later, resplendent as ever in a pencil skirt and white silk blouse under a navy jacket. A year earlier, the fifty-five-year-old director general of MI5 would have stopped at his station for a quick chat before heading to her glass-walled office, but this morning she barely managed to grumble a 'good morning' as she passed.

Harvey decided to let her get settled in before speaking to her. He replied to a few emails and assigned new tasks to his team before heading to the kitchen for a refill. He made one for Ellis, just the way she liked it, then took it to her office and knocked on the door.

Ellis beckoned him in.

"Morning," he said, placing the cup on her coaster. "There's something I need to speak to you about. Have you got a few minutes?"

Ellis continued to type on her computer. "You'll have to make it quick. I have a meeting with the IPCO in less than an hour."

The Investigatory Powers Commissioner's Office was responsible for the coordination and oversight of all of the country's security services. Ellis had been spending a lot of time there recently.

"I'll be as brief as possible. Tom Gray needs our help."

Ellis's head snapped up. "What the hell has he done this time?"

"Nothing. Well, someone attacked him, in Italy."

"And he can't just go to the police because . . . ?"

"He thinks the ESO was behind the assault," Harvey said.

Ellis collapsed in her chair and rubbed her face with her hands. "What makes him think that?"

"The fact that they said 'courtesy of the ESO' before they beat him up," Harvey replied.

"And why would they do that? The most secretive organization on the planet, and they announce themselves before giving someone a bloody nose? Are you serious?"

"I know it sounds off, but there's more. Len Smart and Sonny Baines think the ESO attacked Gray to get him to contact them. It looks like there's some unfinished business."

Ellis knew that Len and Sonny had been pardoned by the US president, as did a handful of others in government. She also knew all about their participation in the events leading up to their initial arrest and prosecution.

"It doesn't make sense," she said. "Every government in the world—including our own—is investigating the ESO. It's a witch hunt on a global scale. If any of their members were still at large, they'd be keeping their heads down, not attacking civilians and telling them who they were. Are you sure it wasn't someone with a grudge against Tom who was using the ESO as an excuse?"

"He doesn't think so. They were American, for a start. He hasn't spent enough time over there to piss anyone off."

Ellis sighed. "What does he want us to do?"

"Give him the names of anyone who could be linked to the ESO."

Ellis chuckled, then turned it into a full-blown guffaw. "Oh, Andrew. Do you realize how stupid that sounds?"

"I don't see why," Harvey said.

"Well, let me enlighten you. For the past three months, I've been under the microscope. Ever since the election that was triggered by President Russell's investigation, the new home secretary has been sweeping clean with his new broom. Over in the States they replaced the heads of the FBI, CIA, NSA, and every other intelligence service en masse. Sebastian Faulkner has been looking for a reason to do the same over here, but our labor laws are a lot more stringent. He has to prove guilt, or at the very least culpability. That's why I've been hauled before the IPCO every day for the last few weeks. They suspect I was taking orders from the ESO and won't rest until either they prove it—which they won't, because it never happened—or I get so frustrated with the entire charade that I step down. And I don't mind telling you, that isn't going to happen."

Harvey was shocked. How anyone could suspect Ellis of collusion with the ESO was beyond him. But then, he'd worked with her for years. The new home secretary was only doing his job. Still, if anyone had asked Harvey to pick a million people suspected of being ESO members, Ellis wouldn't have even come close to making the list.

"I'm sorry," he said. "I had no idea."

"Don't be. It wasn't your fault. However, when it comes to the ESO, you'll forgive me if I don't jump up and down with joy. I've been forensically audited, every bank account scoured for unusual payments or receipts. They've been going through our databases looking for any sign that we were doing searches not strictly in line with legitimate operations, and that's going to take a long time. Expect yourself to be called in for questioning at some point."

"Really? They'd suspect me?"

Ellis nodded. "You, Sarah, Hamad, everyone in the building. If there's the slightest discrepancy with your bank accounts, mortgage payments, anything like that, they'll have probes up your arse before you can so much as blink."

Harvey was stunned. His mind raced to think of any instance where he'd received money that was not work-related, but thankfully he couldn't recall any.

It did, however, remind him of Gray's offer.

"Tom has asked me—or rather, Sarah—to look after Melissa until this is all sorted out. He offered to pay for a nanny as I said I didn't believe Sarah could cope with two kids right now."

"That wouldn't be the smartest move." Ellis frowned. "If word gets out that an operative on your salary was able to afford a nanny, it would be a red flag to a bull."

"Just what I was thinking. I mean, taking the cash to pay for it . . . We could always dip into our savings, short-term."

"Do you think it's wise to get involved with Gray right now?"

"Well, if I'm to be suspected of involvement with the ESO, what better way to prove my innocence than to be seen to be combating them?"

"Except you couldn't say that in an interview. 'Oh, yes, I hired a nanny so that an old friend could take the law into his own hands and kill people he suspects of being in the ESO.' That would go down a treat!"

"Not when you say it that way," Harvey admitted, "but I owe Gray. We both do. And Len and Sonny, too. I couldn't sit back while Melissa might be in danger, and she will be while the ESO's after Tom."

Ellis shook her head slowly.

"It could also prove that you're not under the ESO's influence," Harvey added.

He was unnerved when Ellis stared at him for what seemed like minutes. He knew her analytic mind was working overtime, and he prayed that it was coming to a logical conclusion.

"I'll see what I can do," Ellis eventually said. "I'll get back to you later today."

Harvey took the hint and returned to his own station. He hoped Ellis would come through, but until then, there was an equally difficult challenge to prepare for.

He still had to tell Sarah about the new houseguest.

CHAPTER 11

"Are you sure that moron installed it correctly?" Langton growled.

"Yes, sir. We have control of three cell phones and the laptop was sending data. It just . . . stopped."

"Then why haven't we got anything? Are you telling me these people never go online? It's been twenty-four hours."

"It's hard to tell, sir. I looked through their phone history and there's not a lot of activity to report."

"I'm not interested in history, I want to know why Gray didn't reach out to his friends after the attack."

No answers were forthcoming, so Langton kicked his people into action. "Where's the team now?"

"In a hotel at Lamezia Terme Airport, awaiting further instructions."

"Send them back in. I want them to hit him hard this time. Tell them to hurt the girl or the old couple."

"Roger that," Eckman said. He got on comms to speak to the team in Italy. "Viper One, this is Nest."

"Go, Nest."

"I want you back at Gray's house immediately. The gloves are off. Do what you need to, but keep Gray alive. The kid and the old couple are viable targets."

"Understood. Out."

Langton checked his watch. It would be a couple of hours before they were ready and on the scene. Time for something to eat.

~

"You heard the man," Durston said. "Grab your gear. Let's go!"

He checked that his SIG had a round in the chamber and stowed it in his shoulder holster, then picked up his bag and carried it to the door. Chuck Dubowitz and John Feinberg followed, while Hank Pendleton remained on the bed. The hit he'd taken from Gray had broken a couple of bones, and he would be out of action for a few weeks at least.

"Kick his ass for me," Pendleton said as they left the room.

"We're gonna do more than that," Dubowitz promised. He'd taken a few punches from Gray himself, and it was time for payback.

Feinberg drove, and they reached the outskirts of the town in an hour and twenty minutes. Durston gave him directions to the now-familiar house.

"Park out front," he said. "No need for stealth on this one."

Feinberg drove a few yards past the house, then reversed into the empty driveway, ready for a quick exit.

"Their car's gone."

"We're going in anyway."

The three men piled out and ran for the door. Durston tried the handle, but it was locked. He took a couple of steps back and launched his foot at the lock. The wood splintered, and the door flew inward, quickly followed by the three armed men.

Durston tapped Feinberg on the shoulder and pointed to the stairs. Dubowitz and Durston separated, checking each of the ground-floor rooms as Feinberg handled upstairs.

"Clear!"

"Clear!" Durston echoed.

A minute later, Feinberg came down and announced the upper floor empty.

"Should we wait for them to come back?" Feinberg asked.

"They're not coming back. Their phones are in the living room and the laptop's still on. They've split, and somehow they knew not to talk to anyone."

Durston got on comms and apprised Nest of the situation. He was told to pull back and await further orders.

"Let's go," he said. "We're wasting our time here."

~

"So where the hell is he?"

"We're looking," Eckman said, getting a little pissed off at Danby for constantly trying to run the show. The old man might pay the best salary on the planet, but having him jump in and direct the mission was getting to be a major headache.

"Then look harder. And find out who Gray managed to talk to. Someone gave him instructions not to use his phone or laptop."

Danby turned and stormed out of the room, and the tension dropped considerably.

"Okay," Eckman said to the four men sitting at their stations, "I want you to check all airports and seaports. Check passenger manifests, but also CCTV and compare it with facial recognition. They may have used different papers. Then issue an Interpol BOLO for their car. Send it through the NSA database."

For the moment, those were all the bases he could cover. If these measures didn't produce results, he'd have a lot of explaining to do.

~

"We've got him!"

Eckman ran over to the operative's station and looked at the black-and-white image on his screen. It showed Gray with a young girl standing next to him. "Where?"

"Heathrow Airport. They landed just after 2300 Zulu time last night. This is him at passport control."

"Where did they go from there?"

"That's the bad news," the operative sighed. "He didn't leave the airport."

"What? That's impossible."

"Well, we've been through the CCTV for every exit, and he didn't show."

"What about internal cameras? If he didn't leave by the normal exits, he must have found another way out. Bring up a schematic of that terminal and show me where he was last seen."

The operative searched for the blueprints and displayed them on a separate screen. "The last image of him is here, joining the line for passport control."

"Then check these cameras," Eckman said, pointing at three locations.

Barnaby found the feeds for the ones Eckman had selected and put them up on the big screen. He wound the recordings back to the same time as the one on the still photo, then pressed the Play button. Everyone in the room watched the scenes unfold. After eleven minutes, Eckman yelled for Barnaby to stop. The recordings froze, and Eckman moved closer to the screen.

"There they are. It looks like they're being taken to the interview rooms. Roll that one on."

Barnaby played the recording again, then cranked it up to four times the normal speed. Within a minute, three figures emerged from the room and headed away from the camera. Two of them were Gray and his daughter, but the other wasn't wearing the uniform of a border patrol officer.

"Follow them," Eckman said. "See where they go. And see if you can get a frontal shot. I want to know who the other guy is."

The footage changed as Barnaby switched to different feeds and synchronized the times. He found the trio again and zoomed in on the face of the third person. He ran it through the facial recognition software.

"Shit! It looks like we're not the only ones interested in Tom Gray. The man's name is Andrew Harvey. According to the CIA, Harvey is MI5."

The name was familiar. Eckman told another operative to bring up Gray's file, and it wasn't long before Harvey's name was mentioned as the MI5 officer tasked with negotiating with Gray during his siege. Subsequently, they'd teamed up a couple of times for unofficial business, all of it off the record. Hearsay at best.

"Send me Harvey's file," Eckman said. "I want to have something to go on before I give the old man the bad news."

He sat down at his own terminal and waited for the file to appear. It came through as a link and he clicked it, then told one of the others to get him a coffee. "Black, one sugar."

Eckman read Harvey's file, courtesy of the CIA station in London. He skipped the early years—education, family members, etc.—and went straight to his time at MI5. The file mentioned a few cases in which Harvey had gone above and beyond. He was highly regarded by the members of the US embassy in London.

What Eckman was really looking for was his personal details. He found the section on Harvey's home life. He had a house in Notting Hill, which he shared with his fiancée Sarah Thompson and their daughter Alana. The child was six months old, and Thompson was still on maternity leave. They were due to marry in May, only a few months from now.

"Masters!" Eckman shouted.

Edwin Masters put down the squeezy ball he'd been playing with. "Sir?"

"Find out how soon we can get a dozen men to London."

Masters checked the locations of all the assets and ran a check on available flights into London airports. "We could have the first eight there in six hours, and another four two hours later."

"Get them moving. I'm going to speak to Mr. Danby."

Eckman left and walked up the stairs to the old man's office. He knocked on the door and waited until he heard a bark from inside. He opened the door and walked in, standing in front of the ornate desk.

"Sir, we've discovered that Gray and his daughter arrived in London late last night."

"Late last night? And you're only telling me now?"

"He didn't fly with his own passport. We're checking the passenger manifests now, but it seems he has an alternate identity that we were unaware of."

Danby waved the excuses away. "Where is he now?"

"We're still working on that. I've—"

Danby slammed his bony hand on the desk. "Are you telling me you lost him?"

"He had help when he arrived at the airport. We've only just discovered that he was met at Heathrow by an officer from MI5. His name's Andrew Harvey. They left by a side entrance."

"Do we have access to MI5's systems?"

"No," Eckman said, "and it probably wouldn't do us much good. It seems Gray and Harvey go way back. I think this was done unofficially."

Danby stubbed out his cigarette and lit a new one. "This was supposed to be a simple task. Hit Gray, make him contact Smart and Baines, then follow the trail to Driscoll. Now you've managed to get MI5 involved. Tell me how you plan to unfuck this situation."

"Well . . . I have an idea. Gray obviously knew not to contact Baines and Smart through normal means. My thinking is, if we hit Gray again, there's no reason to suggest he'll break protocol. I think we should try a different tack."

"Such as?"

"His daughter. I've been through Harvey's file, and Gray's, too. These guys are close. I'm confident they'll be in touch again soon, Gray probably using an unregistered cell. I suggest we put a team on Harvey's house and wait for Gray to call, or vice versa. Once we locate Gray, we snatch his daughter."

"That could work," Danby said, "but it needs a little tweaking. Gray's too close to Smart and Baines to give them up. However, I like the idea of using the girl. Pick her up, then convince Gray to speak to his friends, and *they* can give up Driscoll. Baines and Smart have only known her for a few months. Given the choice of Gray's daughter or Driscoll, I'm betting they save the kid."

"I'll get on it right away," Eckman said. "I've already got a dozen assets on their way to London. We'll set things in motion the moment they arrive."

He returned to the control room and went to Art Barnaby's station. "When our people arrive at Heathrow, give them the address of Harvey's house. I want around-the-clock surveillance and an intercept kit available to them. I want to know every word that comes out of that building."

CHAPTER 12

After an hour of being scrutinized by the Investigatory Powers Commissioner's Office, the driving rain and howling wind were almost a relief.

Veronica Ellis considered walking to the Home Office building on Marsham Street, just around the corner from Thames House, but decided against it. She needed to look professional when she spoke to the home secretary, not turn up looking like a drowned rat.

She hailed a taxi and it took her just a few minutes to reach her destination. After getting a receipt for the ride, Ellis dashed into the building and showed her ID to get through security.

One good thing to come out of the whole ESO episode had been the change of government. Not that she'd voted for the incumbents, but at least John Maynard was now off her back forever. She'd worked under a few home secretaries, but Maynard had been the worst by a country mile. His successor, Sebastian Faulkner, was a far better fit for the role. For one thing, he didn't leave her waiting outside his office for a quarter of an hour in a petulant show of power.

Ellis arrived a minute early, and Faulkner's secretary told her to go right in.

Where Maynard had looked and acted like a slob, Faulkner was every inch the ministerial type. His suit was Savile Row and tailored to perfection, and he didn't have a single silver hair out of place.

"Please, take a seat." He smiled and dropped into the chair behind the desk while Ellis sat opposite him.

"Thank you for seeing me," she said. "I understand you'll be quite busy right now."

The ESO scandal had heaped pressure on everyone in government, not least the home secretary. His office was the natural pad from which to launch the investigation into the acceptance of ESO bribes by some of the country's top civil servants.

"Not at all. Though I do have a meeting in fifteen minutes, so I can't dally."

"Then I'll get right to the point. It's about the ESO. I have reason to believe they are active and have attacked a British citizen by the name of Tom Gray."

"And you heard this from . . . ?"

"One of my team. He's friends with Gray."

Ellis laid out what she knew about the altercation in Italy, and how Gray had sought Harvey's help. She also told Faulkner of the connection with Baines and Smart—and ultimately, Eva Driscoll. "I would like permission to help Gray find the men responsible."

"And just how do you plan to help him? I received transcripts of your chats with Sir David over at IPCO, and from what I've read, you continually maintain that you have no knowledge whatsoever about the ESO or their members. Has some new information come to light?"

"No, not at all. I was thinking more along logistical lines."

"Ah, you mean give him access to our databases. Let him use MI5 as his own personal detective agency, is that it?"

This was only her third private meeting with Faulkner, and on the previous occasions he'd acted with dignity and professionalism throughout. She'd expected more of the same today, but it looked as if she'd be leaving disappointed.

"That wasn't what I was suggesting, minister. Gray and his young daughter need our protection, and if we are going to root out the people behind the ESO, then it would make sense to use this opportunity—"

Faulkner stood and brushed out the creases in his jacket. "I'm afraid I can't allow that, Veronica. We have an investigation in progress. Allowing you to run a rogue operation against the same entity we're investigating seems reckless, to say the least." He paused to let her consider the seriousness of what he was saying. "From what I understand, Veronica, Tom Gray wants to help Eva Driscoll take on the ESO single-handedly. I'm not about to condone a full-blown war."

"But if we could just have access to the files you've accumulated so far—"

"So that Gray and Driscoll can use that information as ammunition in their private war? I don't think so. I suggest you have your team take a statement from Mr. Gray and pass it on to us. If we feel it is relevant to our own investigation, we'll take it from there."

Ellis knew the conversation was over. Much as she hated to let Gray down, after all he'd done for her and the rest of the team, she couldn't go against the minister's wishes.

"And just in case you were thinking of offering Gray some . . . unofficial help—might I remind you that every database search is recorded against the user. If Sir David turns up anything that even remotely smells of the ESO, I'll have you up on a charge of treason. Do I make myself clear?"

"Crystal, sir. I just hoped that if I could help bring the ESO to justice, it would end any doubts about my loyalty—and MI5's as a whole."

"You're not the target of some witch hunt. Nor is your department, I assure you. Everyone in a position that could be exploited by the ESO is under the most intense scrutiny. President Russell removed the top three layers of management from his own security services, and while I don't think that is entirely necessary here, we're keeping a close eye on everyone until this matter is resolved. The ESO is weakened, but far from dead. Yet."

Ellis rose and picked up her purse. Much as she wanted to argue her point, Faulkner seemed immovable. "Thank you for your time. I'll see myself out."

She left the office and made her way back to reception. The rain was still in full flow, but Ellis didn't care. She stepped out into the deluge and hunched her shoulders as she began the short walk back to Thames House.

By the time she reached her glass-walled office, Ellis's mood matched the weather.

She clicked the speakerphone on her desk. "Andrew, my office, please." A moment later, she waved him in. "I just spoke to Sebastian Faulkner. We're unable to offer Gray any help whatsoever."

"Not even to look after his daughter?"

Ellis thought for a moment. "That's a different matter. You said Len Smart offered to pay for a nanny, is that correct?"

"That's right. He offered fifty grand in cash."

"Then make sure he pays you by check or bank transfer. You have to be able to explain where the money came from and pay any tax on it. I'd suggest a written contract between you and Smart that makes it look like a loan, complete with a repayment schedule. Either that, or a gift from him. It's unlikely anyone would suspect it originated from the ESO, given Len's history with them."

"Will do," Harvey promised, "though I still haven't told Sarah about the new arrangement."

She stared at him for a long moment. "Well, do that soon. Do I really have to tell you that?"

"I'll call her as soon as I get back to my desk. As for Tom—"

"As I said, we can't offer him any help. Anything we do—anything at all—will be perceived by the Home Office as a deliberate obstruction of its investigation into the ESO." She stood and moved around her desk to usher him out. "You're aware that any search you perform on the database is recorded. Those records are going to be audited down to the tiniest detail, and if anything suggests we're looking for the ESO, you can kiss your career goodbye."

"Okay," Harvey said. "I'll let Tom know this evening. I'd better go and break the news to Sarah."

"Good luck with that."

Harvey turned to leave.

"And, Andrew, tell him I'm sorry. We owe him so much, and I really wish I could do more."

Harvey nodded, then walked back to his desk. Before he spoke to Sarah, he needed to find an agency that could send a nanny at such short notice. He spent twenty minutes looking up contact details, then began ringing around to check on availability. The fourth agency he tried had someone who could start the next day, and Harvey asked for the woman's details. Armed with a name and National Insurance number, he began the vetting process.

"Time to pull back," Durston said over comms. "We're moving out."

Dubowitz acknowledged the order and put his binoculars back in their case. He'd been in a field opposite the cottage for the last three hours, and there'd been no sign of Gray or the Hatchers. "Where are we heading?"

"London. Gray flew there on a false passport. We're going to pay his friend a visit."

Cold as he was, Dubowitz knew their next destination would be even less hospitable. UK winters might not be on the level of those in Minnesota, but it would be a lot worse than southern Italy.

"Send the car. I'm all set."

The rental carrying Feinberg and Durston arrived at the house three minutes later, and Dubowitz got in.

"Are we picking Hank up on the way?"

"No. He's in bad shape. Maybe he can hook up with us in a few days."

They drove to the airport. As instructed, they picked up their tickets at the Alitalia desk, then boarded the first of two flights to London.

Six and a half hours later, they walked into the arrivals area of Heathrow's Terminal 4. Durston found the Hertz desk and picked up the keys to the car that had been ordered in advance, then led the other two out into drizzling rain.

Feinberg drove, following the satnav to a hotel near Holland Park. By the time the trio had checked in, it was almost 8 p.m. Durston contacted Nest for further instructions.

"Cobra One will be in contact with you in an hour," Eckman said. "They'll have an intercept kit and will be stationed near the target building."

Durston wrote down the frequency the other team was using. "What's the mission? Do we hurt this Harvey guy?"

"Negative. I want you to relieve Cobra One at 0800 and keep an eye on the house. Harvey is a friend of Tom Gray. We wait for them to make contact, then snatch Gray's kid."

"And if Gray doesn't get in touch?"

"Then we'll go to plan B. In the meantime, I want details of everyone who visits the house and every call in and out, plus his Internet activity."

"Roger that, Nest. Out."

Durston unclipped his radio and threw it on the bed in disgust. He preferred direct action to pussyfooting around. Surveillance was a pain in the ass, and it looked like this would be a long one. Then again, for the rate he was being paid, another few days of boredom was no great hardship.

"Get your heads down," he told the others. "We'll be on station first thing."

CHAPTER 13

Andrew Harvey parked outside his three-story townhouse and got out. The rain had stopped, and the departing clouds had caused the temperature to drop several degrees. He locked the car and climbed the steps to the house, unsure of how to break the news to Sarah. Despite what he'd told Ellis, he hadn't had the courage to do it over the phone.

"Hi honey, I'm home," he said as he closed the door behind him. Sarah emerged from the kitchen, and the look she gave him said the American TV humor had fallen flat.

"I expected you half an hour ago."

Good start.

"Sorry, darling, but I got caught up at work. You look shattered. Have a sit down; I'll get you a drink."

"Treble gin, neat. And keep your voice down. I just got her to sleep."

Harvey knew she was joking. She was still breastfeeding and hadn't touched a drop of alcohol since the day the doctor had confirmed the pregnancy. He walked past her into the kitchen, giving her a kiss on the way, and put the kettle on.

"Still giving you a hard time?" he asked, rhetorically.

"It's as if her purpose in life is to give me a nervous breakdown. She cries from the moment she wakes to the second she falls asleep again."

Harvey managed a laugh, then quickly straightened his face. "I'm sure there are lots of *goo-goo-gaa-gaa* moments in between."

Sarah sighed and flopped against the sink, and Harvey saw the woman he'd fallen in love with all that time ago. She might be frazzled, but she still glowed in his eyes. Her blond hair was tied back and she'd swapped the business suit for baggy pants and his old rugby shirt, but she remained, to him, the personification of love.

"Sure, but not enough. I just can't understand how women can have three or four kids on the go at one time. It would drive me insane. It must be like trying to herd custard."

Harvey poured water into two cups and added tea bags. "Perhaps you could do with a little help around the house."

"Oh, please, tell me you booked a few weeks' holiday. That would be wonderful. I could sleep again, and—"

"Actually, I was thinking about a nanny. And . . . maybe another kid for Alana to play with."

Sarah looked at him as if he were a stranger who'd just walked in off the street. "Hello? Are you listening to me? I just said I can't cope with one, and you want us to have another? And what's this nanny nonsense? You know we can barely afford the rent on this place. We're dipping into our savings just to pay the bills each month, and you want to bring in hired help?"

Harvey cringed inwardly. *Not the reaction I was looking for.*

"Well . . . hear me out. Len Smart has offered to pay for a nanny, to help take the pressure off you and me."

"Oh, he did, did he? Just out of the blue, he calls and asks if you need money for a nanny?"

Sarah was about to go into full meltdown, something she'd done frequently since Alana's arrival. Harvey pulled her close and hugged her. At first, she resisted, but eventually she collapsed against him and buried her face in his neck. He knew she was exhausted. She desperately needed more time to herself, but in recent months alone-time had been a luxury they couldn't afford. Harvey had used up his parental leave and most of his annual leave for the year. It would be another three months before he could take any more time off work to let her catch up on life. Len's offer was a blessing, if only she could see it in that light.

"Actually, he offered it as part of a package. That's who I saw last night."

Sarah pulled away. "You saw Len? I thought it was a surveillance op."

"I'm sorry. I couldn't tell you at the time. I had to go to Heathrow to meet Tom Gray and his daughter and sneak them out through a service entrance. Some big players are after him."

"Oh, Andrew, please don't tell me you're going to get caught up in something. Trouble follows him around like a shadow."

"I'm not, I promise. He just wanted some help identifying a few potential suspects, but Ellis told me I couldn't offer him help. Officially, at least."

Sarah frowned. "What does that mean?"

"He needs someone to look after Melissa, just for a couple of weeks."

"And you said he could dump her here? On me?"

"He's not dumping her on us. Len suggested a nanny to look after her and I thought it would actually be helpful if the nanny looked after Alana, too. So that's what we came up with. Melissa will join us for a few weeks, and you'll have someone to take care of them both. Win-win."

Sarah started turning a strange shade of crimson, and Harvey steeled himself for the onslaught.

"If you'd asked me first, and I'd agreed, it would be win-win. When you invite a complete stranger into my house, it most definitely is not."

"Melissa is hardly a stranger," Harvey pointed out.

"I'm talking about the nanny!"

"Oh."

She stood, arms folded tight across her chest, and stared at Harvey with a face like thunder. His only hope was to play his trump card.

"Look, I know it isn't the ideal situation, and I could have handled it better, but we owe Tom. Big time."

Sarah's face softened a little. Harvey owed Tom Gray his life, and it was a debt they would never able to repay. They both knew it.

"I suppose a little help around the house wouldn't be such a bad idea," she said with a sigh.

Harvey's face lit up and he went to hug her, but she stopped him by holding her palm up to his face. "Before you get all excited, I want someone we can trust to look after our daughter."

"Don't worry, I've got that covered. Her name is Janice and she starts tomorrow morning."

"You went ahead and did it?" she cried, the color returning to her cheeks.

Harvey put his hands up in mock surrender. "I had no option. You know how long the vetting process takes, so I checked her out myself. She's a career nanny. She'll be perfect."

Sarah looked as if she'd swallowed a wasp. "And I suppose she's twenty-three, Swedish, and built like a runway model."

"You'll be pleased to know she's fifty-four and looks like Winston Churchill. And just think of the sleep you can get while I'm at work."

Sarah mellowed once more, and Harvey sipped his rapidly cooling tea. "Go on, have an early night. I'll take care of Alana if she wakes."

"I will, but don't think you're off the hook that easily."

He sneaked a kiss on her cheek as she passed, then followed her upstairs. Sarah went into their bedroom and closed the door, and Harvey carried on to the next room, where Alana was sleeping like an angel. He wanted to kiss her, too, but she was such a light sleeper that it would probably wake her. Instead, he tucked her in and crept back out of the room, leaving the door slightly ajar.

He could already hear snoring from his own bedroom as he went back downstairs for microwaved leftovers before a much-needed early night.

CHAPTER 14

The rain had decided to stay away, but the crisp, blue January sky meant temperatures would be hovering close to freezing. Durston was grateful not to be at the mercy of the elements. Dubowitz had drawn the short straw and was stationed at the back of the Harvey house, keeping an eye out for Gray.

Durston and Feinberg approached the white van and Durston spoke into the microphone attached to his collar.

"We're here," he said.

The team they were to relieve, Cobra One, had chosen a good location for the op. The house five doors down from Harvey's was being renovated, so no one would suspect one more work vehicle parked in the street.

The back door of the van opened and two men in coveralls got out. Durston and Feinberg took their places. They were similarly dressed in blue overalls, in keeping with the plumbing company's name plastered across the sides of the vehicle. The remaining member of Cobra One had stayed inside the van to perform the handover, and he introduced himself simply as Mitch.

A laptop was open, and Mitch went through a list of photos the team had taken during their stint near Andrew Harvey's home. He compared each picture to a handwritten list on his notepad.

"Andrew Harvey left the house at 0726 hours. He drove away in this car." Mitch scrolled through a series of images until he had Harvey in the center of the screen, getting into a vehicle. As he moved through more images, Durston saw a series of shots depicting a rather large lady as she walked toward Harvey's house. She looked down at her phone, then climbed the steps and rang the bell. The door was answered by a blond in her late thirties.

"We haven't ID'd the visitor yet. I sent the images to Nest. The woman who answered the door is Sarah Thompson, Harvey's fiancée."

The slideshow over, Durston hoped his shift would be a little more exciting than the one the Cobra team had been forced to endure.

Mitch radioed Nest, confirmed his departure, and left the van. Durston signed on and opened the thermos he'd brought with him. The aroma of fresh coffee filled the van.

Half an hour into the op, Nest contacted them.

"We have an ID on the old woman. Her name's Janice Olsen. She works as a nanny through a local agency."

"Roger that."

It wasn't particularly interesting news. What Durston wanted was for Tom Gray to show his face. Unfortunately, he was unlikely to turn up while Harvey was at work, so he resigned himself to another nine hours of boredom.

~

When Sonny's message came through on the Shield app, Tom Gray was ready to move.

"Get your coat on, sweetheart. It's time to go and visit Auntie Sarah."

Thrilled at the prospect of seeing Sarah again, Melissa became a whirlwind of activity, gathering her belongings. Two minutes later, they took the elevator down to the opulent lobby and saw the diminutive figure of Hamad Farsi standing at the reception desk.

"Great to see you again, Tom."

Gray ignored the outstretched hand and pulled him in for a man hug. "You too, Hamad. How's the leg?"

"It's fine. Time's a great healer and all that."

Hamad did indeed look well. Hard to believe that just a couple of years earlier, the MI5 agent had been run down by an SUV full of Russian mobsters and suffered severe pelvic damage.

"Andrew's waiting. We should go."

Hamad nodded to the desk clerk, who walked to an office door and opened it. Hamad led Gray and Melissa through it and took them down narrow corridors until they came to a fire exit. Outside, a black Ford was waiting in a gated courtyard.

Hamad drove them along Piccadilly to Wellington Arch, then headed north. Fifteen minutes later, they stopped outside a curry house on Edgware Road.

"No tail," Hamad said. "Andrew's down that side street. Take Melissa to him and I'll wait here."

Gray helped his daughter out of the car and led her around the corner. Harvey's BMW was where Hamad had said it would be. He opened the back door and threw Melissa's bag in, then put her in the booster seat and fastened her seatbelt.

"You be a good girl for Auntie Sarah, okay?"

"I will, Daddy. How long will you be?"

"A few days," Gray told her. In truth, he had no idea how long it would take to resolve the situation, but he wanted her out of his sight for as little time as possible. "I'll be back for you, I promise."

He kissed her, then closed the door.

Harvey rolled down his window. "I spoke to Veronica. I'm sorry, but we can't help out in any way. The Home Office actually suspects her of being part of the ESO, so if we go looking in that direction, it'll be career-ending."

It wasn't what Gray wanted to hear, but knowing Andrew, he would have done his utmost to help. It left Gray in a tight spot. Identifying the people after him was going to be a job of mammoth proportions.

"Understood. Thanks for trying. Take care of my girl."

Gray tapped the top of the car and walked back to Hamad's vehicle, waving to Melissa as the BMW passed by. In recent years he'd seen more than his fair share of action, but the hardest part wasn't dodging bullets or fighting one-on-one to the death—it was wondering if he'd ever see his daughter again.

His chest felt hollow as he climbed back into Hamad's Ford: a portent of bad times ahead, perhaps. He tried to shake it. It happened every time he had to be apart from Melissa.

"What's the plan?" Gray asked Hamad.

"Len and Sonny booked a couple of rooms at a hotel in Surrey. It's far enough out of the city that no one should be looking for you. We should be there in about an hour."

As they drove southwest, they caught up on the last couple of years, but Gray was more concerned with the immediate future.

~

"Boss," Feinberg said as he snapped away with the digital camera. "Looks like Harvey's back, and he's got company."

Durston moved to the front of the vehicle and saw the MI5 agent with a young girl at his side. He was carrying an overnight bag and walking toward the house.

"Is that Gray's kid?"

"No idea," Feinberg said. "I'll send these to Nest for an ID."

Feinberg downloaded the images he'd taken and sent a request for an immediate workup. The answer was back in five minutes, by which time Harvey had left again.

Alone.

"Viper One, that's Gray's girl, Melissa."

"Roger. Do you want us to go in now?"

"Wait one."

~

"Sir, they have the opportunity. I think we should take it."

Langton looked at Eckman the way an alpha-male lion would eye a rival male. "That's why I get paid to make the important decisions. Have you seen the photos they've been sending through? There's too much foot traffic in the area to hit them in daylight. Let me think for a moment."

Langton left the room and headed to the kitchen, where he ordered his chef to prepare him a coffee. He needed to get the girl somewhere safe, where Gray would never find her. MI5 would be all over the case in minutes, and London would be on effective lockdown until the girl was found. He couldn't let that happen. He needed time to convince Gray to speak to Smart and Baines and get them to give up Driscoll.

A thought struck him, and Langton worked on it as he walked back to the control room.

"Tell Viper One to wait until the nanny leaves in the evening, then tail her and hurt her. Nothing serious, but she must be unable to work tomorrow. Break a leg or something."

"And then?"

"One of our assets in London is female. I want you to create a cover story for her. I want it to look like she's been in the nanny business all her life. When this Olsen woman calls Harvey to say she can't get in tomorrow, he'll look for a replacement. I want you to intercept his call to the employment agency and recommend . . . what's her name?"

"The female asset? Jane Connor."

"Right. Recommend Connor as a replacement, starting tomorrow. Tell her to find an excuse to take the children out for the day. That way, we'll have a few hours before anyone gets suspicious. That'll be plenty of time."

"To do what, sir?"

"Fly them here." Langton smiled.

"You want Connor to bring the Gray girl *here*?"

"It's perfect. This island doesn't officially exist, so there's no way Gray could find her. We send him a snap of his kid on the beach, then make our demands."

"Except we don't have Gray's contact details," Eckman pointed out.

Langton could have kicked himself for missing the obvious. "Then we send the picture to Harvey, and he shows Gray."

"That would mean dumping Harvey's kid in the street," Eckman said.

Langton failed to see a problem with it. "So?"

"So, why not bring her along? Double insurance, if you will."

The house wasn't set up to accommodate a baby, but then again, they would only have to keep the girls alive until Gray had fulfilled his part of the bargain and Driscoll was dead.

"Fine, bring them both. Have the plane standing by to lift off at an hour's notice, and make sure they have diapers and formula on board."

"Sir, the jet's in Washington."

"Then get it closer! Do I have to think of everything?"

Eckman issued orders to the team. Edwin Masters began a search for airports that could take the 737, while Dennis Turner began creating a legend to turn Jane Connor into Andrew Harvey's new nanny.

"Viper One, this is Nest."

Durston listened to the instructions, then acknowledged them and ended the discussion.

"Looks like we're going to a see a little action after all, only it won't be Gray or Harvey," he told Feinberg.

He was unsure why Nest wanted a hit on the nanny, but orders were orders.

"We have to take Janice Olsen out, but make it look like an accident. Not kill her, just make sure she can't work tomorrow. She must be able to call Harvey tonight, so not too rough. Any ideas?"

"A street robbery?" Feinberg suggested.

"In this area? Unlikely. Plus Harvey'll get suspicious if his new nanny's attacked on her first day."

They batted ideas back and forth for a few minutes, before Durston came up with the perfect solution.

CHAPTER 15

Hamad dropped Gray off outside the four-star hotel in the center of Guildford, Surrey. Gray took his suitcase from the trunk and said his goodbyes, then walked into the lobby. He found Len Smart sitting in an armchair, reading his Kindle.

"Are you ever off that thing?"

"Food for the brain, mate. It's scientifically proven that people who read are more intelligent than those who don't. Take Sonny, for example."

"Fair point. So, what're you reading this time? A bit of Proust? Wittgenstein, perhaps?"

"It's *Those that Remain* by Rob Ashman. It's not often I find a serial killer story that I can't put down, but this one's gripping. I've already bought the other two books in the series, so if you could hold off on your crusade for the next couple of days, I'd appreciate it."

"No can do. We need to get cracking."

Len groaned and put his device away, then showed Gray to the room he'd booked for him. Len slotted the card into the door and opened it, and they walked in.

The room was quite large, but full of people. There were two single beds, an armchair, and a desk with a wooden seat. All were occupied.

Sonny stood and did the introductions. "This is Eva, that's Rees, Carl, Farooq, and you know me and Len."

Gray stowed his case at the side of the wardrobe and found himself gaping at Eva. She was absolutely captivating—like a young Deborah Harry, but with a steely quality that he couldn't quite put his finger on.

"Yeah, I was like that when I first met her, too." Sonny grinned.

Gray realized he'd been staring, and Carl put his arm around Eva's shoulder to show where her affections lay.

"Sorry," Gray said. "I was expecting someone a little more . . ."

"Butch?" Eva smiled. "I can break Sonny's face, if that'll help."

"It would, actually."

With the tension eased, Gray took a seat on the bed next to Sonny. "I spoke to Andrew Harvey. We can't expect any help from MI5. We're on our own."

All eyes turned to Eva.

"It was always a long shot," she said. "Though it doesn't leave us with many options. Two I can think of are President Russell and Bill Sanders."

"Just ring up the president, eh?" said Gray.

She shrugged. "He gave us the get-out-of-jail-free cards and he's taken a personal interest in the search for the remaining ESO members. The only difficulty would be getting access to him. I have a feeling that if I call the White House, they'll be in no hurry to put me through to him."

"What does that leave us with?"

"Bill Sanders, director of the CIA until Russell's purge. He ran clandestine operations when Carl and I trained back in 2006."

"Do you think it'll do any good?" Rees Colback asked. "I know he sent Carl to help us last year, but now that he's out in the cold . . ."

"We don't need access to his databases," Carl said. "We just need to know who he reported to."

"Any particular reason he should tell you?" Gray asked. "I mean, if he's a suspect, is he likely to say anything incriminating? For all he knows, you could be working for Russell."

"Maybe out of respect," Eva said. "I had something on him for years. Video recordings that could have ruined him. After he sent Carl to our aid, I handed them over."

"Then he might consider you quits."

"Not quite. I could have told Russell that Sanders was taking orders from the ESO, but I didn't. I had a feeling that information would come in handy one day." Eva turned to Farooq. "Can you set up a VoIP call and disguise our location?"

"Sure. Give me a couple of minutes."

"What's VoIP?" Len asked.

"Voice over Internet Protocol," Farooq said. "I'll use an unregistered cell as a Wi-Fi hotspot and bounce the call signal from my laptop through a hundred countries. By the time they get a trace, it'll be too late."

True to his word, two minutes later, he gave Eva the go-ahead.

Eva dialed the number she'd had Farooq find earlier and waited for the call to connect. She put it on speakerphone.

"Sanders."

"Hi, Bill. Remember me?"

"Sure. You calling to gloat? Rub my face in it?"

"No," Eva said. "I need your help."

"You've got some nerve. I should—"

"You should what? Thank me for saving your ass? You're welcome."

"What are you talking about?"

"You've got two hours to find a burner cell and call me on this number." She read out the digits and the country code. "Two hours."

Eva ended the call.

"Do you think he'll bite?"

"He'll bite. Time to get moving."

Eva and Huff rose and left the room.

"Where're they going?" Gray wanted to know.

"As far as they can in the next two hours," Farooq said. "We don't want him calling while they're at the hotel. Eva'll turn her phone on just before he's due to call, and if Sanders tries to trace her, he'll see that she's heading away from London on the M3."

"Smart move."

"She has her moments."

Sonny and Len ordered room service to each of the rooms they'd booked. It was now a waiting game, and they had less chance of developing an ulcer if they waited on a full stomach.

CHAPTER 16

Bill Sanders put down the phone and took a seat behind his desk.

Of all the people in the world, Eva Driscoll was the last person he'd expected to hear from again. Only months ago she'd been sent to prison for life, yet here she was giving him a number for a British cell phone. He recognized the country code, though it didn't mean she was actually there.

What concerned him most was her message. When she'd handed over the recordings of him making love to her all those years ago, he'd thought his troubles were behind him. But it seemed that Driscoll had held something back, despite promising she had nothing else on him.

What could it be? More copies of the one-time tryst in his lakeside cabin? No, that wasn't her style.

Whatever it was, it would have to wait. He checked the fridge, then went to the garden and told his wife he was heading out for orange juice.

He got in the car and drove to the nearest mall. He knew it had an electronics store, but first he found an ATM and withdrew three hundred bucks. Better to pay cash than have a credit card transaction to link back to him.

With an hour to wait, Sanders bought a newspaper and found a diner, where he ordered bacon and eggs. His wife had him on a sadistic muesli breakfast diet, and what she didn't know wouldn't hurt her. He washed it down with two cups of coffee, then walked to the nearby store and purchased a burner cell, which he took back to his Jeep.

He still had twenty minutes to burn, but that's all he'd done since they'd canned him a few weeks earlier: burn time . . . He had enough money that he'd never have to worry about finding work again. Which was handy, as in Washington being persona non grata was akin to having leprosy. No one wanted to associate with him for fear of being infected with his career-ending disease. He spent his days puttering about the substantial house, checking his investment portfolio, and wishing he had a liking for sports so that he could at least veg out in front of the TV every now and then.

That, and waiting for his turn under the microscope.

He spent a couple of minutes setting up the phone, hoping the fifty bucks of credit would be enough for the international call. Somehow, he didn't expect Driscoll would be talking for long.

A minute ahead of time, he dialed the number she'd given him and waited for her to answer.

"Glad you called," she said. "I need you to give me the names of the top people in the ESO."

No preamble, just give me the impossible. Pure Driscoll.

"I'm afraid I don't know what you're talking about."

"Nice try. The only reason you're not in a cell is because I didn't tell Russell you were an ESO puppet. That's something I can rectify at any moment."

"Think you can prove it?"

"Easy. I'll tell him to look at who put the kill order on me."

"They'll have already looked at that. I'm just waiting for the Feds to turn up."

"Then help me. I'll tell Russell you saved my life. That's got to count for something. Plus, if you help me stop these people, it'll look good on your part."

"Lots of woulds, coulds, and ifs in there."

"Still a lot better than you've got at the moment. These people are *still* active. They just killed Farooq's friend to get to me, and they're not gonna stop until I stop them. And the more killing they do now, the harder the Feds will come down on you for working for them."

Sanders thought about it, though there wasn't much to ponder. Driscoll was right. One look at the database and they would see his name next to the Eva Driscoll termination order. He was facing the rest of his life in prison, and in his current state of health that could be thirty-plus years. If he survived that long inside. A former director of the CIA was bound to be a tempting target for a con looking to make a name for himself.

There was, however, another angle to consider. He didn't have enough cash to disappear for the rest of his life. He had plenty of assets, but the moment he started liquidating them it would flag up on someone's radar. They'd seize everything and accelerate the investigation against him. He needed access to a lot of money, quickly, and there was only one way that was going to happen.

"I'll see what I can do," he told her.

"Don't take too long. I'll text you again later with a new number."

"Wait. It won't be today. Give me twenty-four hours."

The phone went silent, and Sanders wondered if he'd pushed his luck too far.

"Twenty-four hours," Driscoll said, and hung up.

Sanders turned the phone off and removed the battery, then put the pieces in the glove compartment.

Despite what he'd told Driscoll, he still knew a couple of major players in the ESO. They'd been overlooked when Russell had cast his net, and though they were keeping their heads down, they were still men of great influence.

He just had to decide how to play it. If he gave them up, it would certainly go a long way toward having any sentence reduced, and that was on top of Driscoll's promise to square things with the president. It might even get him off the hook altogether. The problem was, giving Driscoll their names would ignite another killing spree. It would be better to take the information to the authorities and be seen as doing his part to help.

On the flip side, he could warn the ESO that Driscoll was on the warpath. They would already know as much, if they were really the ones after her, but they'd look upon Sanders favorably for the heads-up. He could ask for a few million in a Caribbean account and new aliases for him and his wife—his passport already having been confiscated to prevent him leaving the country—so that they could disappear forever, and muddy the trail back to the people at the top. If he couldn't be found, then he couldn't be questioned about the illicit activities the CIA had carried out on behalf of the ESO.

His mind made up, Sanders drove out of the parking lot just as his normal cell phone rang. It was his wife.

"What's taking you so long? Is everything okay?"

"Sure. I got here and the engine light came on. I took it to the garage and it needs an oil change. I'll be back in a couple of hours."

Now wasn't the time to tell her about his plan. He would let her know once he'd spoken to the ESO and details were finalized.

The next step was to contact them. He drove to a neighboring mall, to a rare public telephone, whose number was recognized by the people he needed to call. He dropped a quarter and dialed the number from memory.

"Alldays Travel, Melanie speaking, how can I help you?"

"Hi, Melanie. I'm interested in your summer Cairo package."

"I'm sorry, sir, but we're no longer accepting bookings for that destination. Is there anything else I can interest you in?"

"No, that's all. Thank you."

He replaced the receiver, then stood waiting by the phone. A minute later, it rang.

"Be at the Ha Wing restaurant in Chinatown at six this evening."

The phone went dead. Traffic would be a nightmare at that time of day, so he'd need to get into DC early. He'd give his wife some excuse about meeting with his portfolio manager.

Sanders went into a grocery store and bought orange juice, then headed home for a nervous few hours of waiting.

CHAPTER 17

As she walked down the steps of the Harvey household, Janice Olsen privately celebrated what seemed like one of the better assignments she'd had. The mother was a bit highly strung, but she'd seen that in other first-time parents. She'd guessed Sarah hadn't had much help since the birth, which was soon confirmed by the tearful blond. Once Sarah had gone for a much-needed nap, the rest of the day had been pure bliss. Sure, Alana had cried, but after a change and a feed, Melissa, Alana and she had played happily together for most of the afternoon.

It sure beat some of the families she'd worked for over the years. People who had kids because they were getting on in years and it was the thing to do, not because they actually wanted children. Sarah didn't seem that kind, and now that she had some help around the house, the poor girl would almost certainly cheer up in the coming weeks.

Janice walked around the corner to the main road. She turned right again, then crossed at the red lights and joined the long queue for the bus to take her to her home in Chalk Farm. The commute was something she'd grown used to over the years. Not having a car meant taking either the bus or the Tube everywhere, and as she found the Underground claustrophobic, it was the double-deckers every time.

She arrived home a little after seven. Hers was one of four apartments in a converted duplex. It was small, but at least she had her own entrance and half of the garden to herself.

She put her key in the lock and turned it, then froze. Years earlier she'd been burgled while away on holiday, and ever since, she'd left the hall light on to deter thieves. Now the hall was shrouded in darkness, and she heard the sound of a drawer slamming shut. It came from the bedroom.

The memory of the previous invasion came flooding back. With it came anger at the thought of someone stealing her hard-earned possessions. Not that she had many, but that only made it all the more infuriating.

Janice tiptoed into the kitchen in search of a weapon. The first thing she spotted was the knife rack. She went to reach for the largest blade but thought better of it. She didn't want to kill the burglar, only hurt him enough that he'd never come back. Instead, she picked up the rolling pin. It was made from marble, with wooden handles at each end, heavy enough to do some serious damage if she got the first blow in.

As she left the kitchen, it struck her that she should call the police. Why she hadn't thought of that first, she didn't know. Adrenaline getting the better of her, perhaps. She tucked the rolling pin under her arm and rummaged inside her handbag for her phone. As she did, a figure dressed in black ran at her. She could see her precious laptop in his hand, and the phone was forgotten. She grabbed the handle of the rolling pin and swung out in the same movement, catching him on the upper arm. She heard a scream of pain, then everything went black.

~

Chuck Dubowitz ran down the hallway toward the woman standing by the kitchen door. He carried her laptop in one hand to conceal the lead-filled sap he held in his other. As he got within range, he raised the weapon to strike her, but before he could smash it down on her head, his arm exploded in pain. He howled and instinctively swiped her with a backhand that snapped her head backward. Her skull crashed against the frame of the door, and she collapsed to the floor.

He grasped his upper arm, knowing from experience that the humerus was broken.

"Fuck!"

Dubowitz looked down and saw the rolling pin on the floor next to the unconscious woman. He knelt and checked her pulse, which was strong.

"Payback time!"

He picked the pin up in a gloved hand and brought it down hard on her wrist. The *crack* was enough to tell him he'd achieved his aim.

"Viper One, Viper Two," he moaned over comms.

"Go ahead, Viper Two."

"It's done, but the bitch broke my arm."

"Roger that. See you at the RV."

Dubowitz looked out the back door and saw that the coast was clear. He removed the black balaclava from his head and stuffed it inside his jacket, then manipulated the broken arm so that his hand was in his pocket. Pain shot through his body as he did so, but walking down the street clutching his arm would be noticed, and he didn't want anyone taking an interest in him.

Biting back screams, he picked up the laptop and kept his head down as he walked through the garden to the street, then turned right.

When he reached the corner, Durston was waiting in the car. Dubowitz flopped on to the back seat.

"How bad is it?"

"It hurts like a bitch."

"I contacted Nest. They've arranged for a doc to take a look at it."

As they drove to the doctor's home, Durston debriefed him. Dubowitz said he'd stolen the laptop to make it look like a real robbery, but also to spite the woman for breaking his arm.

"Just don't use it to watch porn," Durston said. "At least not 'til your arm's better, anyway."

"Oh, ha-fucking-ha."

Despite his crude joke, Durston was pissed that he would be another man down for the rest of the mission. At least the nanny wasn't seriously injured and would be able to play her part.

The next step was to wait for the Cobra team to intercept Harvey's calls, then ensure the rest of the op went as planned.

CHAPTER 18

Harvey put the last of the dinner plates into the dishwasher, then poured a glass of red wine and went to join Sarah in the living room. Alana was on the brink of sleep, so he decided against turning the television on.

"How was your day?" he asked quietly as he stroked his daughter's cheek.

"Surprisingly good. I take back everything I said about hiring a nanny. She was a godsend. I barely heard the girls all day and managed to get a couple of hours in the afternoon."

"That's great. With the money Len gave me, we should be able to keep her for another six months at least."

"Oh, that would be wonderful. If only we could get Alana to sleep through the night. I'd love to get back to work by the summer, but my body clock is just so messed up."

Harvey's was the same. He'd done his share of midnight diaper changes, and once he was up he had difficulty getting back to sleep.

"It gets easier, or so I'm told. Here, let me take her upstairs and tuck her in."

Sarah handed Alana to him and he whispered a song as he carried her up to her bedroom. It was right next to theirs, though for the first few weeks the crib had been in their room. That hadn't worked out well, with both parents forced to wake when she started crying.

Harvey placed her in the crib and tucked the cover around her. He quietly sang her a lullaby, then kissed her forehead and went through to check on Melissa. She'd gone to bed an hour earlier and was sleeping with her arms wrapped around one of Alana's teddy bears. Harvey gave her a gentle pat on the head, then returned downstairs.

"What's new at work?" Sarah asked.

"Not much. The cell we're investigating in Luton's been—"

Sarah's phone rang, and she checked the caller ID. "It's Janice."

She said hello and listened for a few moments. "Oh, I'm so sorry . . . Of course, I understand . . . no problem . . . Okay, you take care of yourself and I'll speak to you soon. Bye." Sarah set down her phone and turned to her fiancé. "Poor Janice. When she got home she found a burglar in her apartment. He stole her laptop and a bit of cash. As he tried to get out, he knocked her unconscious. It looks like she fell on her wrist and broke it."

"That's terrible. Has she called the police?"

"Yeah," Sarah said. "They arrived at the same time as the ambulance. They're checking the place over now. She's sitting in A & E, so she won't be home for some time. She said she's sorry for putting us in a spot."

"The main thing is she's okay. Apart from the wrist, obviously. Though I guess she won't be coming in tomorrow."

"No. She called the agency to let them know. Fortunately, they've got an after-hours line. She said we should call and find a replacement for the next few weeks."

Harvey took his phone from his pocket. "I'd better do that now."

"Ready for your performance?" Durston asked.

Feinberg nodded. His English accent was flawless, making him the perfect man for the job. That was the reason for swapping shifts with the Cobra team.

After intercepting the nanny's call to Sarah Thompson's cell phone, Durston knew it wouldn't be long before Harvey called the agency to find a replacement. It was also something of a relief to know that Dubowitz hadn't gone over the top with the old nanny.

"Here we go."

Feinberg adjusted his microphone and clicked on the Accept button.

"Fitch-Barron Employment Agency, David speaking, how may I help you?"

"Hi. This is Andrew Harvey. We got a call from our nanny Janice Olsen just now. She's broken her wrist and won't be able to work for a few weeks."

"Yes, I received a call from her a little earlier," Feinberg said. "A most unfortunate incident."

"It was, yes. The thing is, I'm going to need a replacement. Just until Janice is back on her feet."

"I was just looking into that when you called. Please bear with me a moment." Feinberg tapped a few keys on the laptop next to him. "We do have one lady on our books who could start tomorrow. The others, I'm afraid, are booked solid."

"That's great. Could you give me her name and National Insurance number?"

Feinberg gave him the details.

"And how long has Linda been working through your agency?"

"Since 2014," Feinberg said.

"That's great. Could you give me the names and numbers of two referees, please?"

Feinberg read off the information he'd been given by control. He hadn't been filled in on the facts, but assumed someone at the other end would pretend to be past employers of "Ms. Myers."

"Would you like her to start tomorrow morning? I can give her a call now if you wish."

"If you could, that would be wonderful."

"No problem. I'll speak to her and call you back with confirmation."

"Thanks. Look forward to hearing from you."

Feinberg killed the call. "I'll give it five minutes, then call him back. Do you think he'll check her out tonight?"

"Maybe. It's almost ten o'clock, so he might leave it until he gets to work in the morning. It doesn't matter either way. Her legend's solid as a rock."

~

Harvey took his untouched wine glass through to the kitchen and emptied it down the sink. If he'd had even a sip he wouldn't have ventured behind the wheel of his car, but now he had no excuse for an early night.

He returned to the living room. "I'm heading into the office. I want to check this woman out before she gets here in the morning."

The agency had called back to say Linda Myers could be there at eight o'clock, but he didn't like the idea of her being alone in the house with Sarah and the kids while he went through the vetting process.

"Don't stay too long, sweetheart. Just do a prelim and follow up in the morning."

"Okay."

Both of them knew how long a complete forensic examination would take, but Harvey wanted to at least make a start.

He kissed Sarah and grabbed his coat on the way out. It was a quick drive to Thames House at that time of night, and he parked in his usual spot in the underground parking lot. He passed through security and took the elevator to his floor, then swiped to gain access to the open-plan office.

He powered up his computer and went to make a coffee. By the time he got back, it was ready and waiting for him to enter his credentials.

"Okay, Linda Myers, let's see who you are."

MI5 didn't have a file on every citizen in the country, but they did have access to databases that, together, could paint a decent profile picture. He first inspected the HMRC database. Armed with her name and NI number, it didn't take too long to get an idea of her employment history. It stretched back eleven years, and from the date of birth held against her NI number, he could see that she was thirty-four years of age. He didn't know if that was young for a nanny. They all had to start at some point in their lives. Why not fresh from university?

Next, he checked with the police. She had one speeding ticket, dated eight years earlier, for travelling at ninety on the motorway. She'd gotten three points and a small fine for that transgression. Again, nothing that set alarm bells ringing.

Harvey looked for details of the people she'd previously worked for. One was a barrister, while the other worked in IT. His watch told him it was too late to contact them now, so he made a note on a Post-it to call them in the morning.

After a couple more checks, Harvey felt satisfied that Linda Myers wasn't a wanted serial killer. There was more to look at, but the basics had been covered and he felt comfortable letting her into his home.

He locked the computer rather than shut it off, then swiped his way out and returned to his car. It was almost midnight, and he hoped Alana would allow him a decent night's sleep.

CHAPTER 19

Bill Sanders had only been to Chinatown a couple of times. On both occasions he'd been forced into it by family and friends, but he never would have chosen it for a meet. Of course, no one dictated terms to the ESO.

After an hour of wandering the streets, he had an early dinner at a seafood place near the White House. Not surprisingly, he recognized quite a few of the customers. He also noted the way they spoke in hushed tones, occasionally glancing his way. It was clear they were talking about him. Some of these people he'd once considered friends, others associates, but no longer. They were reveling in his downfall, and doing little to hide it.

Sanders didn't care. If the ESO granted him his wish and helped him disappear, he could spend his days relaxing on a sun-kissed beach while even the VIPs in the room would be forced to work for another couple of decades.

At five thirty he left the restaurant and the gossips and walked to Chinatown. He passed under the Friendship Archway, the giant, ornate gateway that marked the district, then entered the six-story building that housed the chosen restaurant.

A maître d' dressed in traditional Chinese garb welcomed him and asked if he had a reservation. Sanders gave his name, and the host checked it against a list. He clicked his fingers, and a waiter immediately appeared at his side. Orders were passed in staccato Chinese.

"Please, follow Cheung, sir. He will take you to your table."

Sanders tucked in behind the man and was led up a wooden staircase, then along a hallway to a door that had STAFF ONLY written on it. The waiter opened it and ushered Sanders inside.

It was a small, windowless room, occupied by two men dressed in black suits with machine pistols hanging from straps on their shoulders. Both looked American.

The waiter bowed and disappeared.

"Strip," one of the men said when the door closed.

Sanders removed his jacket, tie, and shirt.

"And the rest."

He kicked off his shoes, then his pants, leaving just a pair of boxers and his socks.

"Everything," the second one instructed.

Sanders sighed as he took off the socks and let the boxers drop to the floor. He stood there stark naked while one of them ran a device over his body and the other checked his clothes.

Satisfied that he wasn't wearing a wire, they handed Sanders a white plastic gown. He put it on and buttoned up the front.

His clothes were put in a box, and another door was opened. Sanders walked through and found himself in a space at least eighty feet long and thirty feet wide. The walls were highly polished, paneled oak. A matching table with seats for twenty took up most of the space.

Two men in their thirties sat on one side of the table. One had short black hair parted to the side, while the other was completely bald. Sanders had never seen them before, but they didn't look old enough to be part of the ESO hierarchy.

"Take a seat," the bald one said, pointing to the opposite side of the table.

Sanders obliged.

"Something to drink? Food, perhaps?"

"Just water. The food here disagrees with me. I think it's the MSG."

The one with the side parting rose and grabbed a pitcher of water and a glass. He put it in front of Sanders, then retook his seat.

"I'm John, and this is Harry. What can we help you with today?"

Sanders knew they wouldn't be real names. "No offense, but I wanted to speak to the organ grinder, not his monkeys."

"None taken," John said. "You are speaking to him. He's listening in and has full communication with us." He tapped his ear, and Sanders could see a tiny wire leading from it into the man's jacket. "Please, tell us what's on your mind."

"I will, but first I need your help. After I tell you this, I need assurances that you can get me out of the country."

John listened to his superior's reply coming through his earpiece, then repeated it to Sanders. "And why should we do that?"

"Because the Feds are closing in, and if I go down, my only hope is to turn state's evidence. That's a route I'd prefer not to go down."

"A sensible choice. What would you need in order to disappear?"

"Forty million and new IDs for me and my wife. And you'd need to fake our deaths, obviously."

"Obviously. Anything else?"

Sanders shook his head. "No."

"Okay, that can be arranged. What did you want to share with us?"

"Driscoll. She knows you're still after her, and I wanted to warn you that she's coming for you. She asked me to give her names, but I refused. You know what she did to Mumford."

Sanders waited for a reply, which seemed to take forever in coming.

"What makes her think it was us?"

"She didn't say. Just that a friend of Farooq Naser was killed in an effort to draw her out."

Another long pause. "Are you still in contact with Driscoll?"

"She got in touch with me, but we're supposed to speak again tomorrow."

"Good. John is going to write down some coordinates. I would like you to pass them on to her."

"Coordinates? For what?"

"We weren't the ones who sanctioned this hit on Driscoll. We think it's a rogue element of the old ESO. Someone who doesn't want to let it go. She'll find him there."

That made a lot more sense to Sanders. When Driscoll had suggested the ESO was back to their old tricks so soon, he hadn't thought it likely. With President Russell after their scalps, the ESO's smartest move would be to slink back into the shadows until it blew over, not rekindle the feud.

"What if I can't convince her about this? What if she thinks it's a setup?"

A long silence passed while John listened to his superior. "That's your problem now. If you want our help, you'll have to earn it. The person she's after . . . never really was one of us. We have a long-term strategy, nurtured over generations, but he wanted to achieve everything in his own lifetime. Quick to destroy people, when patience was the prudent approach. It's time to reap what he sowed."

Sanders had a lightbulb moment. "It's Langton, isn't it? He's still alive."

John gave him a curt nod. "For the sake of the service he gave us over the years—and, of course, to prevent him opening his mouth—we let him escape custody. He lives on a private island with everything he could ever wish for. Or so we thought. Everything except vengeance, it seems."

Sanders had thought Langton's death by heart attack a little too convenient at the time. The papers had run the story for a couple of days, then he'd been consigned to history. A few of the outlying news outlets had challenged the official narrative, but never with enough proof to change opinions. The whole world thought him dead and gone, apart from those who had perpetrated the deception.

"I might have a tough time getting her to believe he's still around," Sanders reiterated.

"As I said, that's your problem now. You don't have to tell her it's Langton, just point her in his direction."

Sanders could do that. All she wanted was information on the men behind the attack on Naser's friend. He'd give her the coordinates of the island and his part in this would be over.

"There's one thing you should be aware of," John said. "The island doesn't officially exist. You won't find it on any maps, nautical or otherwise. Try to google it and you'll just see a big blue puddle called the Pacific Ocean."

Suddenly the task didn't seem as straightforward as it had seconds earlier.

How would he persuade Driscoll to fly halfway around the world to an island that wasn't there? This wasn't a Kong movie.

"That's going to be even trickier to sell."

"For forty million and a new life, I'm sure you'll do your best."

Sanders started to speak, but John stood and gestured to the door. The meeting was over.

Sanders walked through the door and found the two armed men still there. He took his clothes from the box and changed, then walked back downstairs and out of the restaurant.

He pictured Driscoll with her burner phone, counting down the time until their next call. Sanders checked his watch. He had twelve hours to come up with a plan.

CHAPTER 20

Jane Connor felt uncomfortable in the clothes she was wearing, but they were necessary if she were to pass as a nanny. Her normal attire was tight jeans and a T-shirt that accentuated her toned body, but today she had on a baggy woolen jumper and a flowing tie-dyed skirt that reached her ankles. On her feet were leather sandals that were headed for the bin the moment the mission was over. To complete the ensemble, she wore glasses and had her hair tied back.

She climbed the steps to the townhouse and rang the bell. It was answered almost immediately by a blond a couple of years her senior.

"Hi," Connor said, and thrust out her hand. "I'm Linda Myers."

The woman took it, and Myers offered a limp handshake.

"Hi. Come in. I'm Sarah."

"Nice place you've got. I wish I could afford a place round here but prices are just crazy right now."

"And getting worse," Sarah agreed. "Let me introduce you to Alana and Melissa."

Myers followed her down the hall and into the kitchen. It really was a nice house, and on first impression, Sarah seemed decent enough.

It was a shame she was going to have to destroy her life.

Melissa was sitting at the kitchen table eating toast and what looked like chocolate spread, while Alana was in her bouncy chair, *goo-goo*ing at an assortment of fluffy animals tantalizingly out of reach.

"Aw, what beautiful girls. You must be so proud."

"I am, but Melissa's just visiting for a couple of weeks. She's a friend of the family."

Myers knew as much but continued to play the innocent. She squatted down next to Gray's daughter. "And what does Melissa like to do?"

"I like drawing and Peppa Pig and cartoons."

"Wow! That's exactly what I liked when I was your age. I think we're going to be great friends."

She took her turn with Alana, making appropriate noises that seemed to put Sarah at ease.

"How long have you been a nanny?"

"Eleven years. I first did it as a favor for a friend who was hurt in a car crash. She was a single mum and didn't have family close by. I just loved the experience. I can't have kids myself, but this more than makes up for it."

"And when you've finished work for the day you can go home and get a good night's sleep."

"There is that, but nothing beats tucking kids in and reading them a bedtime story. That's why I prefer the live-in opportunities, but there are none around at the moment, and I was told this is just a temporary position. A month, is that right?"

"Yes. Our other nanny Janice was injured in a burglary last night."

"Oh, how awful! I hope she's okay."

"She is. She broke her wrist, though. It's hard enough looking after Alana with two hands, never mind one."

Sarah asked a few more questions, digging a little deeper into the Myers legend, but Linda provided all the answers with ease.

"Would you like me to fix lunch?" Myers asked. "I do a mean spag bol."

"Sounds ideal. Turns out that's Melissa's favorite."

"Great. I'll take them out to build up an appetite and bring them back at midday."

"No!" Sarah looked shocked at her own outburst. "I'm sorry. I don't want the girls leaving the house. I know it sounds weird, but I have my reasons."

"That's fine," Myers said, though it was far from okay. A car was waiting around the corner to take her and the kids to the airport. It was eight thirty now, and the plane was scheduled to leave at three in the afternoon. That allowed two hours to get the kids out of the house, another two to get through London traffic to the airport on the south coast, and two and a half hours of contingency thrown in.

She was going to need every second of it.

At some point, she'd need a few minutes to herself to update the team. She'd go to the restroom and bang out a quick text message, then contact the others fifteen minutes later for updated instructions.

She understood the reasoning behind her orders. If Sarah were hurt or killed, MI5 would throw everything it had into finding the girls. That would mean heightened security at every port, making their getaway infinitely more difficult. Better to sneak away and be on the plane before the shit hit the fan.

"Could you clear up the breakfast plates when Melissa's finished?" Sarah asked. "I have to get ready for a hospital appointment at eleven o'clock."

Myers smiled. *Problem solved.*

She hoped.

"Of course," she said. "Do you want me to get them ready and come with you?"

She could see Sarah was conflicted: take the girls, or leave them with the nanny she'd only known for half an hour.

Say no. Say no.

"No. I've no idea how long it'll take, and I don't like the idea of Alana hanging around the hospital. Too many sick people."

"That's fine. I'll make the pasta for lunch and save some for when you get back."

"Perfect. I'll try to be home by two."

Sarah went upstairs, and a couple of minutes later Myers could hear the shower running. She went over to Alana, who had started to fidget and whine, and recognized the smell immediately.

"Melissa, could you show me where Sarah keeps the nappies?"

Melissa jumped off her chair, more than happy to help. She opened a cupboard and pulled out a bag containing everything Myers would need, then went back for the changing mat.

She had no kids of her own, but Myers had been around her sister long enough to know how to change a diaper. Mica had four children, and for a six-year period, shitty diapers had been a daily occurrence.

Myers deftly removed Alana's pants and pulled up her T-shirt, then took off the soiled diaper and cleaned the baby's bottom with wipes.

"Sarah puts powder on," Melissa said, standing close by.

"Does she? Then I think we should do the same."

A couple of minutes later, Alana was dressed again. Melissa tied the disposable diaper up in a scented plastic bag, put it in a box, and closed the lid.

"Can we do drawing now?" Melissa asked.

"That sounds like a fabulous idea."

Myers put Alana back in the bouncy chair while Melissa went to fetch paper and her coloring set.

The next hour flew by. Sarah returned dressed for her appointment, and she gave Myers a tour of the house. She showed her where to find the baby formula, plus the coffee, tea, and sugar, then went upstairs to show her where Alana slept for her lunchtime nap. She also gave Myers her cell number.

"If you have any problems, call me. For anything."

"I'm sure we'll be fine," Myers told her.

Sarah kissed the girls and told Melissa to be good, then took her coat from the stand and put it on. "Remember—any problems, call me."

She left, and Myers waited a few minutes before walking upstairs and calling her colleague.

"Call me back in two minutes, then bring the car round five minutes later."

She hung up, then went back downstairs and sat next to Melissa, who was busy drawing her favorite cartoon character. Moments later, Myers's phone rang.

"Hello? Oh, hello, Sarah . . . Yes, I'm sure Melissa and Alana would love that! Yes, I'll get them ready and drive there now. Okay, bye!" Myers turned to Melissa. "Sarah said you might like to go on an airplane ride. Would you like that?"

Melissa threw down her crayons. "Yes! Yes! Yes!"

"Great! Let's get dressed. It'll be cold. I'll pack a bag for Alana."

Myers took Melissa upstairs and found some outdoor clothes, then chose something warm for the baby. She threw a couple of diapers in a bag and prepared a bottle of formula, then put her coat on and picked Alana up from her chair.

"Come on, then. Let's go."

She opened the door and let Melissa go first, then pulled it closed behind her. She walked down the steps just as two cars stopped outside the house. Myers handed her phone to the driver of the first, then returned to the other vehicle. The phone would be taken to the nearest Tube station and left on a train for the authorities to follow. By the time they found the unwitting person who'd picked it up, she'd be long gone.

"This is my friend Paul. He's going to take us to the airport for our plane ride," Myers said. She held open the rear door and Melissa climbed across and into the car seat. Myers strapped Alana into a reversed child seat in the front, then got in beside Gray's daughter.

"Off we go!"

The driver took them south through London. When he got to the M23, he reset the trip feature on the odometer.

Eleven and a half miles later, he moved to the inside lane. "Looks like there's a problem with the car," he said. "I'll have to pull over."

"Oh no, nothing serious, I hope?"

"I don't know. I'll see when we . . . Hang on, that's my friend John!"

Myers saw the switch vehicle on the hard shoulder waiting for them. Paul pulled in behind it, and Myers got out and spoke to the other driver. She returned to the car.

"Melissa, John is going to give us a lift to the airport. Isn't that nice of him?"

Melissa agreed that it was, and she followed Myers to the people carrier and let the nanny strap her in. Myers returned for Alana, and minutes later they were off again.

The ruse should keep the security services off their tail. Paul would drive the car around for a while, then dump it in a remote location in the countryside and hitch a ride with one of the Cobra team. By the time the authorities found it and realized they'd been tricked, she and the girls would be on the island.

The new driver kept to the seventy-mile-an-hour speed limit. On the way, they had to endure 'are we there yet?' three times, and Alana made her own contribution by filling her diaper and crying for the last twenty minutes of the journey.

When they got to within two miles of Shoreham Airport, Myers told the driver to stop so that she could change the baby. She did so in the back seat, and five minutes later, they pulled up outside the terminal building. Inside, the driver handed over four fake passports. The clerk checked that they matched the passenger manifest, then asked them to take a seat while the pilot readied the plane.

It was a tense fifteen minutes.

Melissa began to get bored, and Alana started crying once more. Myers fed her the formula, which kept her quiet until the pilot turned up. He made a show of checking their documents, then helped carry their bags to the Cessna waiting on the tarmac.

Myers buckled the girls in, then sat up front next to the pilot. She donned her earphones and told him to put it on intercom.

"What's the plan?" she asked.

"Paris Orly. Someone will meet you when we land and take you to a connecting flight."

"Okay. Let's get this thing in the air."

The pilot went through his pre-flight checks, then taxied to the runway. The Cessna thundered down the tarmac and gently climbed before banking left and out over the Channel.

Melissa spent the first half hour staring in fascination out of the window, but she soon got bored.

"I'm hungry."

Myers turned in her seat. "We'll have something to eat when we land, darling. It won't be long."

"You said spag bol. Can we have spag bol?"

"Sure you can."

Myers was already sick of pampering the brat, but she had to keep her happy until they were on the jet. She couldn't afford to have Melissa make a fuss when they transferred planes. She expected the switch to go smoothly, but a child in mid-meltdown would arouse suspicions.

"There's a sandwich in my bag," the pilot said. "It's ham. She can have that."

"Do you want a ham sandwich?" Myers asked Melissa.

"I hate ham!"

Spoiled little . . .

"I'm sorry, darling, but that's all we have. Let's just wait until we land, and I'll get you that spag bol. Maybe some dessert, too. How does that sound?"

Melissa made a face and stared out the window.

Myers wanted to open the door and throw her out, but if she did, she might as well jump herself. She'd been briefed on how important it was to get the two girls to the island. Failure would be met with swift retribution.

"How long?" Myers asked over the intercom.

"Twenty-nine minutes."

It threatened to be the longest half hour of Myers's life. Thankfully, Melissa kept quiet and Alana refrained from producing any more toxic waste.

When they landed in Paris, the Cessna taxied to a remote part of the airport and was met by a car.

"Where are we?" Melissa asked as Myers helped her out of the Cessna.

"We had to stop at another airport, darling. This plane ran out of petrol. We have to go on a bigger one to get home."

If there was one thing she knew about kids, it was how gullible they were. Melissa seemed to accept the explanation and she climbed into the car without complaint.

"Are we going to eat now?" the little girl asked when Myers got in the front passenger seat with Alana.

"Yes. It's on the new plane. As soon as we get on, you can have your dinner."

That seemed to satisfy her. She started humming the theme tune of a cartoon while she looked out the car window as it passed a number of other aircraft. "Can I watch *Peppa Pig*, too?"

"Of course."

It was a short drive to the next plane, a private Boeing 737-700. The steps were already in place, and Myers let Melissa go first while she carried Alana on board. The car's driver helped with the baggage, and an official gave their documents a cursory glance before leaving the plane.

Myers handed Alana to one of two hostesses, who put the baby in a bassinet. Melissa sat in the seat next to Myers, right next to the forward door.

The commercial version of the plane normally had 149 seats, but the cabin had been set out to the boss's specifications, with no expense spared. There were eight soft leather seats in this section of the plane, and through a door to the rear lay three bedrooms, all with en-suite facilities. There was also a bar and kitchen, where the finest food could always be had.

"How long 'til we get there?" Myers asked the hostess, who had brought her a flute of champagne.

"We're scheduled to arrive in Venezuela in ten hours. After we refuel, Caracas to the island will be another nine hours."

"What island?" Melissa asked.

"None of your business, you little shit. Just shut up and don't say a word until we get there."

Tears welled up in the little girl's eyes, and her bottom lip began to wobble.

"In fact, do me a favor," Myers said to the stewardess. "Lock her in one of the bedrooms 'til we get there."

"She should be strapped in a seat for takeoff and landing," said the flight attendant.

"Like I give a shit. Take her there now. I don't want to hear from her."

The flight attendant unclipped Melissa's seat belt and led her toward the rear of the plane. They went through a dividing door to the sleeping quarters, and Melissa was put in the smallest room. It had a double bed, shower and toilet, and a television. The stewardess ushered her inside.

"Stay in here. Don't come out, or she'll probably throw you off the plane." She closed the door and went back to the main cabin. "I can't lock it from the outside."

"Then keep an eye on her. And if she asks for food, give her ham sandwiches, nothing else."

Myers finished her champagne as the plane began to taxi, and once in the air she ordered the beef tenderloin and boiled potatoes.

With the brat out of the way, she was determined to enjoy the next twenty hours of luxury.

CHAPTER 21

Sarah Thompson walked gingerly from the clinic and made her way to the hospital parking lot. She paid for her parking ticket, then got in and drove toward home.

The procedure on her bladder had been less invasive than she'd imagined, but it had still been uncomfortable. They'd inserted the camera up her urethra, pumped her bladder full of solution, and had a look around to determine why she was still having pain after the UTI had apparently cleared up. It hadn't worked. They'd found nothing to suggest a reason for the discomfort, which meant another series of tests in the coming weeks.

The only saving grace was that she now had some help around the house to take the pressure off. At first, she'd been hesitant. The idea of a stranger being in her home with her daughter had initially been a concern, but after a day with Janice, she had already seen the benefits.

Her phone rang as she drove, and Sarah clicked the hands-free button on the steering wheel.

"Hi, it's me. Fancy meeting for lunch?"

Sarah was inclined to turn her down, but she hadn't seen her friend Gillian for more than three months, and it would be good to catch up. She'd put her off a few times, but now she had no real excuse.

"Sure. Where do you fancy?"

Gillian mentioned the name of one of the restaurants at the Royal Albert Hall. Sarah knew it was a bit pricey, but she hadn't treated herself in a long while.

Months, to be exact.

"Okay. I'll be there in about twenty minutes."

Sarah hung up, then went to dial Linda's number to let her know she'd be back late, only to realize that she'd forgotten to get it from her.

The dashboard clock said it was half past twelve. If she took an hour for lunch, she would still be back around two, as she'd told the nanny. She thought about calling Andrew and asking him to look up a number for Linda, but decided to leave it. No need to disturb him about it.

This was one of the rare moments when a landline would have been a good idea, but she and Andrew had never felt the need to get one. In their previous apartment, the landline had been used solely to handle incoming telemarketing calls, a privilege she resented paying eighteen pounds a month for.

She arrived at the restaurant three minutes early, but spent ten minutes finding somewhere to park. When she finally got to the eatery, Gillian was already there.

Sarah ordered a mineral water, while Gillian asked for a half bottle of white wine.

They'd met at yoga class the year before and hit it off, though Sarah hadn't been able to tell her what she did for a living. Apart from getting her into a whole heap of trouble, mentioning that she worked for MI5 would have invited a host of unwelcome questions. Instead, she'd stuck to her cover and told Gillian that she worked as a PA for the owner of a freight company, a story she'd chosen because it was the kind of job nobody would be interested in.

The talk at lunch inevitably turned to Alana, and Sarah explained about her infection and how it had made looking after the baby so much harder. She didn't mention the fact that she'd hired a nanny, as that would have led to awkward questions about how she could afford such a luxury. Instead, she said a neighbor was looking after Alana until she returned.

Gillian started telling her about her boss, a lecherous old man who flirted with her on a daily basis. It was a story that came up every time they got together, and Sarah thought Gillian actually enjoyed the attention, despite constantly complaining about it.

Before Sarah realized, it was a quarter to two.

"I'm sorry, but I really have to go," she said. "Call me next week. We can do this again."

Sarah dashed out to find her car, then cursed the traffic all the way home.

She got to the house at ten minutes after two, and as she put the key in the lock she remembered that Linda had promised spaghetti bolognese for lunch.

She opened the door, and the silence struck her like a hammer. Normally the house was louder than a soccer stadium, but now it was deathly quiet. No cooking smell, either.

"Linda? Melissa?"

Sarah threw off her coat and ran to the kitchen. Coloring books and crayons littered the table, but there was no sign of anyone.

She ran back to the hallway and saw that Melissa's coat was missing, as was Linda's. Anger replaced panic. How dare Linda take the girls out when she'd explicitly told her not to? She reached into her bag for her phone, then slapped herself on the forehead when she remembered she didn't have Linda's number.

She dialed Andrew instead.

"Hi, hon—"

"I need a number for Linda," Sarah blurted out. "I just got home and no one's here and I told her not to take the girls out and I forgot to get her mobile number and I don't know where anyone is."

"Whoa . . . Hold on a sec and I'll get a number for her."

It seemed like an age before Andrew's voice came back on the line. "I'm dialing her number on the other phone. I'm sure there's an innocent explanation. She probably just took them to the shops or—"

"What? What is it?"

"The number went straight to voicemail. Hang on, I'll try again."

Sarah felt like she'd swallowed a bowling ball. Tears began to fill her eyes, and she wiped them away while she waited for her fiancé to respond.

"Same again. Stay where you are, I'm coming home."

CHAPTER 22

When Andrew Harvey got home, he opened the door with his key and found Sarah slumped in the hallway, crying hysterically. He helped her up and led her through to the kitchen, then fetched a bottle of brandy from the liquor cabinet and poured her a small glass.

"Get that down you," he said.

Sarah pushed the drink away and continued to weep.

"Drink it," he insisted.

She relented and took a sip. "Where's my daughter?"

"I don't know. I told Veronica what happened and she got straight on to Special Branch. The police are on their way, and I've got Hamad working on her background as we speak. He's also tracking her phone."

Sarah stared at him for a long moment through bloodshot eyes. "What? You didn't check her out this morning? You said you were going to do it first thing!"

"I . . . I started on it, but something came up and it completely slipped my mind."

"She could be a *murderer* for all we know." Her shoulders began to shudder as she wept anew. "Oh my god. I should never have let you hire her."

"I'm sure it's nothing like that. The agencies do background checks on the staff before they hire them. They have to, it's the law. They wouldn't open themselves up to a lawsuit."

The doorbell rang, and Harvey answered it. The two men introduced themselves as Detective Chief Superintendent Wayland and Assistant Chief Constable Bennett, and Harvey asked for ID before letting them in.

He took them to the kitchen, where Sarah was trying to compose herself.

"I understand you're concerned for your daughter's welfare," Wayland said.

"She's been kidnapped," Sarah said.

"We don't know that," Harvey told Wayland. "We hired a nanny yesterday and she was injured in a burglary last night. I found a replacement, Linda Myers, who started today. My fiancée Sarah had to go to a hospital appointment, and she told Linda not to take the girls out. When she got home, there was no one here."

"Have you tried calling Miss Myers?" Bennett asked.

Sarah gave him the dirtiest of looks. "Of course we tried."

"I called twice," Harvey said, "but it went straight to voicemail. I was just about to call the agency to see if they have any other numbers for her."

"You do that, Mr. Harvey. Meanwhile, I'll have a few words with your wife."

Harvey took himself into the living room and dialed the number for Fitch-Barron.

"Hi. My name's Andrew Harvey, and I'd—"

"Mr. Harvey, thank you for getting back to me. This is Jeremy. We spoke a couple of days ago."

"Yeah. Hi, Jeremy."

"Awful business with Janice. I really hope it hasn't put you out."

"It may have," Harvey replied. "I'm calling about her replacement."

"Yes, I was hoping you might."

"You were?"

"Yes. I think I've found the ideal person. Her name is Diane, and she'll be available from tomorrow morning—"

"Wait," Harvey interrupted. "I'm talking about Linda Myers."

"Who? I'm afraid we don't have anyone by that name on our books."

"Are you sure? I called the out-of-hours team last night and they sent Myers round this morning."

"I'll check the call logs, but I can assure you that no one by the name of Linda Myers works for this agency. I interview and vet everyone myself, and of the twenty-two people we employ, none of them is called Linda, or Myers."

While Jeremy double-checked his records, Harvey tried to think what might have happened. The simplest answer was that someone had intercepted his call to the agency. But who?

They would have needed extremely sophisticated equipment to pull that off, and . . .

Three letters flashed in his mind.

"I've checked the call logs, Mr. Harvey. We only had two calls last night. One was from Janice, explaining that she would be unavailable until further notice, and another nanny rang in to say she wouldn't be working today because of illness."

Harvey hung up and ran to the front door. He'd noticed a plumber's van parked outside his neighbor's house for the past couple of mornings. He knew the couple five doors down were having their roof converted into a loft room, but he'd thought it strange that they'd need a plumber. It was a half-noticed, minor detail. Now it could be vital.

The van was gone, but Harvey realized that he remembered the company name on the side of the vehicle. He called Hamad Farsi and told him to find out everything he could about Flintside Plumbers Limited when he was done tracking Myers's cell phone.

"Hey, we just picked up a signal at McDonald's in Kentish Town. Want me to send a couple of cars over to check it out?"

"Hang on."

Harvey went back into the kitchen and told the two police officers about the discovery. Wayland got on his radio and ordered all available units to the location.

"Never mind, we've got it covered," Harvey told Hamad.

"Flintside doesn't exist," his colleague replied when Harvey got back on the phone. "Nothing with Companies House or HMRC."

His hunch had been correct, but the realization had come far too late. He left the room again. He didn't want the cops hearing his next statement.

"This *has* to be the ESO," he told Hamad quietly. "They intercepted my call to the employment agency and sent one of their people. Forget Kentish Town. That'll be a diversion. I want a BOLO on all ports. They'll have false papers, so go through all CCTV from the airports and check it with facial recognition."

That was enough to get started with. He needed to think straight, and couldn't do it with Sarah in such a state. He needed to be at the office, where he could oversee the operation.

Back in the kitchen, he leaned into Sarah and hugged her. "I'm going to find our daughter," he said. He kissed her on the forehead and made for the door, but Sarah was on his heels.

"I'm coming with you. She's my daughter, too."

Harvey turned and told the police officers where they were going. He assumed they might need to send a crime scene investigator into the house to check for prints or DNA to learn the true identity of Linda Myers, so he simply asked that they make sure the place was locked up tight when they left.

He returned to the door and saw a small pair of wellington boots emblazoned with the face of Peppa Pig.

In all the commotion, he'd forgotten about Melissa.

CHAPTER 23

Harvey ignored the speed limit as he drove to Thames House. Horns blared as he cut through traffic, and he jumped a couple of red lights in his haste to get to headquarters.

"We have to call Tom," Sarah said.

"That's just what they want," Harvey replied as he spun the wheel to nip down a side road. "I think they took the girls to get to him."

"But why?"

"I told you. They're after Eva Driscoll. Tom leads them to Len and Sonny, who in turn lead to her. Only now we've become involved."

"You mean *you've* involved us."

It wasn't the time to argue semantics. There'd be time for recriminations later, once the girls were safe.

"Yes, I got us involved," Harvey said, hoping it would be enough to make her drop the subject.

It was, though he wasn't sure he preferred the silence that ensued. He'd known Sarah long enough, and anger and resentment would be simmering below the surface. He needed to get her mind focused on the solution rather than dwelling on what couldn't be changed. She was a sharp thinker, clinical and tenacious. That was the side of Sarah he needed to see right now.

"We need to think of places they would take the girls," he said. He got no reply and took it to mean she was working on the problem.

What would have normally been a thirty-minute journey was over in twenty, and he dumped the BMW in the underground parking lot and ran up the stairs, with Sarah close behind him.

After swiping into the office, Harvey went straight to Hamad Farsi's station.

"Anything from the ports?"

"Nothing yet. I've got three people downstairs looking at facial recognition and scouring passenger manifests for three people traveling on the same flight and matching their descriptions."

"What about Kentish Town?"

"As you said, a bust. The phone was with some teen who claimed he found it on the floor of a Tube train."

"Okay. Let's get Elaine and Eddie looking at CCTV of the area around my house."

"They're already on it. Elaine started fifteen minutes ago."

Harvey went over to Elaine Solomon's desk. She was in her mid-forties but had the energy and dress sense of someone half her age. Eddie Howe sat opposite her, the perennial energy drink next to his keyboard. Both were engrossed in their screens.

"Anything?" he asked Elaine.

"Nothing concrete, but a couple of possibilities. There are no cameras in the area of your house, but from the main road we can see two cars entered your street about ten minutes after Sarah left for her hospital appointment."

Elaine switched to another screen and showed Harvey the suspect vehicles. They appeared to be following each other as they drove on to his road.

"A few minutes later, both cars reappear at the other end of the street and split up. Eddie's tracking one and I've got the other. It went down Ladbroke Grove and turned right. I'm just searching for the next available camera . . . Got it. Here they are."

Harvey watched the poor-quality images on the screen. The car was heading west, away from the camera.

"Move to the next one."

Elaine clicked through to the next camera, situated at Holland Park Tube station.

"Okay, they've stopped."

Harvey saw one man get out of the front passenger seat and the car drive off. From the angle of the shot, he could only see one other person in the vehicle. "He's going into the station. Which Tube lines feed Holland Park?"

"Central Line."

"Hamad," Harvey shouted across the room, "where did that kid find the phone?"

Hamad looked through a printout. "Central Line. He got on at East Acton, then switched at Tottenham Court Road to the Northern Line. He got off at Camden Town."

"That was the decoy car," Harvey told Elaine. He ran around to Eddie Howe's desk. "Where's the other vehicle?"

"The M4. They joined at junction 1 in Chiswick. They're just approaching the M25 . . . Yes, they went south on the M25. Let me find the camera for the next exit."

Eddie moved to another shot, then synced the times and rolled on a few minutes. Harvey leaned over his shoulder, waiting to see if the suspect vehicle left at junction 14. After ten minutes of searching, it appeared to have stayed on the motorway.

"Hamad, they didn't get off at Heathrow. Concentrate on Gatwick!"

"Andrew, my office."

Harvey turned to see Veronica Ellis standing in the doorway of her glass palace.

"Keep looking," he told Eddie, then jogged over to Ellis's office and closed the door behind him.

"Have they called you?" she asked.

"No, not yet."

"They will. I've instructed Gerald to put a trace on your phone. The moment they get in touch, he'll start tracing them."

If Gerald Small couldn't track them, nobody could. The MI5 technician was without equal in his small department, and phones were his specialty.

"How are you holding up?" Ellis asked.

Harvey knew what she was really asking: *Are you up for this, or are you going to crumble under the pressure?* He was glad she wasn't tearing him a new one for getting tangled up with the ESO. Her warning was still fresh in his mind.

"I'm good." He looked out through the glass wall and saw Sarah leaning over Hamad's desk. "I can't vouch for Sarah, though."

"Let me worry about her," Ellis said. "What progress are the team making?"

Harvey brought her quickly up to speed. "I need to disappear for a couple of hours. Tom has to be told what's happening. I can't call him, for obvious reasons."

"Okay, but when you do, make sure you stress that we've got it covered. I don't want him racking up a huge body count."

That was exactly what Harvey feared, too. Much as he loved Tom Gray, the man was unpredictable, and direct action was his mantra. Not only would Harvey have to break the news that Tom's beloved daughter had been kidnapped, but he'd also have to warn the ex-soldier to show restraint.

It wasn't going to be easy.

Or pleasant.

Harvey went back out on to the office floor and straight to Elaine's desk. "Keep following the decoy car. I want to see where it goes. Maybe we can ID the driver and see where that leads."

"Will do. I already ran the plates and it's a clone, so no luck there."

"Okay. Just see what you can find."

Gareth Bailey came over and handed Harvey some printouts. "I checked into Linda Myers. Her history is cast-iron. Whoever created this legend knew what they were doing."

"Did you speak to the people who provided references?"

"No reply from either number."

Harvey suspected that even if he'd reached the supposed families, they would have been ESO people posing on the other end of the line.

"Thanks." He went to speak to Sarah. "Gareth has everything you could possibly get on Myers. Even if you'd checked it yourself, nothing would have flagged up."

Her face softened imperceptibly, but Harvey knew his decision to hire a nanny would hang over him for a long time to come.

"I have to go and tell Tom," he said. "I'll be back as soon as I can."

She took his hand, but there was little warmth in her touch.

"I'll be here."

CHAPTER 24

Eva Driscoll and Carl Huff had been on the road for almost three hours, battling through heavy traffic most of the way. Since setting off at nine, they'd headed up the M40, then up the M42 and on to the M6. They were now on the outskirts of Birmingham, and the dashboard clock said it was almost time for Bill Sanders to call.

She adjusted her face mask once more. It was flesh-colored latex and fit over her nose down to her chin, with a large slit for the mouth. Up close it was clearly fake, but it altered the lower half of her face enough to fool any facial recognition cameras along the route. Carl was wearing one, too, the long chin making him look like Dan Dare. Harvey had purchased them at a party accessory shop at her request, and she'd cut them to size. They were good enough for this task, but she would need something more convincing at some point.

At Spaghetti Junction, Eva followed the signs for the A38, then got off the roundabout and into a residential area. She parked on a street and put the SIM card and battery back in the new phone, having texted Sanders her new number the previous day before trashing the other burner.

Carl rested his hand on Eva's thigh, and she put her own hand on his. "You've been quiet," he said.

That was one of the things she loved most about Carl. He knew when she wanted a conversation, and when to let her be alone with her thoughts. Some men just chatted for the sake of it, but Carl was smarter, more tuned in to her needs.

Of all the regrets in her life, the biggest by far was her decision to walk away from him a decade earlier. They'd met at the CIA's clandestine services training camp, both raw recruits and each determined to be the best. After a week-long exercise in the field, they'd bumped into each other at a bar, where the beer had been cold and the ambience relaxing. That night, the love-making had been intense.

Relationships between candidates were strictly forbidden, so they'd used all their guile to ensure no one suspected a thing. It clearly hadn't been enough, because Bill Sanders, then the head of the program, had subjected them to a polygraph and intense questioning. They'd naturally denied everything, and their stories had ultimately been accepted, but Eva had learned her lesson. She'd always been a driven, competitive person, much like her late brother. Washing out of the CIA over an impulsive affair was never an option. They agreed to stop seeing each other until the program was over, but when the time came, she'd chosen to walk away without saying goodbye.

Even to this day, she wasn't sure why. Perhaps it had been the fear that her feelings for him would cloud her judgment and make her take her eyes off the prize. She'd been trained to kill, not to love. She couldn't afford to be deep in a mission and have sentiments screw things up. She'd known that her future targets would be someone's father or mother, son or daughter. Even someone's lover. Could she take a life knowing what she was destroying?

She'd walked away from him and not looked back.

Until last year, when Carl had shown up at the most unlikely moment. He'd got close to Edward Langton, heir to the ESO throne and Eva's prime target. What she hadn't known at the time was that he'd been sent by Sanders to keep her alive, not thwart her efforts.

Looking back now, she didn't only see the short, happy period since their reconciliation. She saw the gaping chasm that marked their ten years apart. A decade they could have spent together as lovers rather than being strangers.

She was determined to make up for it. They were both in their early thirties, so they still had a lifetime ahead of them. If only they could be rid of the ESO to enjoy it.

"Just reflecting on how lucky I am to have you," she said, squeezing his hand.

Then Sanders called, destroying the moment.

"I have the information you wanted," he said.

Eva already had a pen and paper ready. "Shoot."

"The person you want has a private island. Here are the coordinates." Sanders read the numbers off and Eva scribbled them down.

"Where is it?"

"The Pacific Ocean. It has no name, but it's roughly 2,500 miles west of Ecuador, and 600 miles northeast of Hiva Oa in the French Polynesian islands."

"Why doesn't it have a name?" Eva asked. "Every inhabited island has a name."

"Not this one. You won't find it on any maps, either. Go ahead, look it up on your phone. Officially, there's nothing there."

"Which makes me think you're yanking my chain. What's the deal? Get me on a plane there and shoot it down over the middle of the ocean? I wasn't born yesterday, Bill."

"I'm on the level," Sanders insisted. "Who sent Carl Huff to look after you last year, eh? It was me."

"Only because if I died, I'd have taken you down with me. Now that you've got the recordings, I'm more use to you dead."

Eva heard him sigh.

"It was never like that. Even if you hadn't made the recordings of us . . . together, I still would have sent Carl. You were always special to me."

"Bullshit," she said. "We're done here."

"Seriously, Eva. I'm a pariah in Washington, with zero influence and one step from jail. You're the only one who can keep me out of prison. Why would I lie to you?"

For any number of reasons.

"Let's say I believed you," she said. "Who's on the island?"

Sanders paused. "Now, *that* you wouldn't believe."

"Try me."

Sanders waited again, as if trying to build the tension. "Henry Langton."

"So, a man who's dead is living on an island that doesn't exist? You've had twenty-four hours, and that's the best you can come up with?"

"I didn't believe it at first, but it makes sense. The ESO wants nothing to do with you. They told me that. All they want to do is lick their wounds and stay out of the spotlight. Langton, however, has other ideas. He blames you for killing his son and wants you dead."

Eva took it all in and processed what she'd heard. Would it be such a leap to believe that Langton had faked his own death? A man with billions to burn—trillions, if the rumors were correct—could easily afford to pay off a few people to make it happen. A couple of prison guards, a coroner, send another corpse to the funeral home, and *voilà* . . .

It sounded plausible, but something didn't smell right.

"How did you find out about Langton?" she asked.

"The ESO told me."

"Who in the ESO?"

"I don't know." Sanders told her how the meeting had gone down. "They said they helped him disappear for two reasons: to stop him from talking to the authorities, and for all his years of service. But now that he's taken up this vendetta against you, they see him as a liability."

"What else can you give me?" Eva asked, conscious that the call had been going on for some time. If they were tracking her, she would soon know about it.

"That's all they gave me. I suggest you take the chance while you can. You—"

She cut him off. "Okay. I'll be in touch."

Eva ended the call and looked around. Seeing no one near, she lowered the window, dropped the phone in the street, and drove quickly back on to the M6, this time heading toward London.

"What do you think?" she asked Carl.

"It all sounded just a little too convenient. Contrived, even."

"Exactly. It has to be a trap."

"So where does that leave us?"

"Back at square one," Eva said.

Five hours later, after stopping off for lunch and sitting in yet another traffic jam, they were on the outskirts of Guildford once more. The roads were becoming familiar, and she found the hotel without the aid of the satnav. When she pulled into the parking lot and stopped the vehicle, she saw a familiar face.

"Time to clear up some unfinished business," Eva said to Carl.

"Isn't that Harvey, the guy you lied to about being the father of your fictitious child?"

"It is."

"Go easy," Carl warned her. "We need him on our side. In fact, why not save it until later, when this is all over?"

"He deserves to know the truth, and if he thinks we've still got a child together, it could cloud his judgment."

Carl sighed. "You're the boss."

They got out of the car. "Hey you," she said.

Andrew Harvey looked over at her, then did a double take.

"Emilie?"

"I told you that wasn't my real name." She smiled. "Call me Eva."

"Right. Len told me. It's just . . . I'll always remember you as Emilie."

Eva sensed that he wasn't that happy to see her.

"You go ahead," she said to Carl. "I won't be a minute."

Huff walked through the entrance and Eva fell in step with Harvey. "You always were the sentimental type," she said, trying to break whatever ice had formed since their last meeting, the previous year. "It's a shame we couldn't have met under different circumstances."

"If you want to trade clichés, it's water under the bridge," he said coldly. "I've moved on."

"I know. How's Alana?"

"Missing." Harvey held her gaze. "The ESO have her."

"What? When?"

"This morning. One of them posed as our new nanny and took Alana when Sarah went for a hospital appointment. I've got MI5, Special Branch, and the Met looking for her."

"Then what are you doing here?" she asked. "Why aren't you at Thames House?"

"Because they took Tom Gray's daughter too. I'm just about to break the news to him."

"Oh, shit. Andrew, I'm so sorry."

Harvey turned and started for the hotel. "Save it," he said over his shoulder.

Eva followed him inside, staying a few steps behind until they reached the room. When he stopped at the door, she brushed past him to put the key card in the lock, then stopped.

"There's something I have to tell you," she said.

"Can it wait? I have to see Tom."

"I'd rather you heard it now."

Harvey stared at her, waiting for her to speak.

"Remember Maria?"

"Our daughter from that brief relationship when you lied to me all those years ago? Of course I remember. That's not something you easily forget. When someone you haven't seen for a decade shows up and says you've got a nine-year-old daughter, you tend to remember."

"Maria's my niece."

Harvey's face sagged and he seemed to be struggling for words.

"I had to get you to help me."

"Do you know what an evil thing that was? How could you do that to anyone?"

"I couldn't leave empty-handed," Eva said, "so I lied. Please don't take it personally."

"You're a real piece of work, you know that?"

He turned away from her to face the door. She pushed it open for him to enter first.

"Andrew," Sonny said. "What are you doing here?"

"I'm here to see Tom."

Gray stood, and Eva could see concern etched on his face.

"What is it?"

"Alana was kidnapped by the ESO."

Gray's hands balled into fists. "Where's Melissa?"

Harvey's silence said it all.

Gray picked up an empty soda bottle and threw it against the wall. It smashed into a thousand pieces. "They've got my daughter?"

"I'm sorry," Harvey said, but Gray was beyond words. He rushed Harvey and grabbed his throat with a single hand.

"Where is she?"

Harvey croaked an inaudible reply. His face began turning red as he clawed at Gray's forearm.

"Enough!" Len moved quickly behind Gray and took him in a headlock.

Sonny joined in, pinching the nerves in Gray's wrist and forcing him to release his grip.

Len spun Gray around and pushed him on to the bed. "Didn't you hear what he said? Alana's missing too."

Gray was panting as if he'd just run a marathon. His face remained scarlet, but Eva could see the fight draining out of him.

"We're in this together," Len said in a more soothing tone. "We need you calm and thinking straight."

Gray tried to get up but Len pushed him back down and stood over him.

"Okay," Gray said, his breathing coming under control. "What are you doing to get them back?" he asked Harvey.

"I've got my colleagues going through CCTV, and the Met are all over it. A detective chief super is running that side of things."

"What are their demands?" Eva asked, earning another glare from Gray.

"They haven't been in contact yet, but they will. I'm sure they took the girls to get you to contact Len and Carl. It's Eva they're after."

"What about Sanders?" Gray asked Eva. "Did he give you anything?"

She pulled the piece of paper from her pocket. "Coordinates to Langton's private island."

"Then what are we waiting for?" Gray asked, standing next to Len. "Wait. Isn't he dead?"

"Sanders says he's still alive, but I think it's a trap," she said. "The coordinates are for an island in the Pacific, but it doesn't officially exist. Farooq, take a look."

She gave the paper to Farooq, who entered the details into a screen on his laptop.

"Nothing there," he confirmed.

"As I said, it's a trap. They get us all on a plane, send us to a remote part of the world hundreds of miles from the nearest flight path or shipping lane, then shoot us down. Game over."

"Then Sanders was a waste of time," Gray said. "Either he made it up, or they lied to him, too." He turned to Harvey. "Does this change anything on your end? Can you get us information on the ESO now that they've got our girls?"

"I don't know. I'll head back and speak to Ellis right now, but if it were an option, I think she would have suggested it already."

"Ask her anyway. In the meantime, what can *we* do?"

Harvey stood in thought. "Nothing," he said eventually. "Just remain out of sight and let us handle it. I'll buy a new burner cell and be in touch every hour."

"If you're going to do that, just give me your own phone," Farooq said.

Harvey handed it over, and Farooq spent a couple of minutes tapping at the screen before handing it back.

"I added an app called Shield. If you need to talk to us, send a message through that. It's more secure than the systems you use at work. I've put our details in the contact list."

"Thanks." Harvey walked to the door, then turned back. "I'm really sorry, Tom. I'll do everything I can to get her back."

"I know you will."

Harvey seemed to take that as encouragement, though Eva thought it sounded more like a threat.

CHAPTER 25

Harvey's eyes were watering, and he knew it was from lack of sleep. He'd been awake for twenty-nine hours now, and was still no closer to finding his daughter and Melissa. His colleagues at MI5 had given up their free time to help, but every lead turned out to be a dead end.

The decoy car driver had dumped his vehicle in a supermarket parking lot and gone inside with a bag. They hadn't seen him come out again. Police had been sent to get in-store CCTV recordings, but the man had obviously cased the place beforehand. He'd disappeared into a camera blind spot and vanished.

The same happened with the man who'd left the phone on the Tube. He'd gotten off after two stops, then walked into a convenience store and disappeared. A follow-up visit by police revealed that the man had walked straight through and out the back exit, much to the annoyance of the shop's owner.

They had concentrated their main efforts on the other car, the one they suspected of carrying the girls. Images captured in London showed a woman and small child in the rear seats, though there had been no clear front view of the interior.

Tracking the car had been easy, but ultimately fruitless. They'd found it abandoned in a lay-by between two sleepy villages in East

Sussex, and while a forensics team was combing the vehicle now, they weren't hopeful.

Harvey was thinking about joining Sarah on a cot in the meeting room when Elaine broke his train of thought.

"Andrew, we've got a hit!"

Harvey hurried to her desk.

"A party matching Myers and the girls took a Cessna from Shoreham Airport to Paris Orly."

Harvey had asked DCS Wayland to send officers to every small port in the country to interrogate the staff. The police had been armed with a recent photo of Melissa and an e-fit of Myers, and it looked to have paid off.

The fact that the girls might be in another country wasn't such good news.

"When was that?"

"Three o'clock yesterday afternoon."

Twenty-one hours ago . . .

"Get the IDs they used and see if they flag anything in Paris. I want the flight plan. And find out who the pilot was. Hamad, contact the DGSI and see if they can track them beyond the airport."

The DGSI, the French equivalent of MI5, had an informal agreement with the Security Service, and on several occasions had shared information. Harvey hoped this would be one of those times.

"The police already have the pilot," Elaine said. "He's being held at a station in Worthing. They plan to transfer him to Paddington Green in the next few hours. Want me to liaise with DCS Wayland on that?"

"Yes, and request updates every thirty minutes."

After repeated dead ends, the investigation had suddenly kicked into gear. The pilot might be a valuable lead, or just an innocent party caught up in the mess.

Time would tell.

The worst part of the discovery was that the girls had been taken out of the country. MI5's remit was to protect the UK from internal foes; anything beyond British territorial waters was a matter for MI6.

Harvey hated the thought of putting his daughter's life in the hands of MI6 and the French intelligence services. Then again, he could easily think of worse scenarios.

On his way to see the boss, he thought about waking Sarah to let her know about the latest development but decided against it. There was nothing she could add to the search right now, so it was better if she slept and returned to the fray refreshed. Likewise Gray. He'd want to know the next steps, and that was up to Ellis.

Harvey knocked on her door and walked in without waiting to be called.

"A new lead suggests they flew to Paris," he said.

Her eyes panned right. The main office was windowless, but if she'd had X-ray vision, she would have been staring at Vauxhall Cross, the home of the Secret Intelligence Service—MI6.

"You understand what that means," Ellis said.

"I know what protocol says, but—"

"But nothing, Andrew." Ellis sat back in her chair. "Look at you. You can barely function. Didn't I tell you to get some sleep last night?"

"You try sleeping when your child is missing!" He immediately regretted the outburst. "I'm sorry."

"I'm ordering you to get some sleep. Where's Sarah?"

"She hit the cots a few hours ago."

"She did the right thing. Go and join her. Even if it's just for a couple of hours. In the meantime, have Hamad collate everything you've got and I'll take it across the river myself."

"They won't give it priority," Harvey said. "It'll be tomorrow before they even contact the French."

"They'll start acting immediately, I assure you."

Harvey wanted to argue but he felt too drained to try. Not even the recent leads had generated enough adrenaline to keep him functioning at full capacity.

"Go on," Ellis insisted. "I'll speak to Hamad. You get your head down."

"I will," Harvey said, "once the file's ready."

He reluctantly left her office and went to give Hamad his instructions. His friend had also pulled an all-nighter, but had sensibly grabbed a few hours' sleep during a quiet period. Harvey now wished he'd done the same.

He passed on Ellis's order, and stood over his friend to make sure every detail was included.

"Andrew."

Ellis was standing in her doorway, and she gestured for him to join her.

"I just got off the phone with Faulkner."

Ellis had been to see the home secretary the previous day to inform him of the situation and the ESO's suspected involvement. He'd promised to get back to her after speaking with the prime minister.

"Is he going to open the ESO files to us?"

"No," Ellis said. "The PM thinks it highly unlikely that an organization like the ESO would send people to harm the daughters of an MI5 operative and a British civilian living in Italy."

"What? Did he even listen to what you told him?"

"I not only told him," Ellis said, "I provided a detailed report. How he can't see the connection is beyond me."

"Well, you know what? I don't give a fuck what the PM thinks. If we get nothing from the DGSI, I'm going to search every database we have for signs of the ESO. They can have my job. I don't care. Nothing's going to—"

Harvey's phone beeped, indicating a new message. He pulled it from his pocket and frowned when he didn't recognize the number. He hit the notification to open it and almost dropped the cell.

It was a picture of Melissa standing on a beach. Next to her, on a blanket, was Alana. Darkness framed them, though a couple of lanterns burned in the background, and waves lapped on a sandy shore.

A beach.

An island!

Melissa looked miserable. Alana appeared to be in mid-wail. Underneath the picture, a message read:

> *You have 24 hours to deliver Driscoll to me. Upload a video to YouTube with the title 'Willoff Georal scandok', and in it give me her location. Any tricks, the girls die. I will reply in the comments with their location when I have Driscoll.*

The name was clearly designed to be hard to trip across. Only someone entering the exact phrase would be likely to find it among the millions—perhaps billions—of videos available on the website.

Harvey handed the phone to Ellis. She took in the picture and handed it back. "Get it to Gerald. Maybe he can trace the origin."

Harvey raced to Gerald Small's office. He found the tech banging away on his keyboard.

"I need you to tell me where this message came from," Harvey said.

Small took the cell and connected a lead to the power socket, then plugged the other end into his laptop. He hit a few keys before opening a command prompt. He typed what looked to Harvey like gibberish, and what appeared on the screen in response wasn't any more legible.

"Sorry, but it's been bounced off so many servers it's impossible to determine where it was sent from."

Damn.

"Not even a rough idea? I need to know where that picture was taken."

"Ah, now, that's a different kettle of fish."

Small opened the image, then brought up another screen next to it. "All pictures have metadata. It tells you things like when it was taken, the F-stop, exposure time, focal length, flash—"

"Can it tell us where it was taken?"

"As I was about to say, even *where* it was taken. Most cameras have a built-in GPS, and the location is embedded along with all the other information . . . if it isn't turned off. Here we go."

Harvey looked at what Small had highlighted on the screen. It was just a series of numbers, separated by a comma.

"Where is that?" he asked.

Small copied the coordinates and pasted them into Google Maps. It centered in on a blue screen. Gerald Small zoomed out until a few islands came into view.

"Hmm. According to this, it was taken in the middle of the Pacific Ocean."

It was too much of a coincidence. "Go back to the coordinates," he said, and unhooked his phone from the lead. He opened the Shield app and typed a message to Eva, asking her for the digits Sanders had given her the day before.

Eva replied within seconds, and Harvey read them out while Small entered them into the map.

"Ask it for directions from one to the other," Harvey said.

Small did as instructed, and a dotted line appeared between the two points.

They were three hundred yards apart.

"Could someone have planted that metadata manually?" Harvey asked.

"No. There's a flag, here, called—appropriately enough—'Has Changed.' It reads 'false' and can't be set manually, so this hasn't been edited."

Harvey sent Eva another message.

The island exists. I'm on my way.

CHAPTER 26

Harvey ran to the meeting room and shook Sarah awake. "I think we've found the girls," he told her, then left her to bring herself to full consciousness. His next stop was Ellis's office.

"Gerald tracked the location the picture was taken in," he said as he burst through the door. "It's an island in the Pacific."

"It really does exist?"

"Apparently so, which means Henry Langton could be alive."

Harvey had already told her and the rest of the team about the coordinates Bill Sanders had given Eva, but that they'd seemed to be a red herring at best. Until the information Gerald Small pulled from the photograph suggested Sanders had been telling the truth after all. "So there's no need to get Six involved," he said. "Or the French."

"Then how exactly do you plan to get them back?" Ellis asked.

"I'm going in with Tom," Harvey said, his voice ripe with defiance.

"The hell you are!"

"Then you tell me how I should handle it. Pass it to Faulkner and let him deal with it? It took him a day to ask the PM a simple question! By the time he makes a decision, the girls will be dead! You saw the message. We've got twenty-four hours."

"You have an alternative," said Ellis.

"What? Hand over Eva and hope this psychopath keeps his word and returns the girls unharmed?"

"I'm offering balance, that's all."

"Thanks," Harvey said, "but that's not going to happen. Langton believes his island is undetectable, and that if he kills the girls, there'll be no blowback. He has no incentive to release them."

Ellis made a face that said she agreed with him.

"Plus, by the time Faulkner convinces the PM to send a team in, it'll be too late. We have to go now."

Ellis stared at him and, after an awkward silence, looked down at her computer and began typing. "I think you're too close to this investigation," she said without looking up. "You're also in no fit state to function properly. I'm ordering you to take seven days' rest, effective immediately. The memo will be with you in the next couple of minutes."

Harvey started to protest, then realized what she was really saying: *Do it, but on your own time.*

"Thank you," he said, and rushed back into the main office. Sarah was waiting for him.

"I'm going to get her," he told her.

"Where is she?"

"About 2,500 miles west of Ecuador. Langton's island is real."

"What? How the hell did they get her there? And why take her there?"

"Langton thinks it's somewhere we can't find her," Harvey said. "Take a look at this."

He showed her the message that had come through earlier. "Gerald was able to locate the place it was taken. It matched the coordinates Eva thought were fake. I'm going to ask Tom to take me in and get the girls back."

"I'm coming, too."

"No! I need you here. If something happens to me . . . at least Alana will still have one parent."

"Fuck you, Andrew Harvey!"

The shout caught everyone's attention, and all eyes turned to them as they stood in the middle of the office, squaring off.

"We haven't got time for this," Harvey said, lowering his voice. "Twenty-four hours. I have to go."

"And I'm coming with you." She grabbed her coat and purse from the back of her chair and walked to the door, waiting for him.

Harvey grabbed his own jacket and they walked down to the parking lot together.

"This isn't some macho 'I'm the alpha male and you're the helpless female' routine," he told her. "I'm genuinely worried about going there."

"Then don't go," Sarah said. "Leave it to the professionals. Tom, Len, Sonny, this is what they do. And from what you've told me about Eva and the others, they've got enough people to do the job."

"But it's my daughter," Harvey said.

"Exactly. And when she gets home, she'll need her father. In person, not a picture on the wall to remember him by."

They got to the car and Harvey drove. They didn't share another word until they reached the hotel in Guildford an hour later.

When they got to the room and knocked on the door, Sonny opened it. Three of them were sitting around Farooq's laptop, while the others were working at a circular table.

Eva stood. "How do you know the island exists?" she asked Harvey.

He showed her the message he'd received and told her what Gerald Small had found in the metadata.

"It was taken three hundred yards from the coordinates Sanders gave you."

"There's no way we'll get there in twenty-four hours," Len said. "You'll have to stall them."

"What do you suggest?"

"Upload a video and tell him that Eva split when the girls went missing. You'll need time to track her down."

"That could work."

"It has to. Tell him you need . . . seventy-two hours. That should give us plenty of time."

Harvey ran through what he wanted to say, then sat in front of the laptop, Sarah standing behind him.

"Remember, you're desperate to get your girl back," Eva said. "Make it realistic."

Harvey took a couple of deep breaths, then nodded to Farooq, who hit the Record button on the built-in camera.

"Message received but twenty-four hours isn't enough. The moment Alana and Melissa disappeared, so did Driscoll. I've got everyone in the team looking for her, but you know how big a task that is. You've been looking for her for months. I'll need at least seventy-two hours to track her down."

Farooq hit the Stop button. "Give me a couple of minutes to create an account and upload it."

"Okay," Eva said. "Back to work."

They returned to what they'd been doing, and Harvey made cups of the hotel room's instant coffee.

"The cheapest we can buy will cost five million," Farooq said. "It would be better to charter one, considering we're in such a hurry."

"What would we be chartering?" Harvey asked.

"A Cessna Citation Sovereign," Rees Colback said. "It's the only plane we can use to get close enough. The closest airport is on Hiva Oa—Atuona Airport. The runway's only 1,200 meters long, so we need a plane that can get us there and land. The Citation's the best fit."

"So we're going," Harvey said.

"*We* are," Eva said. "You're staying here."

"What? I'm not about—"

"Pull your neck in," Gray said. "You're staying here. For a start, we need false passports for the six of us."

"That's my daughter out there!"

Sarah put a hand on his shoulder in what felt like a gesture of solidarity.

"Noted," Gray said. "When was the last time you did a ten-mile swim underwater, at night, in shark territory, carrying a one-hundred-pound kit bag?"

"You know I've never done anything like that,"

"Exactly. We have. We can't just land a plane on Langton's island and expect him to welcome us with open arms. We have to approach by sea, unseen. That takes skills you just don't have."

"Listen to Tom," Sonny added. "You'd be a liability, mate. No offense."

Sarah squeezed his shoulder. "They're right. Leave it to them. They know what they're doing."

Much as he hated to admit it, they had a point. He would gladly have swum through shark-infested waters to save his daughter, but he probably wouldn't have made it.

No, he'd have to put the life of his baby daughter in Tom Gray's hands. In truth, he couldn't have hoped for anyone better.

"At least let me help with the planning," Harvey said.

"No problem," Gray said. "As I mentioned, we need new passports for me, Len, Sonny, Carl, Rees, and Eva. Once you've got them, book plane tickets to Mexico City, leaving tonight. It would be best if we fly from different airports. Use the money Len gave you for the nanny."

"It'll take a couple of days to work up the new papers," Sarah said.

"You've got six hours to get them to us," Eva told her. "The clock is ticking. If we're not in the air tonight, it's game over."

"You go and sort the passports out," Harvey said to Sarah. "I'll call ahead and let Veronica know what we need."

He saw the look she gave him: *Don't you dare disappear on me.*

"I'll be back in a couple of hours," Harvey promised.

"Okay. I'll need passport photos, though."

"Give me an email address and I'll send them to you," Farooq said.

Sarah gave him her contact details, then left.

"We've got a reply!" Farooq announced. "He's agreed to seventy-two hours from now, not a second longer."

"That should be all we need," Gray said.

"So, what's the plan after you get to Mexico?" Harvey asked.

"We'll hire a Citation in advance and use that to fly to Hiva Oa. It's in French Polynesia in the South Pacific, about six hundred miles southwest of Langton's island. Once there, we'll hire a boat to take us to within a hundred miles of the island, then switch to a Zodiac boat. When we get to within ten miles, we go underwater all the way in."

"Sounds like you've got it all covered."

"Not quite. We still need to find a Zodiac, a plane, and enough weapons and ammo to get us through whatever defenses they've got."

"They'll be considerable," Eva said.

The thought of staying behind suddenly didn't seem so terrible. Harvey excused himself and called Ellis to give her a heads-up on the passport request.

"Sarah's on her way back," he said. "She should be there in just over an hour. I need a big favor from you, or this is dead in the water."

"If it's access to the databases—"

"Nothing like that. Driscoll's people need passports to get them to Mexico and beyond. And they need them in the next few hours."

He had to endure silence as Ellis contemplated the request. "How many?"

"Six."

"*Six?* One, I could get away with."

"I know it's a big ask," Harvey said, sounding as contrite as possible, "but without them, the plan falls at the first hurdle."

"I thought you said they already had false passports."

They had indeed.

"Hang on."

Harvey went back into the room and asked Eva why they couldn't use the ones they'd traveled to England on.

"We could," she admitted, "but I hate leaving a trail. Once this is over, I'd prefer to slip away without anyone knowing where I'm going, MI5 included. It wouldn't take much for someone in your organization to look through the Mexico flight manifests and work out what name I'm using."

"Good point, though slightly insulting."

Harvey was rewarded with a smile. "I've trusted few people in the last ten years, and my only regret is not trusting fewer."

He told Ellis what Eva had said and waited once more for her answer.

"Okay, but this is as far as our hand extends. No more favors."

Before Harvey could thank her, the phone went dead.

"Okay," he told the others, "passports are being prepared. I'll have them back here in six hours max. What else do you need that doesn't involve me sacrificing my career?"

"Get on your phone and look for a place in Mexico that sells Zodiacs," Gray said. "They're inflatable craft used by Special Forces for sea excursions. We want the F470 with the aluminum roll-up floor, plus a storage bag. Oh, and a fifty-five-horsepower engine to sling on the back of it."

Harvey got on it, and ten minutes later he had three outlets that could provide what they needed. While he was doing that, Farooq had booked a charter on a Citation.

"The only thing left is the weapons."

"I can get those in Mexico," Eva said. "I'll place an order before we fly."

"Should we ask who from?" Harvey wondered out loud.

"No."

"What are we talking about?" Sonny asked. "A half-dozen AKs of dubious origin?"

"If that's what you want, sure. I was thinking more along the lines of the HK416 or M4A1 with underslung M203 grenade launcher."

Sonny nodded and smiled. "I love it when you talk dirty."

"That's because you're all talk," Len told Sonny.

"Get serious," Gray said. "To recap, as soon as the passports are here, I want to be moving. Once we get to Mexico, we pick up the weapons and drive to the coast to meet the Citation, load it with the gear, and fly to Hiva Oa. Twelve hours to fly to Mexico, another twelve to get to the plane, then eight to ten hours to Hiva Oa. Once we get there we'll hire a local boat, something that can do at least thirty knots, and take that to within a hundred miles of Langton's island. Figure seventeen hours. From there we use the Zodiac the rest of the way. That should take no more than four hours if we can average twenty-five knots, so that's . . ."

"Thirty-four hours to get to Hiva Oa," Huff said, "plus twenty-one hours on the water. Tight but doable."

Gray nodded. "For the final ten miles we could get some DPVs."

"What are they?" Harvey asked.

"Diver propulsion vehicles. Little torpedoes that you hang on to and they pull you through the water. They can do about three knots, so figure three-plus hours until we reach shore. I reckon that's around sixty-eight hours by the time we get the passports and board the planes. Throw in all the other normal delays we're sure to encounter and we should still be on the island before the deadline."

"That time zone's eleven hours behind ours, so we should have the cover of darkness," Sonny said.

"All the better."

Gray got Farooq to work looking for some DPVs that they could pick up in Mexico. He found a few on the coast, one of them just a few miles from Puerto Escondido International Airport, where they would pick up the Citation.

"There's one thing you haven't covered," Harvey said.

"What's that?" Gray asked.

"Your exit strategy. How do you get back out?"

"Langton will have a way to get people and supplies on and off the island," Eva said. "That's our way home, unless we're all dead, in which case your point is moot."

With little else to do, Harvey asked to borrow Sonny's rental to drive back to Thames House. On his way down to the parking lot, he caught a glimpse of himself in a mirror and stopped to study his reflection. It was like looking at another person. Hair unkempt, face etched with fatigue and stress, but underneath, a resolve as strong as steel.

While hope remained, he would never give up.

With the planning complete, there was little to do except prepare mentally for the mission. For Sonny, that meant sleeping. Len buried himself in his Kindle, while Gray went for a walk.

Eva had an entirely different strategy.

She walked back to her hotel room with Carl, and the moment the door was closed she gripped the sides of his head and kissed him longingly. He responded in kind, his hands exploring her body and coming to rest on her hips. His fingers crept up inside her T-shirt and she moaned as they found her breasts. Eva fumbled with his button and fly, and soon had his manhood in her hands.

Thirty minutes later, they lay naked on the bed, spent. She rested her head on his chest, listening to his heart as it settled down after the frenetic workout.

"Do you think we'll be able to—"

Eva put her finger on his lips. She didn't want to talk, not right now, and especially if it was about the upcoming mission. She'd had a sense of foreboding ever since discovering that Henry Langton's island was no ESO fabrication. She couldn't put her finger on it, but there was something dark on the horizon. A little shiver, almost imperceptible, had gone through her when Sanders had mentioned Langton's name.

She didn't want to think about it. Now was the time to luxuriate in Carl's arms, to wallow in his love. She wanted nothing more than to disappear and be alone with him forever, but that was naiveté talking.

While the ESO still existed, there would be no respite. Convincing them to leave her and Carl alone would be a challenge in itself, but she had to try.

Killing Henry Langton was a good place to start.

CHAPTER 27

Harvey returned a little after seven that evening in Sonny's rental. He'd called ahead to warn them of his impending arrival, and all seven were waiting outside the main entrance. They all had their bags at their feet, apart from Farooq.

He handed out their new passports and the electronic boarding passes he'd printed out for their journeys.

"I've arranged for the facial recognition software at the airports to be down while you're there, just in case anyone is tapping into it. It'll go back on twenty minutes before your planes depart, so don't be late boarding. Eva, I've paired you with Len, traveling on a nonstop flight from Heathrow because you have to arrange the weapons. I guessed you'd want to get there first. I know you'd have preferred to go with Carl, but you guys always travel together, as do Len and Sonny. Splitting you up might muddy the water if anyone's still trying to track you."

She nodded. "Good thinking."

"Tom, you and Sonny will be going from Gatwick with a short stop-over at JFK. Carl and Rees are flying from Birmingham via Amsterdam Schiphol. That itinerary will have you arriving a few hours later than the rest, but it was the best I could find."

"That should be okay," said Gray, looking to Carl and Rees. "We can always make up a couple of hours somewhere."

They compared their ETAs and made arrangements to rendezvous once they arrived in Mexico City. Eva had been there before and knew the places to avoid.

Eva took something from her purse and handed it to Harvey.

He looked down at the faded brown porcelain bear with the cracked clock in its midriff. "You want me to get it fixed?"

"No, just hold on to it for me. I'll be back for it."

Harvey was puzzled but slipped it into his coat pocket. "Sure."

They said their goodbyes, and Sonny asked Harvey to turn the rental car back in for him. He'd hired a new one from a different firm, knowing Harvey would need the old one to get home.

Harvey assured him he would, then grabbed Gray for one last word.

"I know what you're going to say," Gray told him. "Don't worry, I'll bring her back."

"Thanks. But actually, I was going to say sorry for getting you and Melissa into this. I never imagined anything like this would happen when I agreed to help Eva last year."

Gray gave him a friendly slap on the arm. "I know you didn't. You're a good man, Andrew. Shit just seems to happen to us."

Harvey pulled a photograph from his pocket and gave it to Gray. "That's Myers, the nanny. Give her a bullet for me."

Gray studied the face, then put the picture in his pocket. "You got it."

He got into the car next to Sonny and gave one last wave as the rental pulled away.

"Don't worry," Farooq told Harvey, "Eva's the best."

Except when it comes to being truthful, Harvey thought. Her "Maria" story still played in his mind, though he'd been relieved to learn that it was all a lie.

It didn't stop it from hurting, though.

"I'll be in the hotel if you need anything," Farooq said. "The others have checked out, but I'll be staying until they confirm that they've got the girls."

"Thanks. You know how to get hold of me if you need me."

Harvey drove back to the office, knowing that the next sixty-five hours were going to be the longest of his life.

~

"Tell me about Eva," Gray said to Sonny.

Sonny shrugged. "She's hot."

Gray gave him a wry smile. He should have expected nothing less from the young Lothario. "I'm serious. How good is she?"

They'd discussed her before, shortly after Len and Sonny had briefly returned to the UK following their release from prison, but they'd talked about the mission and what they'd been through without going into any details about the woman herself.

"She's one you'd want on your side," Sonny told him. "If I had to pick five people for this mission, she'd be in the top three. She's smart, focused, and has a mean killer streak. I told you what she did to Alexander Mumford."

He had indeed, and it was an image that would stay with Gray for the rest of his life.

"I'm just worried that her priorities are different from mine," Gray said. "She wants Langton, and I'd hate to think it was at all costs. We can't just go in there guns blazing. We've got to think about the girls."

"Nah, she's not going to do anything to risk their lives. If it'd make you feel better, why not have a word with her? We'll be on that boat for the best part of a day. Plenty of time to put her straight on the mission parameters."

"I'll do that," Gray said.

~

Eva chose to drive so that she could keep an eye on the traffic behind her. Langton must have suspected that she was in the UK, so there was a chance he'd have people looking for her. So far, though, nothing flagged up as suspicious, and her mask would defeat any traffic cameras.

They got to Heathrow fifteen minutes before the check-in desk opened, and Len turned in the rental car before they handed over their printed boarding passes and passports.

Harvey's people had done a good job: the documents passed muster without any drama. They eased through security, then found a bar to relax in before the flight. They would be in the air for twelve hours, and it would probably be the last real sleep they got before they reached Langton's island.

Len had a pint of ale, while Eva sipped a vodka and tonic. It wouldn't be enough to dull the senses, but it would help her nod off once the wheels were up.

They both kept an eye out for possible threats while they drank. Single men and women without any carry-on luggage set the alarm bells ringing, but none of them fit the profile of hunter-killer.

As boarding time approached, Eva ordered one more while Len chased his down with a whiskey. By the time they were on the plane and in their seats, they were ready to sleep.

They'd checked in within ten minutes of each other so as to appear to be traveling alone. It meant they were sitting apart, too, but as they didn't plan to discuss the mission in front of nosy passengers, it was no big deal.

Once the doors were shut and the plane began to taxi, Eva put the complimentary sleeping mask on and closed her eyes. Sleep came almost instantly, and the next thing she knew she was being gently shaken awake by the flight attendant.

"Miss, we'll be landing soon. You need to put your seatbelt on."

Eva left her seat and went to the bathroom to freshen up. Her short hair didn't need much attention, but she availed herself of the free toothbrush and toothpaste provided.

Once on the ground, Eva made her way to immigration. Before flying, she'd told Len to meet her in the arrivals hall. By the time she got through, he was already waiting, looking suitably refreshed.

"You say this is your first time in Mexico?" she asked him.

"Yeah. Always wanted to come but never got around to it."

"Shame. You'd love it. Unfortunately, we won't be seeing much of it. At least, not the good parts. Let's go rent a car."

It was a short walk to the street where several rental agencies were fighting for trade. She picked a budget place and paid cash for a gray Ford sedan, then drove around the corner and made a phone call. She spoke in Spanish, then hung up after a minute.

"Is that your arms dealer?" Len asked.

"Sort of. More a gangbanger, though. He lives in Ciudad Neza, and as it's dark, I'll drop you off at the hotel first. It's not the kind of place a gringo wants to be sitting in a car alone so early in the morning."

Eva drove into the city and stopped outside the hotel where they'd all arranged to meet.

"I should be back well before the others arrive. If I'm not here by then, go on without me."

"Are you sure you don't want to wait for the others?" Len asked as he got out. "It might be safer if we all went together."

"Trust me, if I don't go there alone, it'll all kick off, as you guys like to say."

Smart gave an approving nod. "You know best."

Eva doubled back past the airport and into one of the roughest neighborhoods in Mexico City. She reached the place she wanted, and saw it hadn't changed much since her last visit.

It was predominately a residential area, but multicolored buildings lined both sides of the main streets, most with awnings advertising everything from phone repairs to local delicacies. At this time of the morning, many of the local undesirables were already out and about.

Eva took a side street to cut across to the next main boulevard. As in the rest of the neighborhood, this street's buildings all had iron bars over their windows to give the occupants the illusion of safety. At the next intersection she crossed into an area even rougher than the rest. In an abandoned parking lot, she saw a dozen gang members leaning and sitting on cars, and their eyes followed her as she passed by.

She stopped two blocks away, outside a building that had been white in its heyday but even in the faint glow of the street light she could see it was now a faded gray after years of neglect and pollution. Two bangers stood outside the door to what claimed to be an engine repair shop. She got out of the car to admiring looks and whistles, but ignored them as she walked past the two punks.

Inside, it was clear that no legitimate business had been conducted here for years. The concrete floor was covered in dust and old plaster, and the walls were bare.

"*Hola*, Minx!"

Eva turned to see Alejandro López emerging from a doorway. She walked over with a smile and embraced him, doing her best to hide her revulsion.

López was one of the up-and-coming figures in Mexico's underworld. He specialized in drugs and guns, two commodities that were always in high demand in the poverty-stricken country. He distributed for the Familia Michoacana cartel; in addition to paying him well, the cartel also acted as a deterrent in case anyone tried to encroach on his territory.

"How long are you staying? Please tell me you have time for that dinner date you keep promising me."

"I'm afraid I'm just passing through. But I'll be coming back this way . . ."

She let the promise hang, and it seemed to satisfy him.

"Come. I'll show you what we have."

López led her through the doorway and into a room with piles of boxes covering makeshift tables. He flipped the lid on the first one. It contained three suppressed HK416 CQB rifles, and they looked brand new. She picked one up and checked the mechanism.

"Nice, eh?"

She nodded and smiled, moving on to the next box, which held the upgraded M4A1s she'd requested. Again, they looked to be in factory condition. There was no point asking where they'd come from, though she had a pretty good idea.

"How many rounds did you manage to get?" she asked.

"Two thousand, just as you asked. I also have the night-vision glasses and eighteen grenades for the M203s. Everything your heart desires."

Lopez's smile reminded her of a reptile, but she returned it with one of her most seductive offerings.

"That's perfect. How much?"

"Fifty grand."

It was daylight robbery, but she was in a pinch and didn't have time to shop around. "If you give me an account number, I'll transfer the money immediately."

Lopez threw his arms wide open. "Minx, you know I only deal in paper money. It hurts me that you would suggest such a thing."

"I'm afraid I had to get here in a hurry and wasn't able to arrange a cash payment. Maybe I could pay you on my way back, eh? For old times' sake? I'll even add another five grand for your trouble."

The smile disappeared. "It's not my trouble, it's yours. Cash on delivery, that's how I operate. What if you take these and get killed? How do I get my money then?"

"You know me, Alejandro, I'm untouchable. I'll have your money in three days at the most."

"Then you'll have your weapons in three days. At the most."

Eva hadn't been expecting him to be so obstinate. She'd dealt with him twice before, and on both occasions, he'd been reasonable. Perhaps his meteoric rise had changed him for the worse.

She had ten grand in cash but would need that for later. "Look, I've got a brand-new rental outside. I can give you that as a down payment."

The reptilian smile returned, and his hand brushed the front of his pants. "I have a better idea."

CHAPTER 28

López whipped out his pistol, a Desert Eagle that held .50 Action Express rounds. The half-inch-diameter bullet was big enough to punch a nickel-sized hole in her front and a fist-sized one out the back.

Eva had seconds to decide what she was going to do. If she wanted to take the weapons and walk away friends, she'd have to put out. Was that a price worth paying to get to Langton? What about to save the two children Langton was holding? If she walked out empty-handed, any chance of rescuing them would be gone.

López stood before her, his legs slightly apart, pistol hanging loosely by his side.

She had no option.

Eva took off her jacket and dropped it on the floor. Underneath, she wore a black T-shirt that hugged her athletic figure. She walked toward him, letting her hips sway subtly.

"You drive a hard bargain," she said. She put her hands on his chest and moved them over his pecs, making all the right noises.

López leaned to the side and put the Desert Eagle on the table, and Eva struck.

She brought up her knee and heard a howl of pain as it connected with his groin. As López doubled over, she pushed him backward and kicked him in the face. While he was still falling to the ground, she picked up the pistol and swung around to face his bodyguards.

She'd counted eight in all; now she could only hope that he'd bothered to fill his magazine.

She dropped the first two closest to her before they could react. The others had been quicker to the draw, and one got off a loose round that missed by a couple of yards. She hit him in the chest with a blast from the hand cannon, then dived behind a table and put two rounds into the legs of another. He fell, screaming, and with her last round she polished him off with a head shot before snatching a Glock from one of the dead. She dived back behind the table and pushed it over.

There were four left, including the two watching the door. The gunfire had brought them running, and she picked them off before they could find cover.

Bullets smashed into the table, sending wood splinters flying. One stabbed her in the cheek, but she didn't have time to do anything about it. One of López's men tried to flank her, but when he broke cover, she put him on the ground with two shots, then fired two more over the top of the table in the direction of the last thug. Her volley was immediately answered, and she pressed herself to the filthy floor until the shooting stopped and she heard the familiar sound of a spent clip clunking to the ground.

Eva rose and centered the sights on the man's chest as he frantically tried to pull a fresh magazine from his waistband. He saw her as she pulled the trigger, dropping to the floor in time to send the bullet skimming off his shoulder.

Her own slide showed the Glock was empty.

Eva hurdled the table and ran at him. He was on one knee, and she saw him push a new mag into the grip and flick the slide forward. She threw Lopez's pistol at his head. It bounced off his back as he ducked, but it gave her all the time she needed. She covered the remaining few yards in a second and launched a flying kick that caught him square on the jaw. He tumbled backward, his pistol falling away, and Eva followed through by landing on his chest with her knee. Before he could buck her off, she had his pistol in hand and gave him one of the rounds in the head.

She heard a groan coming from behind her, and she turned to see López staggering to his feet.

"You should have played nice," she said, and put a bullet through his heart.

She had no time to lose now. Gunshots in this part of town were a nightly occurrence, and it would be a while before the police deemed it serious enough to stick their noses in, but she didn't want to hang around in case López had other men in the area.

She took the three HKs out of their box and put them with the M4A1s, then dragged the box to the door. She checked outside for movement, but apart from a couple of curious bangers, no one was about to rush the place. She went back in and threw on her jacket, then put the rest of the gear into one box and took that with her. She checked again, and a crowd of about ten people had gathered, with a couple of kids in gang colors walking toward the doorway.

Eva dragged the heavier box to the rear of the car and popped the trunk, one eye on the approaching bangers. When they got to within a few yards she leveled the gun at the first one.

"Back off!" she shouted in Spanish.

He stopped in his tracks and put his hands halfway in the air, then looked around at the rest of the onlookers. Eva heard them taunting him, and he looked like he was about to respond to the urgings, so she put a round in his shin.

He dropped, screaming and holding his shattered leg, and the crowd scattered.

Eva knew it wouldn't be long before news reached criminals itching for a fight, so she moved the rifles into the trunk and went back for the rest. Once the car was loaded up, she got in and drove around the stricken punk.

Priority one was getting out of the area. She reached a main street and kept the speed up until she'd put a few miles between her and López's corpse. Distance aside, she knew it wasn't a good idea to hang around the capital. One of the punks might have seen her plates and told the police—which was unlikely—or the cartel. If either were looking for her, it could compromise the mission.

After another mile of checking that she wasn't being chased, she found a gas station and filled the tank, then composed a message to Len, telling him to contact the others and instruct them to rent two cars. She added that she'd contact them again with a meeting place, then sent the message.

She drove south. To meet up with the chartered Citation, they'd have to drive toward Acapulco, then east to Puerto Escondido International Airport. She thought it better to wait outside the city limits than venture back into DF—or *Distrito Federal*, as Mexico City was known to the locals.

After twenty minutes, she came to a shopping mall and pulled into the parking lot. She sent Len another message and included her location, then went to get something to eat.

It was three hours before Carl, Len, and Rees arrived; Gray and Sonny were forty minutes behind them due to a delayed flight. Eva allowed them a few minutes to stock up on food for the journey, then led them out of the parking lot. They would have to drive hard and break the speed limit if they were to get back on track. Twenty-nine hours had expired since the original message from Langton. They had another seven or eight hours to drive to the airport, and they still had to stop and pick up the Zodiac and DPVs. That left only about thirty-four hours. They'd figured ten hours to fly to Hiva Oa and twenty-one to get within ten miles of Langton's island, then another three in the water.

It was going to be close.

CHAPTER 29

Emilio Hernández watched the short-haired woman pull into the mall and park among the other cars. He stopped his vehicle across the road and waited for her next move.

Ten minutes passed before she got out and went into the mall. He started his car, then drove over to within a few spaces of where she'd parked.

Hernández got out and looked over at the mall. There was no sign of the woman, so he walked to her car and knelt down near the front tire. He took a transmitter from his pocket and placed the magnetic side under the chassis. He stood and checked for anyone watching, but he was clear.

It was a textbook maneuver, one he'd done a number of times since leaving the Mexican special forces and becoming a private detective. He had many friends who'd left the military and gone on to do wet work for the cartels, but he much preferred a chance of living past forty.

He'd known too many who hadn't. They'd opted for easy money and a lifestyle built around death, and most had already paid the price.

Not Hernández. He'd gone into business for himself, and while the money wasn't as much as his counterparts made, his was a relatively trouble-free life. In the beginning, most of his jobs had involved tracking wives or husbands, looking for proof of infidelity. Occasionally he'd picked up more lucrative work performing rigorous background checks on employees, but his big break had come when the stranger who'd identified himself as Gómez had walked into his office a year earlier. He'd asked Hernández to look into a missing persons case, and he'd found the woman two days later. That had led to a fifty-thousand-dollar retainer and the promise of more paydays to come.

Today was one such day.

His assignment was simple: follow the woman and report back on her activities every two hours.

Hernández walked back to his car and placed a call. He told Gómez about her visit to the warehouse owned by Alejandro López and the subsequent gunfight.

"Is she unharmed?"

"It seems so," Hernández said. "She took two boxes from the warehouse and drove to a mall. She's inside now."

"Okay. Keep us posted."

It had been a strange op so far. Normally he'd be given details about the subject, and what, in particular, he should be looking for. Not this time. He'd been given a photograph and told to wait at the airport arrivals hall in case she turned up. If she did, he was to follow her and observe.

For five hundred dollars an hour, he wasn't complaining.

He started his car and moved it to another part of the lot, where he could still see her rental. On his next check-in he had nothing new to report, but two hours later, minutes after eleven in the morning, he was on the move again.

He'd seen her meet up with the occupants of two other cars and had taken a few shots with his phone camera before calling it in. Again, he was told to watch where they went.

Hernández plugged his tablet into the car's charger as the other vehicles departed, giving them a three-minute head start. When the moving red dot on the tablet's screen showed her car to be a mile away, he left the parking lot and set off after them. He had no need to keep her in view thanks to the tracker, but he did find himself struggling to keep within range of the transmitter.

Wherever the woman was going, she was in a hurry.

CHAPTER 30

Melissa Gray had never been so scared in all her life.

Her daddy had told her that monsters weren't real. *The only monsters are people*, he'd said, *and I'll protect you from them.*

Only he hadn't. He'd left her with Auntie Sarah, and now she was locked in a dark cupboard, her face crusted with old tears and snot.

She couldn't understand why Linda was being mean to her. She hadn't done anything to upset her, but Linda had turned really horrible on the plane. She wouldn't even talk to her anymore. When Melissa had been let out of the little room after the plane landed, she'd asked Linda where her daddy was. But Linda hadn't answered. Instead, a man had taken her roughly by the hand and dragged her down the steps of the plane and on to the runway. Another woman had brought Alana down the stairs, and Melissa remembered her screaming like she'd never heard a baby scream before.

After being forced to pose for a photograph, they'd been put in a car and driven up to a huge house. Inside had been like a fairy-princess palace from her DVDs, but she hadn't been given a four-poster bed and silk sheets. Instead, they'd thrown her in a bare cupboard and given her an old blanket to sleep on.

The room smelled of polish and disinfectant, and there was a smelly mop and bucket in one corner. She'd spread the blanket on the cold wood floor and wrapped herself inside it, but it had taken a while to get to sleep.

Hunger had been the main reason.

For some reason the woman had offered her a ham sandwich again. Melissa couldn't understand why. She'd already told her that she hated ham.

So she'd gone without.

Now, she would have given anything for a lump of green ham and some moldy bread.

Melissa snuggled into the blanket, sniffing back more tears. She wanted her father, but Linda had said she would never see him again. She closed her eyes and wished him there, but when she opened them, she saw only the blurred outline of the vacuum cleaner in the darkness.

She had no idea how long she'd been there. It could have been hours or days. Melissa didn't really care. She just wanted her daddy to come and take her home.

The door to the cupboard opened, and Melissa squinted as the light hurt her eyes. Standing in the doorway was Linda.

"Where's my daddy?" Melissa asked.

"Dead," Linda said, a wicked smile on her face. "Eat your dinner."

Linda put a plate on the floor. Melissa ignored it, despite the growling in her tummy. "He's not dead! He's gonna come and get me!" She tried to project an air of defiance, but it came out as a frightened squeak.

Linda shook her head sadly. "Actually, there's not a chance in hell he's gonna find you." She pulled out a knife. It had a long, jagged blade, and it glistened in the light from the hallway. "The only thing that's coming to get you is this," she grinned, running her finger up the blade.

Melissa's eyes widened, and she grabbed the blanket and pulled herself into the fetal position, covering her head and crying for her father.

"He's not coming! And you've got two more days before I slit your miserable little throat!"

The door slammed and Melissa cried herself to sleep, the ham sandwich on the plate untouched and forgotten.

CHAPTER 31

Eva pulled up outside the sports-fishing outlet and looked at the clock on the dashboard. After the mad dash south, averaging over 110 kilometers an hour, they'd managed to shave almost four hours off the journey, but now they'd be losing more time.

There was no sign of the owner.

She waited for the other two cars to join her, then suggested a late dinner while they waited to collect the goods Farooq had purchased online. Colback volunteered to wait outside the shop in case the owner turned up.

"Thanks. Text me when he gets here."

The five of them walked to a cantina and ordered local fare, washed down with plenty of coffee. When the waitress wasn't hovering, Gray asked about the layout of the airport.

"It's a small place," Eva told him. "One barrier just off the road, then another at the parking lot. Although it's an international airport, it's mostly smaller domestic flights. Charters, that kind of thing."

"What about security and immigration?"

"Minimal. Plus, the average wage in the region is about seven hundred dollars a month. If we have to slip someone a few extra bucks, so be it."

"I was thinking more about X-ray machines and the like. How are we going to get the weapons through?"

"I don't know about X-ray, but I thought we could buy a spare bag for the Zodiac and put them in there, along with the DPVs."

"And if someone wants to inspect it?" Sonny asked.

"We'll turn up fifteen minutes before the flight is due to leave, explain that we're in a hurry and bribe them to let us through. I'll explain that we've got a connecting flight to catch and can't be delayed. A few hundred dollars should smooth the way."

"I hope so," Gray said.

They finished their meal and walked back to the shop. It was ten after six when the owner showed up and let them in.

"I have the things out the back."

They followed the man through to a storeroom. The Zodiac was stowed away in a thick, black nylon bag. Gray unzipped it and checked the rubber hull. It was unused. The aluminum floor was rolled up inside, also brand new.

Sonny inspected the DPVs and was happy with their condition. The outboard motor was used, but in very good shape. The scuba gear they'd ordered was fresh out of the box.

"We'd like a spare bag for the Zodiac," Eva told the store owner.

He apologized and said he didn't have any new in stock, but offered them one that was encrusted in white salt crystals and had clearly seen better days.

"That'll do."

She paid cash for the old bag, the rest having been covered by credit card online.

With their new toys loaded into the cars, they drove to a remote area and parked. Eva rolled the weapons and ammunition inside the wetsuits, then, with a little help, stuffed the lot into the old bag.

"That'll have to do," she said. It would pass a cursory inspection, but if anyone removed the contents, the mission would be lost.

"How long until the plane's due to leave?" Len asked.

"Forty minutes. We'd better get a move on."

They piled back into the vehicles and prepared for the last ten miles on Mexican soil.

In the lead car, Eva set a sedate pace. She reached the turnoff to the airport with twenty minutes to go and stopped at the barrier ten yards from the main road.

The guard asked for her papers, and she handed him the passport she'd purchased from DeBron months earlier. He checked against a printed list, then raised the wooden barrier to let her through. She waited up the road for the other two cars to clear, then drove around a couple of bends and into a nightmare.

Lieutenant Juan Fonseca threw the butt of his cigarette to the floor as the three cars came into view. The colored plates told him they were rentals, which aroused his suspicions. It wasn't a commercial airport with a rental drop-off point, so he wondered whether they were here for legitimate business, or to make his day.

A six-year veteran of the Federal Police, or *Federales* as the locals called them, Fonseca was always on the lookout for the bust that would catapult his career to the next level. The small airport on the south coast was as good a place as any to find it. There were flights to and from El Salvador and Nicaragua twenty-four hours a day, and anyone leaving or arriving in the next twelve hours would get a taste of his diligence.

He saw the people get out of the cars, and immediately sensed trouble. They were all gringos, and the bags they carried between them didn't look like typical luggage.

Fonseca let them walk into the small terminal building, then gestured for four of his men to follow him inside.

"Good evening," he said to the woman, a real beauty even by American standards. She was standing next to a table that held their collection of bags.

He was surprised when she greeted him in flawless Spanish.

"And what is the purpose of your trip?" he asked.

"Fishing. We've got a connecting flight in ten hours, so we're in a hurry to get on board. If we miss it, we'll be stuck on the island for two wasted days."

"Then I shall be as brief as possible," Fonseca told her.

He nodded to his men, then the baggage on the table. They walked over, motioned for the gringos to move aside, and started opening the bags. Fonseca had his eye on the woman all the time. Not to admire her beauty, but because she suddenly seemed nervous.

His hand crept to the pistol in his hip holster, and he unclipped the stud that held the strap in place. The moment one of his men shouted that he'd discovered something, Fonseca whipped out the pistol and leveled it at the woman's chest.

The two officers next to him raised their rifles, and he barked in English for the passengers to raise their hands and drop to their knees. Fonseca kept his gun trained on the woman as he inched closer to the table. One of his men held up an assault rifle and told him there were more inside, plus a ton of ammunition.

"Cuff them," Fonseca said.

One officer had to go to the vehicles to get more handcuffs, but the travelers were soon all secured. Fonseca called his catch in to his superiors while his men performed body searches. He was told to bring the passengers in for questioning, something he was looking forward to.

A pile of cell phones grew on the table, along with wallets, loose cash, passports, and a pistol.

Fonseca picked up a passport and flicked through it. "What was the plan?" he asked the woman. "Swap these for drugs down in El Salvador?"

She said nothing, but it didn't matter. He would have plenty of time with her over the coming days.

"Get them in the cars," Fonseca barked.

His men marched the prisoners out to the two armored vehicles and put three in each. Fonseca sat in front, smiling at the prospect of another promotion.

∼

Emilio Hernández drove past the turn to the airport as the three cars disappeared around a corner. He pulled over at the side of the road and took out his binoculars. Through a gap between two trees he saw them pull up at the terminal building.

Hernández took out his phone and called Gómez.

"They're at Puerto Escondido Airport. I'm guessing they're catching a flight. Do you want me to follow them?"

"No. We'll be in touch."

It looked like the job was over. It had been a long day, and he yawned as he thought about the drive home. The prospect of another ten to twelve hours on the road didn't appeal, so he used his phone to look up hotels in the area. He'd earned enough in the last eighteen hours to afford a decent one.

After finding a place to stay, Hernández took one last look at the airport, then did a double take. He picked up the binoculars and gazed at the terminal.

The woman was being led outside by a large group of *Federales*. In custody with her were the other five men in her posse.

He called Gómez and told him what was happening.

"Wait there and keep me updated."

"They're moving," Hernández said. "Should I follow?"

"No, stay right where you are. Let me know when they come back."

Hernández was about to ask why they would possibly be returning, but the phone went dead. So much for crashing in a cushy hotel bed . . .

He dug into a bag of chips, broke the seal on a fresh bottle of water, and settled in to wait.

~

Eva had never seen such a look of anger in a man's eyes.

Gray was looking at her with pure malevolence. If his hands weren't shackled to the seat, she knew he'd be at her throat by now.

"I'm so sorry," she said, and earned a baton in the ribs for her efforts.

"*Silencio!*"

Gray averted his gaze, not even trying to hide his disgust.

She couldn't blame him. He'd lost any chance of rescuing his daughter, and now faced the prospect of a lifetime in a Mexican prison.

They all did.

She tried to think what she could have done differently, but with time at such a premium there was little more she could have done. It wasn't as if she could call ahead and promise bribes when they turned up. The plan had been hastily put together, and some things simply had to be left to chance.

Their luck had run out.

Eva thought about what to tell the police. They'd try to paint her and the men as gun runners. At best. The worst-case scenario was being charged with attempting to exchange the weapons for drugs, which would mean a longer sentence.

The police were unlikely to believe that they were heading to a fictitious island to kill a man who'd been dead for six months.

Above the roar of the tires and the armored vehicle's big diesel engine, Eva heard a phone ring in the front of the vehicle. The man who'd arrested them answered it, and she learned that his name was Fonseca.

The conversation was one-sided, and it ended with a string of expletives. Fonseca barked an order, and the vehicle screeched to a halt. There was a conversation between Fonseca and the driver, then Eva felt the car begin to move again. It turned around, and they started heading back in the direction they'd come from.

She didn't think much of it. Perhaps Fonseca had been ordered to take them to an alternative police station, or had been told to drive them all the way back to Mexico City.

Either way, it was delaying the inevitable.

The armored car bounced along for about ten minutes before it came to a stop. She heard the front doors open and slam shut again, then the rear door was opened and the last rays of sunlight spilled into the gloomy interior.

"Out!"

Eva was glad to be out of the vehicle, which smelled of sweat and gun oil. She expected to see a police station, but instead was shocked to be standing outside the terminal of the airport.

"I'm sorry to have disrupted your mission, captain," Fonseca said. His voice told her that he wasn't sorry at all, only pissed off.

"You had no way of knowing," Eva said, keeping up whatever pretense was in play.

Fonseca had clearly been given orders to let them go—and indeed, to help them on their way. His men were lugging the heavy bags to the waiting Cessna Citation Sovereign, stowing some in the hold and taking the rest into the cabin.

The handcuffs were removed, and their personal possessions returned to them. Eva walked on to the plane without another word, and as soon as the last member of the team was on board, the doors closed and the Cessna began to taxi.

"What the hell's going on?" Gray asked her. "Why did they let us go?"

Eva looked out a window, still having a hard time believing it herself.

"I have no idea."

~

Hernández was surprised to see the *Federales* return so soon. He watched them drive straight through the checkpoint, then pull up outside the terminal building. The prisoners were helped out of the vehicles, and their restraints removed.

He called Gómez. "They're back. It looks like the *Federales* are letting them go. Yes, they're helping them carry their luggage to the plane."

"Okay, call me when they're in the air," Gómez replied.

Ten minutes later, he saw the aircraft climb into the sky, and he informed his client.

"Thank you. Your mission is complete. Payment will be wired to your account in one hour."

As he put the phone away, Hernández wondered what the woman had done to deserve his scrutiny and the intervention of persons unknown. Someone wanted her on that plane. Someone with enough power to overrule the *Federales*.

He drank the last of his water and started the car.

Sometimes it was best not to know.

CHAPTER 32

"You must have some idea," Gray insisted.

"It has to be the ESO," Eva said. "They must have had someone tailing us to make sure we got to the island. Maybe they want Langton dead just as much as we do."

"Then why not kill him themselves?"

It was a good question. They had a lot more firepower available to them, and it wouldn't take much for them to hit the island with a few fighter-bombers and send a few hundred people in to mop up afterwards.

"Sanders told me that the ESO isn't interested in me, but maybe they thought I was still after them. This could be their way of ensuring I get closure. I get to take out Langton, and that's the end of it. If they killed him themselves and told me that he'd been the one that had tried to flush me out they would have had a hard time convincing me. I guess they want me to see for myself."

"That makes sense," Sonny said. "Shame they couldn't help us a little more, though. A private jet from Heathrow all the way to Hiva Oa would have been nice."

"Yeah," Len agreed. "It would have spared us that brown-trouser moment, too."

The tension was broken as everyone laughed.

Everyone except Gray.

He was still brooding over the fact that the whole operation could have been blown by Eva's arrogance. He tried to temper his emotions by thinking about what he would have done differently, but he couldn't find an obvious answer. Fighting their way into the airport and on to the plane would have been futile. The Mexican Air Force would have intercepted them in minutes and shot them down. Scouting the area first would also have been of little benefit. They would have seen the police and had to proceed anyway, or lose the window of opportunity.

Gray got up and found a bottle of whiskey in the galley. He poured himself a couple of fingers, then took the bottle back in case anyone else was interested. Len and Sonny both had a shot, but the others were settling in for some sleep.

Gray polished off the glass, then got his head down, too.

It seemed like seconds later that the copilot walked into the cabin and announced that they would be landing in half an hour. A favorable tailwind and Eva's insistence that the pilot redline the engines all the way had reduced the flight time by ninety minutes.

Gray drank some water, then went into the bathroom and freshened up. When he returned to his seat, he saw nothing out his window except blue above and below. It was a magnificent spectacle. If it weren't for the fact that he would soon have to swim ten miles under that freezing water, he might have enjoyed the view.

"How do you plan to get past immigration and security here?" Gray asked Eva. "The same Hail Mary?"

"We don't have much choice, though I have a feeling it'll be a lot easier this time."

Her guess was well founded.

The plane landed smoothly and taxied to the front of the terminal. When they took their bags inside, they were asked the reason for their visit. Eva told them it was fishing, and that seemed to suffice. The security staff didn't even make a cursory inspection of the baggage.

Gray asked about hiring a couple of taxis and was told that two would arrive from Atuona in about twenty minutes. They decided to wait outside the airport building, just in case anyone started taking an interest in their bags.

Twenty minutes turned out to be nearly forty, but the vehicles that arrived were in good condition and big enough to carry the six of them and their equipment.

It was a short journey. They parked outside a restaurant that wouldn't open for another half an hour, probably to cater for the early-morning fishing trade. Eva announced that she was heading to the harbor to look at the boat Farooq had sourced in advance.

Gray said he'd go with her. They asked the taxi driver for directions before setting off on the fifteen-minute walk.

"I wanted to apologize," Gray said when they were out of earshot of the others. "There wasn't much else you could have done at Puerto Escondido. I overreacted."

"You were concerned for your daughter. I would have reacted the same way."

Gray wasn't so sure. There was a huge difference between imagining what you would do in a certain situation, and actually living it. Gray had almost lost his daughter once, and he'd sworn never to put her in harm's way again.

He thought perhaps that was why he was being so hard on himself and taking it out on Eva. He'd failed Melissa, and didn't dare imagine what she was going through at that moment.

One thing was certain: from this point on, he wouldn't leave her safety in anyone else's hands.

"I appreciate what you've done to get us this far," he said to Eva, "but from now on, we'll do things my way."

It was enough to raise one eyebrow.

"What I mean is, it's my daughter on that island. When we get to Langton, he's all yours, but this needs to be done with military precision. Len and Sonny know the drill, but I've never worked with you three. They both speak highly of you, and I've no doubt you can handle yourself, but it's my daughter's life at stake."

"And if I think your plan is complete bullshit?"

"Then say so," Gray said. "I don't claim to have all the answers, but we have to go in there with everyone on the same page. In the regiment, we had what we called 'Chinese parliaments.'" He shrugged at her reaction to the term. "Everyone got a say, but I made the overall decision."

"Suits me," Eva said. "Just as long as I get Langton."

"Done."

He'd been expecting a lot more resistance, but was happy to have got the conversation out of the way.

It was a pleasant stroll to the harbor. Farooq had told them to look for someone by the name of Jed, who owned a boat used for deep-sea fishing. He'd agreed to meet them early to discuss the charter, but as yet nothing was confirmed. There were a dozen vessels moored, and they found the *Morbius* easily enough.

Jed was sitting at the stern, a cigarette dangling from his mouth as he tied a lure to a line. He looked to be about sixty, with leathery skin that told of many days under a fierce sun. They introduced themselves and, as previously agreed, Eva handled the negotiations.

"We're here to rent *Morbius* for two days," she said. "I understand it's one of the faster boats on the island."

"Nope." Jed removed the cigarette from his mouth and spat over the side. "It's *the* fastest. She'll do thirty-five knots with a tailwind and a flat sea."

"Sounds like she's just what we're looking for. How much would it be?"

Jed eyed the pair. "Two days, you say? Let's see. Leave at nine be back by dusk, times two . . ."

"No, we'll be staying at sea for two full days."

Jed looked at Eva as if trying to decide whether she was joking or terminally stupid.

"What you see is what you get," he said, tossing the butt into the sea. "Seating for eight people and no bunks. It's a day cruiser, lady."

"That's fine," she said. "We don't need beds."

"No toilet, either. You'll have to piss over the side. In your case, I could find a bucket."

Eva's face lit up. "Wouldn't have it any other way."

Clearly thinking her crazy, Jed scratched his stubbly cheek as he thought of a price. "Three thousand," he said. "US dollars."

"Sounds reasonable." It was a lot less than she'd been prepared to pay for his services. "Do you have GPS?"

"Yep."

"What about fuel?" Eva asked. "Can she handle a long cruise?"

"How far were you thinking? Twenty miles out?"

"A bit closer to five hundred. One thousand round trip."

Jed laughed, but when he saw that he was the only one, he turned serious.

"What's five hundred miles out there that you'd want to see? If you want to get to another island, you can take a plane."

"Not another island. Actually, we want you to drop us off in an inflatable raft roughly five hundred miles northeast of here."

"Lady, there's nothing there. If I drop you off, you'd be dead in a couple of days."

"Let us worry about that. If I offered four grand, would that ease your conscience?"

Jed shook his head. "When you captain a ship, you have certain responsibilities—"

"Five grand, final offer."

Jed sighed. "I gotta be crazy."

"It helps," she said. "We'll be ready to go in an hour."

"What? An hour?"

"No time like the present. We'll get our gear and the others. See you later."

She turned and walked away before Jed could protest at the short notice. Gray fell into step.

"It's not going to be easy assembling the Zodiac on that small deck," he said.

"That's the least of our worries. With all the equipment, that thing's gonna ride low in the water. One big wave and we're swimming the rest of the way."

"Maybe we should build the Zodiac before we set off and tow it behind us. We could dump some of the gear in it, too."

"Sounds like a plan," Eva said.

They were back at the restaurant fifteen minutes later. The others were tucking into a breakfast buffet, and Eva and Gray joined them.

"We'll be casting off in an hour," Gray said. "I'll order a couple of taxis to get our gear to the harbor, then we'll have to inflate the Zodiac. We can't do it on the boat."

He spoke to the waitress and she promised to call two cabs for the short journey. The gear was too heavy to carry all that way.

They finished their last hot meal for a while, then waited outside for the cars to arrive. Sonny excused himself, saying he was going to get supplies for the journey.

"We're going to have to think on our feet once we get to the island," Gray said. "We have no idea what the terrain will be like. The picture of Alana and Melissa showed a beach, but that could go right round the island or just be a small cove. The rest could be vertical cliffs for all we know."

"We also have to consider his defenses," Eva pointed out. "He's the richest guy on the planet, so if you can think of it, he's probably got it. Think surface-to-air missiles, helicopters, a small army, everything."

"The best way to defend an island is to know who's coming," Gray said. "He'll probably have radar. That's why I want to swim the last ten miles. We should have a small enough signature at that range. Any closer and we risk being seen."

"If we're talking sea defenses, then we have to consider the possibility of sonobuoys," Len suggested. "It's a lot easier and more efficient than having patrol boats cruising up and down the coast."

"Good thinking," Gray said. "If he has them, they'll probably be within a hundred yards of the coast. When we get to ten yards out, we'll crab along the coast, just in case there's a welcoming committee."

The taxis arrived just as Sonny returned with bottled water and a bag full of chocolate and energy bars, and they loaded up the baggage. Three minutes later, they were at the harbor.

Jed was carrying two big cans of gas to the boat, and he looked displeased at the amount of baggage they'd brought along.

"Don't worry," Gray told him, "we're gonna tow the inflatable behind us."

They got to work unpacking the Zodiac. They laid out the rubber hull, then inserted the aluminum floor before using a two-handled manual pump to inflate it. They took turns, and within twenty minutes it was ready to go into the water. Jed threw them a rope to tie it off and secured the other end to a cleat on the stern. They packed most of the scuba gear in the Zodiac and tied it down securely.

Gray took Sonny aside.

"Do me a favor. Nip back into town and get us a dozen thick plastic bags and some tape. We need to waterproof the weapons for the swim."

"Shit. I'd forgotten about that."

"Me too," Gray said. "Jog on, then."

While Sonny ran the errand, Gray helped the others get everything else stowed away. By the time Sonny returned, they were ready to go.

The boat had two bench seats, one running either side, and half of the deck was covered by the roof of an open cabin. They took their seats, and Jed cast off, then climbed a ladder to the wheelhouse.

It gave the others a chance to talk among themselves, but for now they sat in silent contemplation. The mission had been on their minds for the last forty-eight hours, but now it was becoming real. They had a grueling boat ride ahead of them, and they'd need to use that time well to cover anything they'd overlooked. Because once they were in the Zodiac skimming their way to Langton's island, it would be too late.

CHAPTER 33

After seventeen hours plowing through the South Pacific, the team was weary. They'd taken a battering as the craft clattered into the tops of four-foot seas, but the thought of the action to come helped focus their minds. They'd managed to grab a couple of hours of sleep each and had eaten their fill of chocolate bars and bananas to top up their energy levels and block their pipes. The last thing they wanted was to take a dump in the middle of the operation.

Jed gave them a warning that they'd be in position in half an hour, and Gray told everyone to get into their wetsuits. Once dressed, they began waterproofing the weapons. A rifle went into each bag, along with spare magazines and a set of NVGs, or night-vision glasses. After taping up the necks of the bags, Gray reminded them what the mission was all about.

"We're here for the kids, first and foremost. Eva can have Langton once the girls are safe, but we need to do this as quietly as possible. If we can, we skirt around any opposition forces, understood?"

He got nods from everyone.

"We're here," Jed called from his perch on top of the open cabin. His reaction to seeing them dressed in scuba gear and carrying plastic-wrapped rifles was priceless, but no one offered an explanation. What could they say? More importantly, who was going to believe him? What they were about to do was unlikely to make the news.

Gray checked the time and saw that they had only eight hours until the deadline.

It was going to be close.

Jed cut the engine, and Len and Rees pulled the Zodiac alongside. Sonny jumped aboard and tied a second rope through a rubber hoop at the inflatable's stern. He threw the other end to Len, who fastened it to the *Morbius*. Once they were all in, Jed appeared at the side of the boat.

He looked nervous, and Gray guessed why. He'd just seen them prepare for war and was probably wondering if they were planning to leave any witnesses behind.

"No need to hang around for us," Gray said, flicking off a quick salute. "We'll make our own way back. Thanks for the ride."

Jed shook his head and began pulling in the mooring lines. "What about your clothes and personal effects?" he asked.

"If you can store them for a few days, that would be great. If no one picks them up within a week, they're yours."

Len started up the outboard motor, and the inflatable bucked at the sudden acceleration. Within minutes, the *Morbius* had shrunk to a dot in the distance.

Gray felt nervous, scared, but that was normal. He'd been into battle many times, and the feeling had been a constant companion on each op. The trick was to use it to his advantage, focusing his mind to concentrate not on what might go wrong, but on how to do his job effectively.

Only this time it was different. It wasn't merely an assault on an enemy position or targeting supply lines; if he failed in this mission, his daughter would die.

He glanced down at the GPS strapped to his wrist and told Len to correct his course a few degrees to starboard. Once the green line indicating their direction passed over the red dot that represented the island, he signaled full steam ahead.

Powering through the swell at twenty-five knots in pitch darkness was a terrifying experience. Occasionally, an unseen rogue wave would roll into their path, and they'd hit it full on, jolting everyone aboard and earning Len more than his share of curses.

It went on for four hours, and by the time they reached the transition point, their arms were numb from gripping the handles of the Zodiac.

Len cut the engine and they donned their scuba gear. Each had a tank of oxygen and a rebreather mask, which would eliminate any telltale bubbles as they neared the shore. They'd brought along six DPVs. The Sea-Doo RS3s were about eighteen inches in length and had a top speed of three knots. In open water, they were meant more as an aid to the swimmer's flippers than as a propulsion device. There were more powerful models available that would have taken them to the island in a quarter of the time, but they weighed around thirty kilos each and it would have been impossible to transport them this far.

"Remember," Gray said, "once we get within ten yards of the beach, turn right and go a hundred yards farther up the coast."

"Got it."

Sticking together in the darkness would be a huge problem, so Gray had asked Jed for some rope. He hadn't had any fit for purpose, but had given them the line from one of his fishing reels and cut it into eight-foot lengths. These were tied to the handles of the DPVs so that all six units were connected.

Preparations complete, Gray thought about a last few words, but he could see they all had their game faces on. He simply nodded and said, "Let's go."

They fell backward off the inflatable and let it drift out of the way, then got in line and set off into the darkness, all traveling three feet below the surface of the ocean. There was no point trying to anchor the

Zodiac for the return journey. If Langton had a way to get on to the island, there had to be a way to get off.

Gray had one eye on the GPS on his wrist, but was constantly sweeping the waters below him for signs of sharks. Not that he had much chance of seeing one in the inky darkness. The waters around French Polynesia were teeming with shortfin makos and oceanic whitetips, two species of shark that could seriously ruin their day. Tiger sharks had also been seen in the waters, and Gray now regretted looking up the information before leaving the UK.

Sometimes, ignorance is bliss.

Fortunately, they encountered nothing larger than a sea turtle on their way to the island. As they neared land, an array of corals festooned the ocean floor, barely visible through the crystal waters below them and populated by an assortment of sea creatures. It would have been a sight to stop and admire on a peaceful sunny day, but they had bigger fish to fry.

A few minutes later, from his angle a yard below the surface, Gray could see the shoreline ahead. He stopped in the water and the others followed his lead when he angled right and followed the near-silent engine of the Sea-Doo. After a couple of minutes, he stopped the engine and removed his weight belt. Until now, its purpose had been to keep him from breaching the surface, but now he attached it to the Sea-Doo's handle and let the DPV sink to the bottom.

As he raised his head above the surface, the first explosion shook the water.

CHAPTER 34

When Michael Olivera received the call to check out an alarm in sector four, he couldn't wait to get there and investigate. After all the action he'd seen in Iraq and Afghanistan with the 75th Ranger Regiment, he couldn't believe any place could be so quiet and boring. The island was certainly idyllic, with the huge house, golf course, swimming pool, and beautiful beaches, but the twelve-hour shifts, seven days a week for two months at a time, were beginning to wear at his sanity. Sure, the compound had all the luxuries you could think of, but they were off limits to everyone but Mr. Danby.

In another few days, Olivera would rotate back to the world. A boat would bring in another thirty men to relieve them, and he could go and spend sixty days catching up on beer and women, two things forbidden while on duty. His neighbor in Sacramento was taping the football playoffs for him, and he had a huge Amazon Prime Video library to get through before he returned for another eight weeks of sheer boredom. Having a TV would have relieved some of the tedium, but no personal electronics were allowed. One ex-soldier caught trying to sneak a phone on board the ship as it left the west coast of the US had been turned away, missing out entirely on the three-grand-a-day gig. For that money, Olivera was happy to stick to books and porn magazines.

"On my way," he told Nest, the apt name for the control room, which was located within the house at the center of the small island that towered above the terrain. The entire island measured only two miles across and three miles in length, and the house sat on the summit of an extinct volcano. A single, winding road led up to the front of the building, which looked like a colonial mansion.

He had no idea who Danby was, though he'd been told he was an ex-NSA adviser. Olivera had done a search on him after getting home on his first shore leave, but Google had no record of the man. He'd also tried to find the island on maps but, lacking coordinates, he'd been unsuccessful. All he knew was that it took ten days to get there by sea, and the course changed each trip. Best he could figure, they were on one of the 118 islands in French Polynesia, but damned if he could narrow it down to the exact one.

Olivera told his three subordinates to get in the open-topped Jeep, and he drove them down to the beach. This area was one of ten sectors the island had been split into, and Nest had reported a hit on a couple of sonobuoys in the area. The beach in this cove was three hundred yards long, so he asked whether Nest could narrow it down a little.

When the instructions came back, Olivera drove to the specified location and played the vehicle-mounted spotlight over the water.

It looked as calm as ever.

"Nest, are you sure about the location? There's nothing here."

"Roger, that's the spot. We got a decent hit off units 238 and 239."

Olivera checked his tablet again and confirmed that he'd come to the right place.

"Cover your ears, Nest. If anyone's in the water, I'm gonna wake 'em up."

He pulled the pin of a grenade and tossed it into the water. A fountain erupted, but the ocean quickly settled back to its usual tidal pattern. He gave it a minute, then unclipped another grenade and threw it farther out to sea. This time, the spotlight caught movement, and Olivera followed the shape for a few seconds before losing it.

"It was a mako," he told Nest.

One reason the beaches were off limits was the number of sharks that inhabited the reef half a mile out. It wasn't uncommon for large predators to activate the buoy alarms, especially when they were thrashing around while feeding. Tonight, one had strayed too far toward shore, and Olivera had just given it the mother of all headaches.

"Roger that. There's nothing else showing. Stand down."

With the morning's excitement already over, Olivera ordered his disappointed troops back into the Jeep and they drove inland to continue their patrol.

CHAPTER 35

"Damn, that was close," Rees whispered.

They were treading water a hundred yards from where the grenades had exploded, and five yards from a sheer rock face. Far enough away that they wouldn't easily be spotted from the beach.

"Good call, Tom," Len added. "That could have been us."

Gray was happy that he'd foreseen the danger, but he needed their luck to hold out a little longer.

"We're not there yet," he said. To their left was the beach, while ten yards to their right was a rocky outcrop. "How should we go in?"

"If they're expecting an attack from the sea, they'll have trip wires or motion sensors on or near the beach."

"Maybe," Gray said, "or they might think the sonobuoys are enough."

"When you've got as much money as Langton, there's no such thing as overkill."

Gray didn't doubt Eva's words. She knew more about the old man than he did.

"Okay, we go over the rocks, but be on the lookout for anything manmade."

They swam slowly to the outcrop, where they dumped their flippers into a crevice and removed the plastic covers from their weapons. With his NVGs on, Gray scanned the climb ahead closely. It appeared to be about sixty yards to the top, but he could see plenty of handholds even after the boulders transitioned to a smooth cliff face.

"Sonny, up you go."

Sonny climbed on to the nearest rock, then slung the HK over his shoulder and made his way up the cliff like a mountain goat on a promise. When he got to the top, he paused, stuck his head over the summit, and scanned the other side. Seconds later, he motioned for the rest to follow.

It had been a while since Gray had been mountain climbing, and he felt it. The others were quickly leaving him behind, but he told himself it wasn't a race. He took his time, making sure he got good handholds before inching closer to the top.

When he got there, he was blowing harder than he'd expected.

"Tom, I think you're—"

"—getting too old for this shit," Gray said, finishing Len's sentence for him and catching his breath. He made a promise to himself that when he got back, he would add upper-body work to his daily exercise routine. A three-mile jog clearly wasn't enough.

While he got his breath back, Gray looked up at the mountaintop mansion, its roof visible above the nearby treetops. It appeared to be a bit more than half a mile away, as the crow flies.

"Ready when you are," Eva said.

"I've been thinking," Gray said. "We should split up."

"Seriously?" she asked. "We've got no comms. How do we stay in touch?"

"It doesn't matter. I just think it gives us two chances to reach the girls. If one team trips an alarm, the others are still on mission. If we get caught together, it's over."

"Do you want the first team that reaches the house to wait or go on in?"

Gray thought it through and decided to have them wait. If one team got there intact, the other might, too.

"If you're there first and hear the other team engaging, go in. We'll do the same. Otherwise, meet you there."

Gray selected Len and Sonny to go with him, and they set off first. He chose a straight path to the house, which led through thick foliage. He was working on the assumption that any cameras or tripwires would be set in the most accessible places, though skipping the trails would make for slow going. It also meant that if anyone was listening for them, their movement through the vegetation could give them away.

Gray checked his watch. Langton had threatened to kill the girls in the next forty-five minutes if Harvey didn't give up Eva's location.

They'd moved two hundred yards through the foliage when the sound of gunshots reached them. It was coming from up ahead, and he didn't need to tell Sonny and Len to join him.

They ran through the trees. Their presence was known, so there was no further need to remain quiet.

The gunfire grew louder and more intense. Gray could see muzzle flashes coming from his right and left, and it was clear that his friends needed help. It looked to be three against eight or more. He signaled for Sonny and Len to follow closely as he aimed to flank the island's defenders.

An explosion ripped a tree apart as Eva's team sent a grenade from an M203 toward the enemy, but the incoming fire didn't falter. That told Gray that they were facing seasoned fighters.

Through his NVGs, he could now see the closest of the defending force. To his surprise, they were only ten yards away, nearly invisible in the greenery and darkness.

At least, the defenders he knew about.

Gray waited for Sonny and Len to get in position, then opened up on the nearest figure. Through his NVGs, he saw a puff of green explode from the man's head, and Gray moved forward in search of the next target. A hail of bullets slammed into the tree next to Gray, sending splinters flying. He answered with a round from the underslung M203 and saw body parts separate in the air. Len and Sonny also engaged the opposition; with fire coming from two directions, it wasn't long before the last defender was mopped up.

"Eva!" Gray shouted.

The other team ran over, swapping out magazines on the move.

"What the hell happened?"

"They must have cameras," Eva said. "We were in cover and silent when they opened up."

A groan came from behind them, and Gray jogged over to find that one of Langton's men was seriously wounded but still alive. He'd taken rounds to the abdomen, and blood was bubbling from his mouth. He was going to die, and it would be painful to the end.

"How many men on the island?" Gray asked. "Tell me and I'll send for help."

"Fuck you . . ."

"Please yourself."

Gray ripped the comms pack from the man's belt and pressed the Send button. "I need twenty men here, now!"

He waited, looking at the rest of his team, wondering whether the people on the other end of the radio would detect the ruse.

"I'm not sending everyone. Eight are on their way."

That was all Gray needed to know. He put a bullet in the survivor's head, then put on the earpiece and stuffed the enemy radio into his wetsuit. The others had gathered radios for themselves, and Gray led them in the direction of the house.

"There are more on the way. Eight of them. Let's try and find a road and get to the house as soon as we can."

CHAPTER 36

"What the hell is going on?" Langton demanded as he kicked open the door to the control room. "I heard gunfire!"

"Sir, we have intruders on the island."

"Intruders? Who? How many?"

"At least half a dozen. One of them's a woman."

Langton looked up at the large screen on the wall. "Show me."

Eckman played the recording he'd made when the trio had first been caught on camera and Langton recognized her face instantly.

Driscoll.

"Why the hell didn't you call me?"

"We've been busy organizing the defenses. We engaged them and had them pinned down, but Oscar One reported at least three more on his left flank."

Langton wondered how the hell Driscoll had been able to find him, but it was a question that would have to wait until later. Right now, he needed to stop her.

"Where is she now?"

"We don't know, and Oscar One isn't responding."

"You don't know? We've got a hundred cameras on this rock. Find her!"

The team flicked through the array of cameras. Sixteen at a time could be seen on the big screen, and they soon detected movement.

"She's three hundred yards from the house," Art Barnaby said.

"How many men have we got left?" Langton asked.

"Twenty-two. Eight are on their way to intercept them as we speak."

"Send another ten and leave four to protect the house. Send two of those to me now."

~

They found a road leading to the house, and Gray put his hand up to listen to what was being said over comms.

"They've got eighteen more men coming our way now," he told the group, "and they know where we are."

"Then let's give them a warm welcome," Len said.

Back in the day, they'd have had the chance to choose their ordnance before departing on the mission, and Claymore anti-personnel mines would have been near the top of the list. Now, however, there was little time to do much more than dig in defensively or push the attack.

Gray preferred the latter. The house was now only three hundred yards away, and his daughter likely in it, but the numbers remained in the enemy's favor.

He had to even the odds a little.

"Let's get two grenade launchers up the road as fast as we can. Once we see them coming, we let 'em have it. The rest of us will stay in the trees and move up on their left and right."

Eva and Rees Colback had two of the M4A1s, and they jogged up the road a hundred yards, sticking to the trees and ready to dive for cover at the first sign of trouble. It wasn't long before they found it. Four men ran into view, and the instant they appeared, grenades flew their way. All four were blown off their feet, the two moaning survivors finished off with bursts from the rifles.

Gray and the others took the opportunity to move up. They'd split into pairs, two on each side of the road, ten yards into the treeline. It wasn't long before they found targets.

Gray saw three men creeping along the side of the road, and he and Len tore into them. The targets dropped to the floor, one looking for cover, the other two dead.

Twelve defenders remained, and they all opened up at once. Gray's team answered immediately with volleys of their own, and Gray added a couple of M203 grenades to the mix, the resulting screams confirming hits on two of them.

Gray saw movement out of the corner of his eye. "They're trying to flank us!"

He sent another grenade in the direction of the flankers and followed up with a burst of 5.56mm, and four more men fell. The numbers were now in their favor, and Eva and Colback piled on the pressure with their grenade launchers. They took out two more, leaving only a quartet between Gray and his daughter.

That's when time stood still.

In green-tinged slow motion, he saw a man thirty yards away stand and hoist a large tube on to his shoulder. Gray raised his rifle and fired, the bullet hitting the man in the chest, but not before an RPG round flew with a fiery tail across the road and into the trees.

The resulting explosion was devastating.

"*LEN!*"

Sonny ran to where his best friend had been taking cover.

His body language said it all.

After looking down at Len Smart's body for a few seconds, Sonny marched directly at the enemy line, spraying them with lead and turning the air blue with his language. Gray and the others covered him, all the while shouting for him to get down, but Sonny wasn't listening.

Gray used the last of his grenades and emptied his magazine into the enemy, then stooped to switch it out, but by that time it was all over. His explosives had done most of the damage. Sonny cleaned up.

Gray jogged over to him as Sonny inserted a new magazine and emptied it into the corpse lying next to the RPG-7. When the firing pin clicked on an empty chamber, Sonny reached for another mag.

Gray put his hand on Sonny's shoulder. "Save it. We're not done yet."

Sonny spun, and Gray barely recognized him. His youthful looks had fled, his face contorted in fury.

"Sonny! Listen! We need you."

Sonny clapped him on the arm and turned, walking toward the house.

Gray turned to find the others, and saw Eva standing where Sonny had moments earlier. He trotted over to her and saw the reason why.

Carl Huff was lying a few yards from Len Smart, the two of them on either side of a crater. Len had lost his legs below the knees, and half of Carl's face was missing.

A thousand emotions flooded through Gray's body, anger and grief battling for dominance. His hands began to shake, and he gripped his rifle tightly so that it wouldn't show.

"We've got to go," he said. "We'll mourn them after the battle, not during."

Eva took a deep breath and nodded once. "Let's go get them."

CHAPTER 37

They got to within fifty yards of the house before they came under fire
again. Two men were using huge ornamental lions as cover outside the
main entrance, and their first volley missed Gray by inches.

"Spread out!"

The quartet dispersed so that they had a better angle on the shoot-
ers, and Gray threw himself behind a tree and returned fire. Eva used
the last of her grenades to take one of them out. The one that remained
tried to backpedal into the house, firing as he went, but Sonny hit him
in the chest with a three-round burst.

Gray sprang to his feet. He sprinted to the door and put the muzzle
of the rifle through the opening. He knew there were at least two more
guards standing between him and his daughter. He had no idea how
many other people might be in the house.

Sonny tapped him on the shoulder, the signal to go in. Gray stepped
inside and Sonny followed. Eva and Colback were not far behind. Gray
gestured for them to check the rooms on the right while he and Sonny
went left.

The first room Gray and Sonny came to was a reception room that
looked like something from a royal palace. It was sixty feet long, and
at the far end was a door. Gray skirted the antique furniture, checking

behind the sofa as he went, but the room was empty. He got to the door and put his back to the wall as he tested the handle. Open. Gray kicked it and stepped back to allow Sonny to check for targets.

"Clear!"

They heard gunfire from somewhere in the house, and the pair ran toward it. They were back in the entrance hall when another burst rang out. They crossed into another reception room decked out like the first, and saw Eva emerge from a doorway.

~

The moment Eva and Colback approached the door, they heard raised voices inside. Eva kicked it in and stepped into the room, just in time to see one of the people inside reach for a pistol. She put a burst in his chest and dropped him, and the others in the room threw their hands up in surrender. They looked to be techies, and posed no immediate threat.

"How many are there?" she shouted. "How many left?"

"F–f–four. Two soldiers, Linda Myers, and the old man. Oh, and the housekeeping staff."

"Where?"

"Housekeeping? In the basement."

"The others!" Eva barked.

"I don't know."

Eva looked at the screens they monitored. She'd seen similar operations rooms at CIA headquarters, and they served one purpose. These were the men who had tracked Farooq to Lyon and had been instrumental in the kidnapping of the two girls. If it weren't for them, Langton would be blind, impotent, and she and Carl would be sitting in a Munich café enjoying lunch right now. Instead, the only man she'd ever loved was lying dead with half his brains missing. They might only be armed with computers and radios, but they were still responsible for Carl's death—as culpable as the man who had fired the rocket that killed him.

Eva pointed her rifle at the youngest one. "How much is he paying you?"

"T—two grand a day," he stuttered.

"When you get to hell, ask yourself if it was worth it."

The analyst started pleading for his life, but Eva had already tuned him out. She'd been trained to kill, not empathize or exercise her conscience. She'd made her decision, and no amount of begging was going to change her mind. She emptied the magazine into the techs, each bullet a small slug of revenge.

"They were unarmed!"

Eva looked at Colback with contempt. "These people were Langton's eyes and ears. They guided those men in to kill me in Lyon. They found Farooq and reignited all this. The girls were put in danger because of their actions. Do I have to go on?"

"I was just saying that—"

"Well, don't. If you dance with the devil, you get burned."

She walked out of the room, leaving Colback shaking his head.

~

"Did you find the girls?" Gray asked Eva.

She shook her head. "That was the control room," she said. "Only two men left, plus Myers, Langton, and the household staff."

"Where are they?"

"The staff are in the basement. No idea about the others."

"You two clear the ground floor," Gray said. "Sonny and I will take upstairs."

Gray took the lead up the marble staircase, looking up while Sonny covered their rear. At the top he had two choices: left or right. He went left, hugging the wall and focusing on the doors to either side.

It was the wrong decision.

Sonny let off a burst in the opposite direction just as a bullet slammed into the wall next to Gray's head. He turned and saw someone he'd been hoping to meet disappearing through a doorway.

Linda Myers.

Sonny was already on his way, and Gray tucked in on Sonny's left as they crept along the landing. When they came to the door, it was slightly ajar. He told Sonny to get on the other side of the doorway, then pushed it open with the barrel of his rifle.

Shots rang out, and Sonny stuck the nose of his HK into the doorway and emptied half a magazine. Gray joined in, and when Sonny stopped firing he took a couple of steps into the room looking for Myers.

He saw a woman's arm sticking out behind a sofa. Gray approached, rifle at the ready, and he gradually saw the rest of her. Myers was lying on her back, her right hand on her throat as she tried to stem the flow of blood.

Gray stood over her as her fading eyes stared at him with defiance. It wasn't how he'd wanted her to be when he faced her, helpless on the floor with her life ebbing away. He'd imagined getting his hands around her throat and taking her life while she was able to defend herself, not watching her bleed out on a very expensive carpet.

Regardless, she'd taken his daughter and would pay for it.

"This is from Andrew," he said, and put a round in her left knee. Her face contorted, but she didn't have the strength to move.

Sonny came and stood next to him. "Is this Myers?"

Gray nodded, and Sonny put a bullet in her other kneecap. "That's for Len."

He turned and walked back to the door, leaving Gray alone with her.

"Normally I'd put one in your head," said Gray, "but you don't deserve it. I want you to die slowly, in as much pain as possible."

He fired one more round straight through her belly button, guaranteeing that her last moments would be intolerable.

He walked back out of the room, to where Sonny was waiting, then pointed down the corridor.

There was work still to be done.

Gray was just about to try the knob of the next door when he heard shouting coming from the ground floor.

"Drop your weapons or the girls die!"

Gray and Sonny ran to the balcony and stood at the railing, looking down at the grand hallway below. Colback and Eva had their rifles aimed at two of Langton's men.

One was holding Alana and had a knife to her throat, and the other had a pistol pointed at Melissa's head. Ten yards to their right, the man he guessed must be Langton stood with his hands on his hips.

"Let them go," Eva said, her aim never wavering. "It's me you want."

Langton laughed. "Really? Hand over my only insurance? I don't think so. What I will do is let you tell me how you found me."

From his vantage point, Gray looked down at the classic standoff. If Driscoll were to shoot, Alana would be okay but Melissa's fate was far from certain. Unless it was a perfect shot that closed down the man's brain instantly, the dying man's reflexes would kill his little girl.

He had to end this without gunfire.

An idea came to him. It was crazy, but worth a try. If it failed, they could always resort to plan A: shoot the fuckers. He whispered instructions to Sonny and watched his friend disappear to carry them out.

"The photo you sent of the girls had GPS coordinates in the metadata," Gray said to Langton as he walked down the stairs, gun locked on the man holding Melissa.

"Ah, you must be Tom Gray. I must reproach Myers for her mistake. Not quite the camera expert she claimed to be."

"Then you'd better hurry. She's only got a few seconds left."

Gray reached the bottom of the stairs and slung his rifle over his shoulder, knowing Eva and Colback had the guards covered.

"Daddy!"

The cry broke Gray's heart, but he knew it wouldn't be long before she was in his arms once more.

"Stay still, darling. It'll all be over soon."

They heard a whistle, and when Gray looked up, Sonny threw Myers's phone down to him. Gray opened it and turned on the camera, setting it to record.

He stood facing the men holding the children. "Is this the man who pays you?" he asked, pointing at Langton.

One of them nodded.

"Good. Because in about one minute, Eva's going to kill him. Then you have to decide what you're going to do. You can either kill the girls, in which case you not only won't get paid, but you'll be dead, too. I'll be recording it, and I'll make sure the video goes viral. I don't know if you've got wives, or mothers, or children, but they'll remember you as baby killers. Or you can let the girls go. We'll let you leave the island with whatever you can carry to make up for lost wages. You should be able to get a few million for some of these pictures on the wall."

The two men looked at each other.

"Don't even think about it," growled Langton. "You work for *me*!"

The men were clearly undecided.

"I'll give you a ten-million-dollar bonus," Langton said, clearly realizing how precarious his position was.

"Not much good to 'em if they're dead." Gray turned back to the soldiers. "Fifteen seconds left. Live well or die horribly, the choice is yours."

The one holding Alana tightened the grip on his knife for a few seconds, then let it drop to the floor. Melissa's captor released his grip, and she ran to Gray.

"Cowards!" Langton yelled, and pulled a pistol from inside his immaculately tailored suit jacket. He raised it and aimed at Eva, but Sonny was quicker. He let off a round that caught the old man in the shoulder, sending him spinning. Langton hit the wall and the gun flew out of his hand. He slid down, clutching his arm.

The two remaining soldiers looked apprehensive. Eva and Colback still had their guns trained on them, their fingers itchy on the triggers.

"Toss your weapons," Gray told them. "Eva, let them go."

Eva lowered her weapon and watched the two men visibly relax. One of them held out Alana, and Colback took the baby from him.

Gray hugged his daughter, tears welling in his eyes.

"Daddy, she said you weren't coming." She was crying as she spoke, and it was a heartbreaking sound.

"I know, darling, but she was wrong. I'll never leave you, ever again."

Eva stood next to Gray. "Clever move, but just so you know, we could have taken them."

"And you could have killed my daughter. My way worked better. Besides, they were just earning a living, same as when you hired Sonny and Len."

At the mention of Len's name, Gray felt a hole in the center of his chest. With his daughter finally safe, his grief for his old friend threatened to overwhelm him.

Eva had walked over to Langton and now stood in front of him. "Get out," she told the others. "This one's mine."

Gray looked over and saw the look in her eyes. He knew what was coming, and he didn't want Melissa to witness it.

"Stay here, darling," he said to his daughter.

He strolled over to Eva and stood next to her. "Consider yourself lucky," he said to Langton in a soft voice his daughter wouldn't hear. "I promised Eva that I would leave you to her. I guess she's gonna do some fucked-up things to you, but if I had my way, it would be a lot worse.

Before she starts, though, I'm going to your quarters and I'm going to help myself to your stuff. All those precious trinkets you've traded for human life and misery are now mine. I'm a nobody, someone who's done nothing to deserve them, but I'm taking them and there's nothing you can do about it."

Langton said nothing, but his sheen of arrogance had been wiped away.

Gray managed a half laugh. "Doesn't it feel terrible to be powerless," he said. "You've had everyone on this planet dancing to your tune for all these years, and now *you're* the one on the receiving end of a shafting. You think we're scum, worthless peons, but now we're going to walk away with everything dear to you. I hope you choke on that thought before you die."

Gray turned to Eva. "Give us five minutes."

He walked over to take Melissa's hand, then spoke to what was left of Langton's security force. "Show me his room."

The two men led Gray and Melissa up the stairs. Gray had his gun handy in case they tried anything, but they seemed content with the situation they'd found themselves in.

On the landing, they indicated three doors. Gray chose not to go into the room where Myers would now be lying dead. Instead, he chose the third door, which opened into a bedroom.

"Have a look around for anything pretty," he said to Melissa.

They pulled open drawers and cupboards but found very little inside. He looked for a safe, while Melissa explored an adjoining dressing room. Gray looked behind every picture on the wall, but none concealed a safe of any description.

"Daddy, this is nice."

Gray followed her into the dressing room and saw her holding up an old-fashioned pocket watch.

"Where did you get that?"

"In here."

Gray looked in the drawer and saw at least three dozen more watches. Underneath each was a piece of paper. He took out the one that had been underneath the pocket watch and saw that it was a certificate of authenticity. He knew nothing about timepieces, but guessed it might be worth a few thousand dollars, especially with the accompanying paperwork.

He found a small carry-on bag in the corner of the dressing room and emptied the drawer into it.

He considered looking for some clothes to replace the wetsuit he was wearing, but Langton's would have been too small. He would have to put up with it for now.

"That should do," he said. "Let's go home."

He threw the bag over his shoulder and held her hand as he led her back downstairs. Eva hadn't moved an inch. He heard a noise behind him and turned to see the two surviving members of Langton's security team walking down the stairs. They had their own bounty wrapped in silk sheets, and seemed almost buoyant as they headed for the door.

"Hey, do me a favor," he said to them. "Go and find some clothes for me and the others. This thing's beginning to chafe. Also, I need a changing kit for the baby and a couple of body bags."

One of them dropped his loot and jogged back up the stairs, while Gray spoke to the other.

"How do we get off this island? Is there a boat or something?"

"Better. There's a private jet on the north of the island."

"And the pilots? Don't tell me we killed them."

"No, they stay in a residence by the runway."

"Great. Meet us there."

"Will do. And . . . I'm sorry. That wasn't what I signed up for."

"I know." Gray had banked on the two men to be working for Langton to earn a dollar, not because they wanted to kill innocents for fun. His guess had been right.

"You'll find a few vehicles around the back of the house," the man added. "Out the door and turn right. The keys are in the Jeeps."

"Which way to the airfield?"

"Follow the road until you come to a fork, and go left."

Gray thanked him and joined up with Sonny and Colback, who was doing his best to comfort the screaming baby.

"We've got transport home," Gray told them. "We're taking Len and Carl with us."

"I'll help you," Sonny said.

"Okay, but first let's get these two to the plane."

Gray told Eva the plan, and she nodded before dragging Langton to his feet and pushing him through a doorway. She closed the door quietly, and as Gray left the house, he heard the faintest of screams coming from the depths of the mansion.

Eva had been keen to get started, and he didn't envy Henry Langton one bit.

They followed the directions Gray had been given and found four Jeeps lined up at the rear of the building. Sonny drove, and five minutes later they'd navigated the dark roads and found the airport.

Gray had been expecting something along the lines of the Citation they'd used the previous day, not the full-blown passenger jet parked next to a simple, two-story structure.

Gray told Melissa to wait in the car, and knocked on the house's door. A light came on upstairs, and a minute later the door was opened by a sleepy-eyed man in his fifties.

"Get the plane ready," Gray said. "We're leaving."

"What?" the man asked, rubbing his eyes. "I didn't receive any orders. Plus I need personal authorization from Danby." He looked Gray up and down, as if noticing the wetsuit and bare feet for the first time.

"He's dead," Gray said, bringing the M4A1 into view. "Want to join him?"

The man put his hands up and backed into the room, shaking his head now that he was wide awake. Gray followed him in.

"You'll be taking us to Heathrow, England."

"Okay, but we'll need to refuel her first."

"No problem. Once that's done, go down to the house and collect anything you want. Call it severance pay. Just don't try to call anyone. One of my men will be with you, so no funny business."

"Understood. I'll have to go and wake John. He's the pilot."

"Then let's go."

Gray followed him up the steps and waited while he knocked on a door. The man who opened it was also in his late forties to early fifties.

"Have you got any idea what time it—"

The copilot cut him off and explained the situation. The captain declared it quite unorthodox, but once he found out about the free pickings back at the main house, his manner improved.

"How long before we can get in the air?" Gray asked.

"A couple of hours," the captain said in an English public school accent. "We'll need to pump her full of Jet A-1, which takes about twenty minutes. Then we have to perform our preflight checks. You do realize that we'll have to stop for more fuel on the way, don't you?"

"That's fine, just as long as it's a quick turnaround."

"It usually is. We'll contact Panama and let them know we're coming."

"Good. I'll let you get changed."

Gray started back down the steps, then stopped. "I don't suppose you've got anything to eat here? We're starving."

"Kitchen's downstairs, first on the right. There's some spaghetti left over from last night, if that's any good."

"That'll do nicely."

Gray went to find the food and put a big bowl of it in the microwave, then went to fetch his daughter.

"Daddy, I'm sooooo hungry."

"Then you come with me. I've got the perfect thing."

He took her into the house and sat her at the small kitchen table. When the microwave pinged, he put the bowl in front of her and gave her a fork and spoon. "Dig in, darling. I just have to go and make a phone call."

CHAPTER 38

Andrew Harvey felt as tense as Sarah looked. Only Veronica Ellis seemed to be in control of her emotions as they sat in her glass palace, waiting for the phone call.

The deadline had passed fifteen minutes earlier. An hour ago, he'd added a new comment to the YouTube video, asking for another twenty-four hours and claiming that he'd been chasing down some strong leads.

He'd refreshed the page every ten seconds, looking for a reply, but to no avail.

"What if they didn't get there in time?" Sarah asked.

"It's Tom we're talking about. He'll get there."

"But what if something went wrong? What if—"

Andrew jumped as the phone in his hand started playing a tune. He looked at the caller ID and saw a familiar number. He knew he'd seen it recently and tried to remember where.

The answer leapt out and shocked him.

"It's Myers," he said. The cell phone continued to sing out to him, and he reluctantly hit the Connect button and put the call on speaker.

"About bloody time," Gray said. "I thought you were never gonna answer."

"Oh, thank God!" Sarah said, the tears finally coming after days on edge. She threw her arms around her fiancé.

"Are the girls okay?" Andrew asked, still hugging Sarah tightly.

"They're fine. A little hungry, but we're working on that as we speak."

There was a collective sigh in the room. After almost three days of waiting, it was a huge relief to finally have some good news.

"I can't thank you enough," Andrew said. "Do you have a way to get off the island, or do you need our help?"

"No, we're gonna take the old man's private jet. They're getting it ready as we speak. I think it'll be about ten hours to Panama, a couple of hours to refuel, then twelve to Heathrow. Expect us there at about three tomorrow afternoon."

"We'll be there waiting for you," Andrew said. "Is there anything you need?"

The phone went quiet for a few moments. "Two coffins."

Ellis's hands went to her mouth, and Andrew bowed his head. "Who didn't make it?"

"Carl and Len."

Andrew choked back a cry. When he'd seen them off three days earlier, his thoughts had only been for his daughter's safe return; it never once crossed his mind that his friends might not make it back.

"How did it happen?"

"I'll tell you when we get home. See you tomorrow."

Gray hung up.

They sat in silence for a while, each coming to terms with the news in their own way.

"I can't believe Len's gone," Andrew said. "I always thought those guys were invincible."

"Me too," Sarah agreed.

"Tom must hate me for getting them involved in this."

Gray had certainly sounded cold and distant during the call. Perhaps his relief at getting his daughter back had been tempered by Len's death . . . or maybe it was loathing that Andrew had heard.

"He might now," Ellis said, "but in time he'll see that it was what Len would have wanted. He died doing what he did best. He was a true soldier."

Andrew nodded, but the feeling of guilt just wouldn't leave him. Every time he looked at his daughter, he would remember the sacrifice Len had made to reunite them.

"Go and check the flight plan with Heathrow to get an ETA," Ellis said, "and arrange for someone to collect the bodies at the airport. They'll also need accommodation when they get back. Sarah, you sort that out."

They both left Ellis's office and went back to their stations, but not before they shared another hug and broke the news to the rest of the team.

CHAPTER 39

Bill Sanders tossed the last of the suitcases into the back of the SUV and slammed the door closed. His wife Joanne was standing by the front door of their house, and she looked as if she was trying to remember whether she'd packed everything.

"Will you just get in the car!"

Given the choice, he would have left everything he owned, but Joanne had a sentimental streak that bordered on insanity. She'd insisted on bringing framed photos dating back years, while he only wanted to put the past behind him.

The contact from the ESO had come twenty-four hours earlier in the form of an advertising flyer. When it had dropped through the mail slot, he'd gotten in his car and driven to the mall to make a call to the fictitious travel agency he used to contact the ESO.

Minutes later, he'd been given his itinerary. They were to go to a local heliport and be flown to a regional airport, where they'd pick up their new papers and fly by private jet to Antigua.

A hotel had been booked in their names and paid for by the ESO, and a local high-end real estate agent would meet them that evening to discuss their needs.

Joanne finally got in beside him, and he pulled out of the driveway.

"Did you remember to turn off the furnace?"

"What the hell does it matter? In a couple of hours, we'll be officially dead. Who are they going to send the utility bill to?"

Sanders hadn't been given details as to how their deaths would be faked, only that it would happen that day. He suspected they would dress up the corpses of a couple of homeless people, put their bodies in a vehicle, and push it into a lake. Give it a few months, and there would be nothing more than bones left.

They would have to do something about their teeth, but a little creative dentistry would fix that.

On the freeway, his wife was already planning their new home.

"It has to have a pool, and a separate wing for the staff to sleep in."

"We'll find out what's available when we get there."

Joanne had wanted to search online for properties in St. John's, Antigua, but having that in their web-search history hours before disappearing would raise too many questions. He'd managed to convince her to be patient, which hadn't been easy. With forty million in the bank, she was desperate to go on a shopping spree.

It was an hour to the heliport, and when they arrived they were met by a man in a suit. He didn't introduce himself, but helped to load their bags into the chopper. Once in the air, he handed over brand-new US passports and gave them the name of the hotel they'd be staying at once they arrived in their island paradise.

"We've booked you into a suite for two months. That should be plenty of time to choose your new home. You'll also have a personal concierge to provide anything you desire. If you need to speak to us, he'll pass on your requests."

It seemed they'd thought of everything. Sanders squeezed his wife's hand and gave her a reassuring smile.

It was a short hop to the airport, and the mystery man loaded their luggage into a car and they drove to a hangar. Inside was a white Learjet, and they walked up the steps and into the luxurious cabin. There were four seats, and a beautiful young lady asked them if they would like champagne before takeoff. The couple gratefully indulged.

Twenty minutes later they were in the air. The hostess offered them something to eat, and both settled on the steak option.

Sanders poured another glass of champagne and sat back in his chair. After all the uncertainty of the last few months, the pressure was finally off. He had enough to buy a house more than big enough for their needs, and at their age, about a million bucks a year to live on.

The food arrived, and both tucked in. The steak was succulent, the sauce divine, and they polished it off with the last of the champagne. The stewardess brought another bottle and popped the cork.

"To a new life," Sanders said, raising his glass.

Joanne smiled as she raised hers, and they polished the drinks off in seconds.

Sanders felt comfortable enough to chat about their future. The last few days, he'd been worried that the ESO wouldn't keep their end of the bargain, but now they were mere hours from a new beginning. They spoke about the new house they wanted, the clubs she was looking forward to joining, and his desire to do some decent deep-sea fishing.

His eyes suddenly felt heavy. He saw Joanne yawning, which set him off, too. He'd never been one to nap during the day, and he'd only been awake for nine hours. He put it down to the champagne and heavy meal.

Then the pain came. It started in his arm, then migrated to his chest and jaw. The base of his skull ached, and he had a coppery taste in his mouth. He tried to say something to Joanne but could see that she was in much the same state. She clutched at her chest and doubled over in her seat.

Sanders tried to get the stewardess's attention, but the woman just stood there, an impassive look on her face. He wanted to shout to her, but his throat was so constricted he could barely breathe.

Too late, he realized that the ESO had chosen not to fake his death. They were doing it for real.

It was his last thought before the darkness enveloped him.

~

The stewardess called the cockpit, and the copilot came out to inspect the two bodies. Both had pain etched on their faces, the result of the poison she had added to their meal. He went back to the cockpit and told the captain to reduce altitude to five thousand feet, then waited until the plane had leveled off at that height.

"Get the door," he said to the stewardess.

She went to the front of the cabin and opened it, holding tight to a handle on the wall to avoid being sucked out as the wind blew into the confined space.

The copilot dragged both corpses to the door and looked out. They were above the Atlantic and heading towards deeper water, but there was more to do. He went to the rear of the plane and opened a locker. Inside were two vests, both loaded with lead weights. He dragged them to the front and put them on the bodies, then one after the other he pushed Sanders and his wife out of the aircraft.

He locked the door and returned to the cockpit. Once he was strapped in his seat again, the captain turned back to the airport, their mission completed.

CHAPTER 40

Tom Gray performed the slow march in time with the other five pall-bearers, the coffin on his shoulder no weight at all. Behind them, a procession of forty people shuffled along, the wind tearing at their clothes.

They reached the grave, and the coffin was placed on a platform that would soon be lowered into the ground. Gray took his place between Melissa and Sally, Len's only surviving relative. She'd flown over from Australia on hearing the news. Next to Melissa was Gill, the long-serving receptionist at Minotaur Solutions.

The vicar began speaking, but Gray heard little of his sermon. His mind was filled with images of Len enjoying life. Many people had seen him as aloof, austere, but with his close friends he was a different person. He'd had a rich—though dry—sense of humor that hadn't been expressed as often as Gray would have liked. He had also been a brutally loyal friend.

Sally let out a sniffle. Gray didn't know if it was a reaction to the terrible weather or a show of sadness, but he took her hand anyway. She squeezed back tightly.

They sung a hymn, then the vicar said his last words before concluding the service. A lone trumpeter played "Amazing Grace," and Gray almost fell apart. The tears he'd promised not to shed came flooding out, and by the end of the solo, there wasn't a dry eye in the graveyard.

As the coffin descended into the ground, it felt like it was dragging Gray's soul with it. When it was finally out of sight, he turned with the others and walked back to the church parking lot.

They thanked the vicar, then got into the waiting limousines that would take them to the wake.

It was held in the basement of a pub a few hundred yards from the now-empty offices of Minotaur Solutions. It had been Len's regular hangout, and the owner had been honored to offer his services.

When they arrived, there was already a large group waiting. Most had served in the regiment with Len, Gray, and Sonny. Others were people whose acquaintance he'd made after leaving the army.

Some of the guests, Sally included, were astonished at the upbeat atmosphere in the cellar bar. Gray had to explain to her that, in true regimental tradition, they didn't mourn a brother's passing, but instead celebrated his life as if he were still among them. It was like attending a normal party, except no one got to meet the host.

As more and more people came to offer Sally their condolences and regale her with stories from Len's past, Gray excused himself and went to get a drink.

Sonny was already at the bar.

"Decent turnout."

"It is," Gray agreed. There were at least a hundred people in the place.

"Where's Melissa?" Sonny asked.

"She went home with Sarah and Andrew."

When Sonny gave him a concerned look, Gray shrugged it off. "Andrew has a couple of his armed colleagues stationed outside the house, and she has a panic button, just in case. I don't think anyone's going to try anything tonight."

"Andrew not staying, then?"

"He'll be back," Gray said. "He's just going to make sure everything's in place first."

Music began blasting from half a dozen speakers, and Sonny had to lean in close to make himself heard.

"Where have you been the last few days?"

"Yeah, sorry about that. I had to make plans."

"Such as?"

"I'll tell you when Andrew gets here."

Eva arrived and ordered a bottle of beer from the free bar. She clinked the neck against their drinks.

"To life," she said, and swallowed half the brew.

They echoed the toast and ordered a fresh round.

"Is everything arranged?" Gray asked her.

"Just about. I'm waiting for the paperwork to take Carl back home. The funeral's in six days."

"I'm sure Andrew could help smooth that through," Sonny suggested.

"He already has. He said I could pick up the documents tomorrow."

"That's good."

They stood around in silence for a while, until some of Gray's former colleagues came over to offer their condolences. Carl Levine and the bear-like Jeff Campbell had turned up, and they all caught up on old times. It had been a long time since they'd seen each other, and they spent a good half hour chatting about what they'd been up to since they'd helped bring James Farrar to justice six years earlier.

Gray was on his fifth bottle when Andrew arrived. Gray set his beer aside, made his excuses to the guests at the bar, and dragged Andrew and Sonny to a quiet corner.

"I'm leaving in a couple of days," Gray told them.

"Back to Italy," Andrew said, nodding.

"No. Just . . . leaving. I won't be back. This is the last you'll see of me."

Sonny looked hurt. "But you'll be in touch, right?"

"I'm afraid not. It's time I took Melissa away from all this, and that means we have to disappear for good. I'm sorry."

Sonny looked crestfallen. "Wow. I mean . . . are you going to stay around until they read Len's will? I'm sure he left you something."

"You take it," Gray said. "I've instructed my lawyer, Ryan Amos, to draft a letter renouncing any claim to Len's inheritance and giving it all to you."

"Are you sure? He had a couple of million stashed away. That's not to be sniffed at."

"I'm sure." Gray smiled, fingering the lapel of Sonny's suit jacket. "You keep it. Buy yourself a decent suit."

"Cheeky sod. This cost me three hundred quid."

"I rest my case."

"Seriously, though," Andrew said, "what are you going to do for money?"

"That's no longer an issue. When we left Langton's place, I snagged a few of his watches. I had them valued the other day, and we'll never want for money again. One of them was something called a Patek Philippe Henry Graves Supercomplication."

"Never heard of it."

"Nor had I, but the last time it was auctioned, four years ago, it fetched over twenty-four million dollars. That was one of the cheaper ones in his collection."

"Holy shit!"

"That's what I thought," Gray said. "It'll keep us going for a few years, and I'll leave the others to Melissa when I'm gone. So yeah, we're good for money."

"What about papers?" Andrew asked. "I'm sure after everything you've done for us, Veronica would be able to arrange something."

"Thanks, but I've got that covered. If MI5 know my new identity, I'll never be free of . . . all this. Every time the phone rings, I'll wonder if it's you asking for a favor, and I can't live like that. I'm sure you understand."

"I do," Harvey said.

A large man came staggering over and put his arms around Gray's shoulders.

"Hey, Tom, long time no see."

"Hi, Taff. Glad you could make it."

"I wouldn't have missed it for the world," the Welshman said.

"This is Andrew. You know Sonny."

"Of course I know Sonny. The only dwarf to pass selection!"

"You making fun of my height?" Sonny asked, adopting an aggressive stance.

"What height? You haven't got any height. Here, take this tenner and go and buy yourself some height, then come back here and I'll make fun of it!"

Andrew looked worried, as if it was all going to kick off, but Sonny grabbed the money and planted a kiss on Taff's cheek. "Ta very much!"

"Lighten up, Andrew," Sonny said, "the fighting doesn't start until at least seven o'clock."

Taff went off in search of entertainment, leaving the trio alone once more.

"I still can't believe it," Sonny said. "This is like . . . the end of an era. First Len gone, now you. It's gonna take some getting used to."

"It will," Gray agreed, "but we all have to move on. You've got plenty of money, and with those newfound cooking skills you've been bragging about, you can open a restaurant or something. Go find yourself an island paradise, spend your days on the beach being attended to by lovely maidens in skimpy bikinis, and cook your heart out at night."

"When you put it that way, it doesn't sound so bad."

Gray slapped him on the shoulder. "It doesn't, does it? Let's go and mingle."

For the next six hours, Gray chatted with his old friends. Many wanted him to retell the story of how he'd kidnapped the five repeat offenders all those years ago, or how he'd managed to get the MI5 agent out of Tagrilistan. That hadn't made the newspapers, but little went on in the world that didn't get back to Hereford, especially when ex-22 members were involved.

By the time it came to say goodnight, Gray was as drunk as he'd ever been in his life. As the wake organizer, he was one of the last to leave. His only companion at the end was Sonny, who, if anything, was even worse for wear.

"They might be the best . . . *burrrp* . . . soldiers in the world, but they're a bunch of messy bastards."

Sonny swept a clumsy arm toward the dance floor, which was slick with spilled beer and spirits. The remnants of the food fight that had taken place two hours earlier covered the nearby tables and chairs.

Sonny reached into his pocket and, with some difficulty, extracted his wallet. He took his time counting out a few notes and threw them on the table.

"Give that . . . to the . . . landlord. I'm gonna call . . . Hughie and Ralph . . . on the big white telephone."

While Sonny went to throw up, Gray's wavering hand eventually latched on to a rum and coke, and he held it up in the air.

"To you, big man."

He tossed the drink down his throat and slammed the glass back down on the table.

I need to call them, too.

He staggered to the restroom, bouncing off every wall on the way, and discovered Sonny asleep with his head on the toilet. For some reason, it was the funniest thing he'd ever seen, and he leaned against the cubicle door and laughed until it hurt. Eventually, he managed to pull out his phone and take a picture for posterity.

The urge to vomit had gone for now, so he helped Sonny to his feet and half-dragged him up the stairs. The cold air hit him like a freight train, and it sobered him up a little.

He called Andrew and asked if he and Sarah could look after Melissa that night. He didn't want his daughter seeing him in such a state. Andrew agreed, and Gray hailed a taxi, pushed Sonny aboard, and asked the driver to drop them off at The Ritz.

CHAPTER 41

It had been three days since Len's funeral, but Gray still couldn't face a beer. Instead, he ordered an exorbitantly overpriced Coke from the airport bar and a fruit juice for Melissa. Eva sipped a glass of white wine.

True to his word, he'd checked out of the hotel the next morning and, after picking Melissa up from Andrew's house, checked into another one booked under Eva's assumed name.

When picking up Melissa, his final goodbye to Sarah had been emotional, but she'd understood his reasoning. For her part, she'd decided never to use a nanny or babysitter again. Veronica Ellis had passed on her good wishes, and Gray asked them to say goodbye to Hamad Farsi for him.

He'd spent the next two days searching for private watch collectors on the Internet. As he'd expected, it hadn't been easy. In the end, he'd asked Farooq to help, and had been rewarded with the names of three people in the US who would pay top dollar for the items in Langton's collection. He'd emailed all three of them, asking if they would be interested in a couple of the timepieces, and their replies had been instant. A bidding war soon ensued, and arrangements had been made to meet the winner in New York to make the exchange. In a few days' time, he would be two watches lighter and have a hundred grand in cash and another forty million wired to a numbered account in the Cayman Islands. The only downside was that he'd been forced to wear an old-fashioned, three-piece suit to get them through customs. He had a pocket watch on a gold chain in his vest pocket, and an extremely rare Patek Philippe on his wrist.

First, though, he had to say goodbye to one more person.

Tom Gray.

Eva had agreed to take him to see DeBron Harris in Louisville. She'd called ahead and made arrangements, and he and Melissa would be given US passports in their new names, plus a prepaid credit card and social security numbers. Everything he would need to disappear into the open.

He still hadn't decided on a destination, though. For simplicity he would have preferred an English-speaking country, but the idea of Melissa learning a second language while still in her formative years also appealed.

He had plenty of time to decide.

He'd decided to take Melissa to Disney World in Florida for a couple of weeks, to try to get rid of the nightmares she'd been having. She'd told him what she'd been through on Langton's island, and he imagined that would be enough to induce some kind of mental trauma in one so young. After Disney World, he'd take her to see a therapist if her condition didn't improve. He didn't have much time for psychologists himself, but would do anything to ease the painful memories in his daughter's mind.

The screen showed that their plane was boarding, and he, Eva, and Melissa walked to the gate like one happy family.

Twelve hours later, they booked into separate rooms at the Best Western JFK Airport hotel. Thankfully, the customs official had taken little interest in his watches.

In the morning, Eva knocked on their door and presented Melissa with a giant teddy bear and Gray with a pair of airline tickets.

"We leave in three hours," she said. "I thought it best to book us a hotel in Louisville for tonight, and you can make your own way from there."

That sounded good to Gray. He didn't want to pick up the new IDs and then get back on a plane. It was tiring enough for him to do it, never mind Melissa.

He showered and dressed, then they took a cab to LaGuardia where they boarded the two-and-a-half-hour flight to Louisville. When they landed, Eva rented a car.

The neighborhood she drove him to was rough in the extreme, but Eva assured him that they would be fine.

She was right.

They were in and out of DeBron's place in a couple of hours. At Gray's insistence, Eva left the room while his papers were created. He didn't want anyone knowing his new identity, not even her. At his request, DeBron swore never to give the information to anyone, including to Eva.

They reached the hotel around dinnertime.

"Any plans?" Eva asked as he tucked into his steak.

"Plenty, but I'm not sharing them. What you don't know, you can't tell."

"Very wise."

"I'm sorry I won't be at the funeral," Gray said. "Carl was a good man. I just think Melissa's seen enough death."

"I understand. I hope this horrible experience doesn't affect her long-term."

Gray hoped so too, but only time would tell.

They shared small talk for the next hour, steering the conversation away from their recent exploits for Melissa's sake, and when they parted that night, Eva promised to pop in and say goodbye before she left in the morning.

～

When Gray woke, he immediately felt refreshed and invigorated, as if he had something good to look forward to. When he took in his surroundings, he knew what it was. Today was the first day of his new life, and he was keen to get on with it.

He showered and dressed before waking Melissa, and on the way down to breakfast he knocked on Eva's door.

There was no answer.

He assumed she would already be in the restaurant, but when they got there, she was nowhere to be seen.

After filling up on bacon and eggs, Gray walked back through the reception area and was called over by the desk clerk.

"Mister Gray, we have a message for you."

She handed him a sealed envelope, and he opened it.

I hate long goodbyes. Take care, Tom Gray.

E.

Gray smiled. He hadn't really been looking forward to it either.

"She also asked me to tell you that she settled the bill," the clerk said.

Gray thanked her and took Melissa back to the room. He packed their bags, then changed into the three-piece suit once more. No way was he checking the watches through in luggage. The rest of the timepieces were in a safe deposit box in London, and he would let the buyer know about them later that day. If he wanted to purchase them all, the transaction would be done in the UK to avoid import and export duty, and Gray's lawyer would ensure the majority of the money was put aside for Melissa.

"What are we doing today, Daddy?"

"We're going to New York, honey."

"But we went there yesterday," she moaned.

"I know, but this time we're going to see some of the sights. We can climb to the top of the Empire State Building and the Statue of Liberty, then go to the zoo in Central Park. How does that sound?"

"Yeah! I love the zoo!"

"Great! We'll stay there for a couple of days, then I'll take you to meet an old friend of mine."

He just hoped Mickey Mouse had the stamina to put up with her for two weeks.

CHAPTER 42

Eva Driscoll sat outside the *parrilla* and checked the menu. One of the best things about Argentina was the steak, and this was her fifth in the four days she'd been in Buenos Aires. She ordered the tenderloin, medium, with sweetbreads and baked potato.

She felt a pang in her chest as the waiter walked away. Carl had loved his steak, too, but they would never share another.

The funeral two weeks earlier had been a typically solemn affair. Carl was survived by his mother, and only ten mourners had attended, Eva included. She'd introduced herself as an old colleague to avoid any unwanted questioning, though everyone seemed more preoccupied with wondering who had arranged and paid for the service.

After seeing him laid to rest, Eva had taken the first flight to Montevideo, Uruguay. It wasn't the chicest of places, but it was home to Javier Bustamante. If DeBron Harris was the go-to guy for counterfeit US passports, Javier was his South American equivalent. Armed with a new name and papers, she'd spent a couple of days in the Uruguayan capital before taking a leisurely boat ride over to Buenos Aires.

She flicked her hair off her shoulders. It was growing out nicely, and she intended to wear it long for the foreseeable future. She thought it suited her new persona, that of Señorita Lucía Sánchez. All she needed to do now was find a place to rent, and she could slip into her new lifestyle. She still had to come up with a personal history for herself, though. A wealthy widow would be the simplest—living life without a care now that her husband was gone.

It brought another stab of grief. She and Carl hadn't spoken of marriage, but she knew the possibility had been lurking in the background. They'd talked about the future, but matrimony had been the one subject they'd never broached.

Now it was too late.

She thought about the bear he'd bought her at the flea market, the one she'd given to Harvey for safe-keeping. It had been the simplest trinket, but had epitomized his love for her. With him gone, she'd decided not to ask for it back. It would only remind her of her loss each and every day, and that was no way to spend the rest of her life. It was better that Sarah and Harvey keep it to remind them of the man who'd sacrificed his life to bring their daughter back.

Her food arrived, but Eva had lost her appetite. She picked at the plate but couldn't get Carl's face out of her mind. She called the waiter over and ordered a double vodka and tonic, hoping it would take her somewhere more pleasant.

"Señorita Sánchez, you have a phone call."

Eva looked up at the waiter, who was holding out a cordless phone. She couldn't think how anyone would know her new identity. She'd only had it for a few days and had checked into the hotel using an old alias.

"Are you sure it's for me?"

He shrugged. "That's what he said."

Eva took the phone and put it to her ear. "Hello?" she said in Spanish.

"Miss Driscoll, it's good to finally speak to you."

"Who is this?" she asked, but had a feeling she already knew. She looked around but couldn't see anyone staring at her. Still, her body had already entered fight-or-flight mode.

"I think you know the answer to that question. If it clears things up, though, we're the people who are thankful for your efforts in French Polynesia recently."

"Okay, you have my attention. What do you want?"

"Just to make sure we have a mutual understanding. Henry Langton . . . overstepped the mark. His actions were not in keeping with the standards we uphold."

"Standards that include having my brother murdered and trying to kill me and Rees Colback?"

"You were never meant to be involved," the voice said. It had an echo to it, as if he were speaking from inside a tin can.

"Is that supposed to make me feel better?" Eva was gripping the phone so tightly, her knuckles were white, and she had a hard time keeping her voice down. "Are you saying you had every right to kill Jeff?"

"As I said, Langton did not always act with our full authority. He may have been our leader, but he lost sight of what the organization stands for."

"I don't think he did. World domination at any cost seems pretty simple to me. Kickstart illegal wars in the Middle East to benefit the fossil fuel industry and the military–industrial complex. Pay to ensure that legislation is passed allowing banks to print trillions of dollars with a few key taps, and then lend that money to the masses so that they can work their entire lives in servitude trying to pay it off. And all the while your media outlets ignore the entire scam and instead pitch black against white, left against right, Democrat against Republican. The sheep take the bait and have too much going on to realize they're being manipulated like puppets, working their entire lives simply to enrich you and your cronies."

"That was quite a speech, Miss Driscoll, and accurate in some respects. Only, our plan has been in play for a number of years and will be for the next hundred at least. Sadly, Henry Langton couldn't wait. He wanted to see it come to fruition in his lifetime and accelerated the program too quickly. We were willing to wait for North Korea to implode, which it would have done in another twenty to thirty years, but Henry wanted to see it wiped off the face of the earth. If his candidate had won the last election, it would be a graveyard by now. He'd lined up both candidates for the next election, but as you know, they're out of the running. Maybe that was for the best."

"I still don't understand why you're calling me," she said.

"To extend an olive branch. This could easily have been a drive-by shooting or suicide bombing. You would never have seen it coming. We want to assure you that we have no intention of coming after you again. Henry Langton acted foolishly, and thanks to you, he paid the price. We'd like that to be the end of it. We go our separate ways and hope our paths never cross again."

He had a point. They could have shot her in the back of the head long before now, and there were plenty of tall buildings around her for a sniper to lie in wait.

"You seem unsure of our proposal," the voice said. "As a token of our sincerity, check your bank account."

He read off some numbers, and Eva recognized them as the account where the vast majority of her funds were held. Money she'd stolen from the CIA. Effectively, the ESO's money.

"Don't worry, we haven't taken anything. In fact, we added a little bonus. It's our way of apologizing for your brother's death, and a thank you for ridding us of Henry Langton. The balance should now read one hundred million. That should be enough to keep you going for the rest of your life."

It was all too good to be true. In addition, the fact that they'd found her so quickly was disturbing. She hadn't even used the Sánchez papers yet, which could only mean that the ESO had Javier Bustamante in their pocket. They must also have someone following her around, which was even more disturbing. Her tradecraft was first-rate, so whoever was following her must have been her equal at the very least. They knew where she was and had got the number for the steak bar, which meant someone was tailing her.

They were close.

She looked around once more but could see no one. In fact, nothing had pinged her radar for the last week.

"Your answer, Miss Driscoll?"

"Sorry, what?"

"Do we have a deal? We don't come after you, you don't come after us."

"Yeah, deal. Only, on one condition. Stop following me. Your men are good, but one day they'll make a mistake. If I see anyone acting suspicious within a mile of me, all bets are off."

"That seems more than reasonable. We only used them to get your attention, and now that we have, I'll simply wish you a long and happy life."

The phone went dead, and Eva slowly placed it on the table. She considered leaving immediately, but needed time to think, so she picked up her knife and fork and tucked into the steak. It was cold, but she needed sustenance.

She also needed to get out of the country if she had any hopes of making a fresh start away from the ESO. But where to? And new IDs were a must. She could go back and see DeBron, but something told her that her European connection would be a better idea.

She'd fooled them once with her old-lady routine, so it could work again. If not, she would find another way to lose them.

With her immediate plans in her head, she stuck a handful of pesos under the plate, then picked up her bag and casually threw it over her shoulder before heading back to her hotel.

~

Vincent May hit the End button on the call.

"What do you think?" the new head of the ESO asked the other four men in the room.

"She knows a lot," one offered. "Is it really wise to let her go?"

"Of course it is!" another snapped. "Do you want to end up like Mumford? I'd rather keep my balls where God intended, thank you very much."

"Gentlemen, we've discussed this. Our priority is to undo the godawful mess Langton created, and regain control. Hopefully, we've got her off our backs for the next couple of years."

"We should have killed her while we had the chance. Now she's on notice. It'll be impossible to get close to her again. She's like an attack dog. We're deluding ourselves if we think we can control her."

"Even attack dogs have their uses," May said.

The predicament Langton had left them in could put their plans back by years. They would have to keep their heads down until the next election, when the liberal Leo Russell would be ousted. Once their own man was in the White House, they would end the witch hunt and get things back on track.

"It was a wise move to contact her," another of May's colleagues said. "We don't need her interfering with what's coming up. Hopefully the pittance we threw at her will keep her out of our hair."

May's decision to track Driscoll from the UK had been vindicated. They had discovered who was supplying her with passports, and DeBron Harris and Javier Bustamante were now in the ESO's pocket. Both had been given cash and promises of immunity from future prosecutions in return for their cooperation. May had also found the new IDs that Tom Gray and her other friends were living under, and that information would be filed away for now.

"How soon after the election do we strike?" a member of the board asked.

"There's no rush," May said. "Let them think we've forgotten about them. When they're back in their comfort zones, we'll pick them off one by one."

AUTHOR'S NOTE

If you would like to be informed of new releases, just send an email with "Driscoll" in the subject line to alanmac@ntlworld.com to be added to the mailing list. You can find details of all nine of Alan's books at www.alanmcdermottbooks.co.uk.

ACKNOWLEDGMENTS

When writing about MI5, one has to take certain liberties; the organization isn't known for opening its doors to the public. I would therefore like to thank Matt Johnson for his help in making this book more realistic than it would otherwise have been. Not only is Matt a great author, he's also a top bloke.

ABOUT THE AUTHOR

Photo © 2017 Darlene McDermott

Alan McDermott is a husband and a father to beautiful twin girls, and currently lives in the south of England. Born in West Germany to Scottish parents, Alan spent his early years moving from town to town as his father was posted to different army units around the United Kingdom. Alan has had a number of jobs since leaving school, including working on a cruise ship in Hong Kong and Singapore, where he met his wife, and as a software developer creating clinical applications for the National Health Service. Alan gave up his day job in December 2014 to become a full-time author. Alan's writing career began in 2011 with the action thriller *Gray Justice*, his first full-length novel.